Two Weeks Every Summer
STORIES FROM CAMP MEETING

by

Carolyn Steele Agosta

Published by Carolyn Steele Agosta, North Carolina.
Visit my website at http://www.carolynsteeleagosta.com

First paperback edition: July 2020
First Kindle edition: July 2020

The characters and events portrayed in this book are fictitious. I have used Rock Spring Campground and the history of the Denver, NC, area as inspiration only. I have also borrowed some interesting first or last names from the area, but strictly in fictitious ways – at no time are they meant to represent any real person, living or dead. The stories are from my fevered brain only, they do not involve a retelling of anyone's personal anecdotes or family secrets.

Agosta, Carolyn Steele, 1952-
Two Weeks Every Summer, Stories from Camp Meeting /
by Carolyn Steele Agosta, 1st ed.

ISBN: 978-0-9829561-3-7

Dedication

To my family, who have always given their full support,
and filled my life with love and laughter.

Table of Contents

A word from the Author

Camp meeting is a phenomenon going back to the early 19th century and the Second Great Awakening of the Protestant Christian religions, held for worship, preaching and communion. Over time it has evolved into a combination of religious revival, family reunion, community history and a pretty good smack of small-town carnival. Revivals and camp meetings continue to be held by various denominations to this day, and in some areas of the mid-Atlantic, these led to the development of seasonal cottages for meetings. The cottages might range from simple wood shacks to the very elegant and elaborate Victorian cottages at Martha's Vineyard, Massachusetts.

I encountered camp meeting for the first time when I moved to North Carolina from Michigan in 1975. Rock Spring campground, in Denver, North Carolina, consists of nearly 300 wooden shacks (called 'tents', in memory of the original accommodations) built in three concentric rings around a central arbor, or open-air church setting with rough-hewn pews, a pulpit and stage.

I was fascinated by the history of the place, as well as the opportunity for lots of drama caused by the coming together of various generations, family members, old friends, sometimes old enemies, and primitive living conditions. Year after year, people choose to come here for two weeks during the hottest part of hot North Carolina summers, with no air conditioning. Many expect to follow the traditions of summers past, while others simply enjoy the present moment. Two of my sisters own a tent and I've been able to visit camp meeting and see for myself how some of these dramas might play out. I love the community atmosphere and the music and decided I must capture a bit of that before it disappears forever. Modern progress can be a constant pressure on both the evolution and survival of camp meetings.

As these stories go to press, we are in the midst of the 2020 Covid-19 quarantine and there has not yet been a decision whether camp meeting will go forward this year. There have been only two times that Rock Spring camp meeting has not been held, in its 190-year history. Once, during the Civil War, when Yankee soldiers were in the area, and once in the 1940's, during a polio epidemic. My bet is that it will go forward, perhaps under different circumstances than usual. At a time when people need to believe that a 'new normal' is possible, I'm pretty sure they'll find a way.

I hope you enjoy the stories. I sure enjoyed writing them.

Carolyn Steele Agosta

June 8, 2020

Little Week
2018

RAY CANSLER COULDN'T SLEEP. For the past half hour, he'd tried to calm his mind and slide back into peaceful oblivion, but he just couldn't. Every time he shut his eyes, another thought would pop back up. Lists of things to do. Today was Move-In Day, the last Saturday of July, when he and Mary Lou would bring everything over to their tent at the campground and prepare for two weeks of Heaven. Well, two weeks of camp meeting.

To him, camp meeting was much more than a religious gathering. It was a touchstone where he renewed his faith in Life. Over the space of his seventy-two years, he'd discovered that God's ways were sometimes puzzling, and his wife's often completely baffling, but the campground and he agreed just fine.

Finally, Mary Lou awoke and they packed his old pick-up truck with cleaning supplies, and headed right over. Power and water had been turned on a couple of weeks ago, and there was already a fair bit of activity at the campground. People worked on updates to their tents, a clean-up crew labored at The Shack, and a couple of men mowed the grass.

As soon as they got there, Mary Lou hooked up the CD player and put on the first of many Beatles CDs that would be the soundtrack to their work. The first song was *I Saw Her Standing There,* and Ray smiled. He hadn't always been a fan of the Beatles, but her relentless playing of their music had gradually won him over, and this song always seemed like he could have written it himself. He'd fallen in love with Mary Lou at camp meeting, when she was seventeen, a little ball of fire. He was twenty-three and just out of the military. He'd fallen *hard.*

Now she stood before him, hands on hips, and her head tipped back to meet his gaze. "Are you just going to stand there? Lots to do."

"Yeah, boss," he replied. "I was just fixin' to."

They removed the tarps over the open-slatted walls and folded them away until the end of Big Week. Then, by long-standing tradition and unvarying routine, Mary Lou went upstairs to sweep and clean, and he began working downstairs. From time to time, she would call down with some kind of observation or cryptic comment. "Fan paddles front bedroom – warped!", or "Mud dauber nests, back bedroom! Three!", and possibly his favorite for this year, "Red and blue…no, yellow and blue… White!".

"You bet," Ray said. Eventually he'd find out what that meant.

By noon, the tent was clean, and they were filthy. They sat in companionable silence on the backporch step, sipping iced tea and munching bologna sandwiches. In the background, *I'm Happy Just to Dance with You* played, and a cooling breeze ran through the tent. Mary Lou said, "That was fun." She always thought everything was fun.

After lunch, he made a trip back to the house and found their son Wade already there, ready to help load the truck with furnishings that had spent the winter in the garage. Old wooden swings for the front and back porches, two long, narrow tables to be end-to-end so that the entire family could be seated, some mismatched wooden kitchen chairs. They loaded item after item - small painted dressers for the bedrooms, queen-sized air mattresses, Mary Lou's antique Hoover cabinet for the kitchen, a small refrigerator.

They returned to the campground and unloaded, while she carried in armloads of sheets and towels, pillows and quilts, and gradually everything began to take shape. The finishing touches were a small bookcase with board games and paperback books, a child's playpen in a corner near the staircase, and electric fans on stands.

The place now felt like home, but Mary Lou still had one thing on her list. Their tent, as did most at the campground, shared common side walls with their neighbors, like townhomes. Front and back walls had open slats to let air through, while side walls were covered with solid sheets of plywood. And she wasn't about to let those walls stand undecorated.

Years ago, she'd dug up family photos taken through the decades and framed them. Group shots, showing the whole family lined up on the front porch of the tent, dating back to the 1920s. There were enough to cover every inch of available space, even up the stairway wall.

Ray always grumbled about unpacking and hanging them, as his contribution toward the unvarying routine, but he also quietly enjoyed gazing at them. He liked to think about the relatives who had gone before, now gone on to eternity.

He got a kick out of tracing the family resemblances – the wide Cansler grin and out-jutted chin, the way so many of the women tilted their heads to one side. And he enjoyed seeing the change of fashions, from old-timey suspenders and whiskers to crewcuts and jeans, from bell-bottoms to bike shorts.

He could even spot his own self – a frowning infant in his mother's arms in '46, later a skinny adolescent, and eventually a father hoisting his own child to his shoulder. How could all that time pass so quickly?

He and Mary Lou worked in tandem, unwrapping and hanging the picture frames, but then as usual she had him take about half of them down and rehang them in some other order. This year, she was intent on a chronological scheme.

Finally they finished, and she stepped back and exclaimed, "Look!"

"What?"

"Wizard of Oz." She pointed. "Look – left to right, black-and-white to full color. From Kansas to Emerald City."

"Well, I'll be," Ray said. "Hey, who do you propose for the role of the Wicked Witch?" She laughed and swatted his arm.

He could have stood there all day, just looking, but Mary Lou began gathering up the discarded bubble wrap and cartons, and handed them over to be carried out to the truck.

"That was fun," she said.

On Sunday, after family dinner at home, they loaded the truck for a final trip. They would arrive at the campground, carry in clothes and groceries, and then they were done. Little Week could begin.

Each day of the two weeks of camp meeting would see planned activities, all of them based on years of traditions. Even their meals were the same, from one year to the next. Ray had no intention on missing out on any of his favorites. Fried chicken, potato salad, homemade peach ice cream, country style steak, and more, plus gallons of sweet iced tea.

And each evening they'd continue one of their favorite rituals, a stroll through the campground just before dark. Between each of the three concentric squares of tents were grassy areas called passways, and it was a given that they and many others would be walking those passways, checking to see who had arrived and who had yet to arrive, stopping to visit with old friends, meeting a new son-in-law or grandbaby, and noticing how much the 'small fry' had grown since last year.

And he wouldn't forget his own little ritual, the greeting of the old oak trees, as if they were long-lost friends. He checked them for signs of age or disease and made mental notes as to which needed a little loving attention. The oaks, scattered throughout the area, predated the campground, and he hated to lose even one. They were like living tethers, holding the campground in place and not letting it disappear as so many other good things had over the years.

Finally, as dusk fell, he and Mary Lou would end up back at the tent for a nice quiet evening. No TV at camp meeting, and no computers. Very little use, even, of their cell phones. Let others get mesmerized by television shows or video games, he and Mary Lou would relax the way people did in the olden days. He'd read the local paper, and she'd have her nose in a book. Later in the week, once the kids arrived, they might play some board games, but these first few days were always very quiet and peaceful.

Evening arrived. They had completed all that had to be done and could sit and rock, while *Yesterday* played in the background. He stretched and sighed in pure contentment.

"I love the peacefulness here," he told Mary Lou. "No politics on the news, no telemarketers. Simpler times. Like the good old days, when camp meeting began."

She put down her book and looked at him affectionately. "Oh, honey. You always say that. I know you love to reminisce but come on. Things were tough in the old days. Drought, boll weevils, disease. Just think of all the things that have happened since 1830. The Civil War, two world wars, the Depression, the atomic bomb. September 11. Life isn't simple, now or in the past. The past just looks simpler because we know how things turned out."

"But it was different, you know. Not so much noise. Not so much coming *at* you all the time. Peace and quiet."

"Quiet, maybe. I don't know about *peace*. People still had their troubles and strifes. Money problems, marriage problems, children who died young, or who ran around and got in trouble. Camp meeting itself wasn't so peaceful, you know, in the early days. Lots of Bible-thumping back then." She sighed. "Don't get me wrong – I loved the calm, easy time we had today, too. But you know and I know that once the kids arrive, all heck will break loose. They bring the modern world with them." She flashed a grin and added, "So, my dear, you best enjoy this peacefulness while you can!"

"I suppose. I just like thinking about the fact that despite all the changes in the world, camp meeting has remained pretty much the same."

"Yes, well, for two weeks every summer, at least."

They soon made their way went upstairs and got ready for bed. As they lay on the air mattress, holding hands and looking up at the slow-moving ceiling fan and the underside of the tin roof, Mary Lou said, "Copper wire. And some epoxy."

"Sure thing," Ray concurred. *Another mystery.*

Just before they fell asleep, Mary Lou said, "Today was fun."

Over the next three days, they finished settling in. Made trips to the hardware store and the garden supply and antique store where Mary Lou bought three old bowling balls. Before the day was done, the fan was fixed and the mud dauber nest removed, and geraniums planted at the base of the nearest oak.

She painted the bowling balls to look like two ladybugs and a bumblebee. Ray watched dubiously. "They're gonna roll all over," he said.

"Won't. We'll bury them halfway."

"When you say 'we', I know you mean me."

"But you're so strong and handsome."

She grinned and he saw that seventeen-year-old again. He'd had to wait four years to make her his wife, and he'd never regretted it once. *She Loves You* played in the background, and there was fried shrimp and hush puppies for dinner.

On Thursday morning, their mystery neighbors moved in. The Triplett family owned the tent next to Ray's, but didn't use it themselves anymore, and every year some other family would rent it out during camp meeting. He was upstairs, topping up the air mattresses, when he saw a van pull into the field across the road and watched as two young men climbed out. Both had long wavy hair, beards, and colorful tattoos. Oh Lordy, he thought. *What in Sam Hill is this?*

He watched them open the back of the van and begin unloading tables and chairs. Soon he could hear them moving around in the upstairs room of the tent next door, talking to each other in deep voices that carried through the thin plywood wall. He headed downstairs but Mary Lou had already hurried out and offered to help. She would, he thought. She'd never met a stranger in her life. Soon, she was volunteering him to help tote baskets and bundles, boxes and bits. Guitar cases, too, he saw. The two fellows had terrible New York accents. Or maybe New Jersey, he wasn't sure. And they started out cussing a lot, but eventually began policing themselves when they saw Mary Lou wince.

"Dis place is crazy," one said, the one with the snake lady tattooed on one arm and a t-shirt that read *I Was Drunk at the Time*. Ray didn't know whether that was referring to the tattoo or something else. Maybe the nose ring. "Never seen nuttin' like it. We hoid it was tents, but dese is more like cabins."

"Well, originally, people did stay in tents, way back in the 1830s," Mary Lou explained. "So we still call them that."

She already had a pitcher of iced tea in her hand. Any minute now, Ray figured, and she'd be breaking out the cheese straws. She was saying, "Do y'all live in the area?"

"Oh, naw, we're just helpin' out," said the other, the one with a row of small hoops piercing his ear. Just the one ear. "Dis ain't our kinda place." He looked at his pal and they both laughed. "Our grandma's stayin', not us." He set down the big cooler chest he'd been carrying and opened it, taking out a bottle of beer.

"Beer's not allowed at the campground," Ray said, revolted and fascinated in equal parts.

"Bettah drink it quick, then, huh?" the second fellow said, and laughed again. "Want one?"

Ray shook his head and shot a glance at Mary Lou, trying to figure a way to scoot her out of there. Naturally, she was delighted with these two new friends. "Well, who's your grandma?," she asked. "She from around here? I wonder if I know her." Mary Lou had that big smile on her face, the one that said I Just Love Everybody, Because I'm Innocent as Heck. Ray wondered if anyone sold t-shirts with those words.

Eventually the van was empty and the two fellows, now known as Mike and Tony, left after thanking Ray and Mary Lou for their assistance, and taking a couple of beers with them. There's still some left in the cooler, he thought. I could report it.

"Lisa King," Mary Lou told him. "Two years ahead of me in high school. Beautiful prom dress. Silver and aqua. Married a pilot from New Jersey."

"Oh, her," Ray replied. "They're her sons?"

"Grandsons. Twins. Fraternal."

"Good grief."

Mary Lou went back into their tent, humming *With a Little Help from My Friends*. She stood at the sink, peeling potatoes with a dreamy look on her face. After a while, she said, "Lisa and I double-dated a few times. It was fun."

That evening, Wade and his family came for dinner and to stay through Little Sunday. The three children – Alison, Becky and Colin – would sleep upstairs in the second bedroom, and Wade and Joni would have to make do in the living room. It was a tight fit, but they were used to it. Back in the old days, when his folks were still alive, they'd crammed the whole extended family into the tent, seven or eight to a room, the womenfolk up in the sleeping loft and the men downstairs. People didn't cotton to such crowding nowadays, so their daughter's family wouldn't arrive until Big Week.

The kids would spend most of their time outdoors, anyway. Alison was seventeen, old enough to pretend to be bored and young enough to secretly hope to meet some handsome young man. Becky was fourteen and absolutely prime age to get all caught up in walking the passways with her giggling girlfriends. Colin just wanted to play all day. He was eleven and had big plans for fishing with Grandpa and going to the Shack for sno-cones.

Ray sure loved Little Week. Fewer people, more free time.

The weekend went by too fast. The women-folk played cutthroat games of Skip-Bo and gave each other manicures while Ray, Wade and Colin went out fishing on the lake. Colin caught two pretty fair-sized bass and they had them for dinner on Saturday, along with cheesy potatoes and fried okra.

The woman Mary Lou remembered – Lisa King, now Lisa D'Angelo – arrived on Friday along with her father, Deke, who was in his late eighties and pretty frail. Ray's feelings about the Tattoo Twins began to change as he saw them tenderly steering their grandfather from the car to the tent. "Dis way, Grandpa. Lean on me. Nope, nope, nope, gotta move your feet. Dat's it, dat's right. Atta boy."

Mary Lou absolutely doted on them, and the two young men ended up spending more time at camp meeting than they'd probably expected, sitting on their grandma's back porch and egging Mary Lou and Lisa to tell stories of their high school days.

The twins even entertained everyone in the evening with their guitars, singing close harmony. "Grandma's a freak for da Everly Brothers and Buddy Holly," they explained. "She made us learn all dese." And they very creditably performed *All I Have to Do is Dream, Cathy's*

Clown, It's So Easy, and several more. Mary Lou asked if they knew any Beatles songs and they obliged with *We Can Work It Out*. Mary Lou was in heaven.

Well, Ray thought, it goes to show you never can tell.

Little Week ended with Little Sunday, of course, but on the evening before, everyone at the campground gathered at the arbor for the Big Sing, when professional singing groups from all over the southeast came to perform. The Cockerill Family. Terry Dunn and the Hillside Boys. Marian Jackson. The Hamiltons.

He and Mary Lou and the family sat on one of the benches inside the arbor, surrounded by hundreds of other people. Outside of the arbor, out on the grass, were probably another couple hundred more, sitting in lawn chairs and fanning themselves with cardboard fans passed out by the local Methodist church.

Children chased fireflies and babies were handed around like appetizers at a cocktail party. One by one, the various music groups performed old timey gospel music, accompanied by guitars or electric keyboards. The three generations of the Cockerill family sang some original songs they'd written, and various members played guitar, bass fiddle, banjo, keyboard and even a mandolin.

The patriarch of the Hamiltons had a slightly comical appearance, thanks to his bowl haircut and rotund figure. He reminded Ray of Baby Huey – but when the family began to sing *O Holy Night*, the fellow went into a high tenor solo, that brought chills to Ray's spine and tears to his eyes.

What a gift, he thought, to be able to sing like that and touch people's emotions. He wouldn't have missed out on The Big Sing for all the money in the world.

Soon after the concert ended, Wade and his family left because he had to be back at work early on Monday. They'd return in the evenings when they could, and would definitely be there for Big Sunday.

Alone together in their tent that night, Ray lay next to Mary Lou, feeling bone-deep contentment. They held hands and looked up at the ceiling, and Ray said, "This past week as been about as good as it gets. Practically perfect." *Eleanor Rigby* played softly in the background.

"It was fun," Mary Lou agreed. "But we still have Big Week, when Bethany's family comes. Three grandkids under the age of five. Yikes." She rolled over toward him, tucking her head against his shoulder. Just before he fell asleep, he heard her say, "Baby swings. Corn on the cob. Bubbles."

"Bubbles," he agreed. At last, a list he understood.

The Minister's Wife
1830

A NOONTIME SOMNOLENCE LAY over the individual groups of men, women and children gathered at the oak grove. All morning they had been busy – the men pacing out distances and bickering with all the calm reasonableness of any group of men, each of whom knows the one best way to do anything – deciding where to place the central arbor and along which axis to line up the individual lots.

They referred frequently to a drawing that Reverend Henry Ames had made after visiting the camp meeting ground near Thomsonville. Finally, agreement was met, and they marked the spaces with wooden stakes and twine. The reverend called a break for lunch, said grace, and gratefully joined his wife and children for a picnic on a quilt under the shade of one of the oak trees. The others settled in like manner and soon all were engaged in the serious business of eating.

"Are you content with how it's ending up?" Martha Ames quietly asked her husband. "Is it even close to what you envisioned?"

"Oh, yes," Henry replied, with a short laugh. "The trustees decided everything months ago. But you know how it is, everyone wants a chance to have their own say about it first."

He bit happily into a ham biscuit and relaxed against the tree trunk, taking time to chew and swallow. "I'm just glad to see it's finally truly happening. Just think! A permanent location for camp meeting, after more than thirty years of moving from this place to that. I tell you, Martha, this means a big change for the Methodists of this county. It will draw people to the area. Eighty-eight tent lots already sold! By next year, we'll be able to finish paying for the land and make a start on the permanent arbor. I am so thankful – "

"Ma! Peter took three ham biscuits and I haven't even had two!"

Martha glanced with annoyance at her two oldest children. "Peter! What have I told you about being greedy? And Dovey, what have I told *you* about complaining all the time?" It figured, she thought. It did seem like every time she reached a moment of peacefulness, one of the children had to interrupt. Usually Dovey. Her seventeen-year-old daughter was going through a spell of being dissatisfied with everything. It's something they all go through, Martha thought, but I'm ready for it to be over.

She sat up and attended to the children, making sure Dovey got a second biscuit, reminding twelve-year-old Matthew that other people were thirsty too and not to hog the water jug, wiping jam off two year-old Daniel's face, and rescuing the hard-boiled eggs from nine-year-old Juliet and seven-year-old Miranda.

A sudden rise in murmuring voices drew her attention to the edge of the field near the fresh-water spring. People around them were sitting up and paying attention as three men came riding into the grove.

Henry hastily brushed himself off and got to his feet. He waved his hat at the newcomers, and said to his wife, "It's Bishop Poovey himself! And the circuit rider from Ohio that I told you about – Reverend Edwards. And Mr Shelton, too. They're here early!"

Martha got to her feet, as did most of the others. Some of the children began to run about. Dovey slowly rose, smoothing her dress and hair, with a sudden bloom to her cheeks.

Bishop Poovey was an old friend. He and Henry had ridden circuit together, years ago. Mr Shelton was the local farmer who'd sold the grove to the trustees. He wasn't ordained, but was always ready to assist whenever preachers came into the area. The Reverend Mr Edwards, though, whose fame preceded him, was new to the area. They had all been looking forward to finally seeing the great preacher.

He's every bit as good-looking as I've heard, Martha thought as he came further into view. Wide shoulders, black wavy hair, dark eyes under strong black brows.

"Ma! Ma! Gotta go squat." Daniel's high piping voice carried through the air. "Go squat *now*."

Martha turned to Dovey. "Go take him into the woods. Over there."

"Ma!" Dovey's voice was an agonized whisper. "Everybody heard him! They'll all know where we're going."

"So? Everyone has to go squat some time. Now hurry!"

Dovey stalked off across the rough grass, dragging her baby brother by the hand, her back rigid with mortification. Martha shook her head and turned her attention back to the newcomers.

Henry stood before them and motioned for his two older sons to take the horses. The men climbed down and began shaking hands all around. A large tree stump stood nearby and Henry climbed up on it and addressed the crowd, introducing the bishop and Reverend Edwards to all that had gathered, and inviting the men to speak.

Bishop Poovey went first, congratulating the men on setting forth on this great project, one that would help bring the word of the Lord to many, many people in the years to come. He probably knew they were all more interested in hearing from the second man, so he kept his remarks short and relinquished his platform.

Reverend Edwards climbed up onto the stump and stood surveying the folks before him. A breeze disordered the curly black locks on his forehead, and played with his tie, but he paid no attention. His gaze, Martha realized, seemed to lock for a second with the eyes of every person there. She felt a shiver run through her as she met his scrutiny, and then his observation passed on. Even her younger daughters stood still for a moment and stared back at the man. Martha had a fleeting wish that their pinafores were cleaner.

"The Lord is good to us," the man said, in a deep voice that carried easily through the grove. "He is so good to us every day. We have the sunshine he made, and the trees and grass, the fresh water that sustains us. He gives it all to us freely. Today, you are taking those gifts and creating a holy place, one that will nourish mankind for generations ahead. But can you do more? Is this day's effort enough?"

He paused, surveying the crowd.

"The Lord asks you to work with the same kind of vigor *every* day, not just once in a while. Not just on Sundays, but every day, in every moment, to live the kind of life, to be the kind of person who does honor to all His gifts. We are to spread His word with every utterance we make. For in the Bible, it says 'Go into all the world and proclaim the gospel to the whole creation. Whoever believes and is baptized will be saved, but whoever does not believe will be condemned.'"

He stopped and let his gaze rove over the crowd again, and when he spoke next, his voice was quiet so that everyone became as silent as possible, wanting to hear. "Do you believe? Do you truly believe? Do you hold that belief deep in your soul, so that it can never be shaken?" Gradually, he raised the volume of his voice, although to Martha, it seemed not louder, but deeper within her body. "*Do* you believe? Does the Lord have hold of your heart? *Do* you willingly offer your strength to the service of the Lord? Can he count on you? Are you *thankful* for all that He has given you? Will you give back to his people even *one-tenth* of everything you've received through the goodness of the Lord? Are you *ready to serve*? Will you serve with *me*? Will you serve with *Bishop Poovey* and *Reverend Ames*? Will you serve alongside and *for* your fellow man?"

A woman's voice rang out across the field. "I will!" And then another voice and another, shouting "I will!" Martha found herself shouting "I will! I will!" and felt tears running down her cheeks. Half-blinded, she glanced down at her children, and then saw Dovey, standing near the woods, further back from the rest of the crowd, down on her knees with her hands in the air. Martha couldn't hear her, but she knew the words Dovey was calling. "I will! I will! Amen!"

Come evening, they returned home and, since it was Saturday, Henry marched all the boys off to the wash house while Martha corralled the girls in the kitchen. Everyone would get a bath. In the summertime, a cool bath was a pleasant sensation, instead of the shivering experience of winter when water was heated on the stove and went cold by the time the bather got out.

Martha hustled the girls through their baths, towel-dried and braided the younger girls' hair, and sent them to bed. Dovey, for once, went quickly and quietly to bed after her bath, and Martha enjoyed the all-too-rare experience of a few quiet minutes for herself. She finished bathing, put on her nightdress and dressing gown, and emptied the hip bath.

Henry was already in bed when she came up and she jumped in quickly and put her cold toes on his. "Oof, woman!" he exclaimed, flinching, but he drew her close afterward and placed his feet against hers. "You're lucky I like you," he said softly. "What a day!"

She nodded and found the warm place on his shoulder where she liked to rest her head. "You men got so much done. The brush arbor, the log seats…"

"No, I meant the preaching. Edwards is a powerful speaker. And he talks just as Godly when he's off the pulpit as on."

Martha knew Henry's opinion of preachers who spoke one way in public and quite a different way in private. "He does seem a good man."

"A man of God. He'll go far in the conference. I suspect they'll offer him his own pulpit soon, although a speaker of that dimension will always be in demand for revivals and special needs. The Bishop has hinted that he might stay here in the Bennetton district."

Henry waited for Martha to say something, but when she didn't, he added, "He should marry soon. A man like that needs a good wife at home."

"But will he have a home? What if he stays on the circuit?"

"I kept riding circuit after we were married."

"That was different. I was able to live with my brothers' families."

"Dovey could live with us."

Martha sat up and stared at her husband in the sliver of moonlight that came through the window. "Dovey! Who said anything about her? She's only seventeen!"

"Same age you were."

Martha threw herself back on her pillow. "She's not ready."

"Why not? You've taught her everything about housekeeping. And she's a minister's daughter. She'll know what kind of life to expect."

Ha! Martha thought. No woman ever really knows what to expect. She sure hadn't. Not about her wedding night, or her first pregnancy, and certainly not about childbirth. And a minister's wife was held to a higher standard. She had to be thrifty, but still always have a well-turned-out family, no matter how quickly her children outgrew their clothes. She had to be prepared to serve meals at a moment's notice to anyone her husband brought home, from a bishop to a tramp to an entire family passing through the area. Sometimes all at once. She was expected to do her own cooking and cleaning without servants, to teach her daughters to read and do sums, to give up her own little vanities and pridefulness, to have unswerving faith through all her own doubts.

Martha remembered the bleak times, after little Nathan's death when he was six, falling off a wagon and dashing his head against a rock. And when Mary died of the fever, only two years old. Martha was expected to recover from these heartaches, and to be able to sit with any other woman who went through them and needed comforting.

Life as a minister's wife was not easy. And though Dovey had been a daily witness to her mother's responsibilities and had learned at least the basics of being a good homemaker, Martha seriously doubted whether she'd ever given thought to tackling those responsibilities on her own. Being a minister's daughter had not kept her from longing for pretty, fashionable dresses like the visitors to the church sometimes wore, or from glancing at herself a little too often in the mirror. No, Dovey was not ready. And she, Martha, was not ready either.

Over the next few days, the crowds began to arrive from every road and lane and path, until the grove, which had looked so vast when empty, began to seem like a gypsy camp. For the most part, those who had purchased titles to a lot set up camp right away, either with a covered wagon pulled into their allotted space, or a tent strung from two poles, or even a quickly built lean-to, with straw or wood shavings on the ground. Outside of the ring of purchased lots, there quickly grew a more helter-skelter arrangement of wagons, tents, and other rugged shelters. Some family groups pitched their tents together, in a sort of pavilion with sections for women and men.

On the very outskirts, the negroes made shelters of brush and colorful crazy quilts. Many families had brought two or three slaves. A woman to help with the cooking and minding the babies, and a man or two to help with the livestock – the cows, chickens, ducks, horses and mules that were part of the traveling parade.

Martha's brothers, who ran the McLeod Brothers dry-goods business, traveling the stagecoach road between Salisbury and Bennetton, brought a small crew of slaves to help finish clearing some of the unwanted pine trees, and to cut firewood, and make additional log seats in the area around the arbor. The darkies, same as the white folks, were excited to be at an event which promised so much drama and novelty in their otherwise routine lives.

The center of attention, of course, was the arbor. Here, the preachers began to reach out to their audiences. Prayers were said and songs were sung. Many in the congregation were quite familiar with a number of hymns, from frequent practice, but they also enjoyed learning new songs, led by song leaders who sang a line at a time for them to repeat. Hour after hour, people stayed in the arbor to hear the preachers read scripture and exhort the people to live better lives.

Henry, of course, was among the pastors speaking. Often, at revivals like this, he spoke early in the day, when people were bright and fresh, because his style was friendly and relaxed. "I'm not a thunderer," he'd explained once to his children. "I'm like the gentle rain that brings a fresh breeze on a hot day. I'm there to soften people up before the thunderers crack open their hardened minds and hearts."

The children had their own opinion of their father's 'gentle rain'. They had often felt it falling on their heads for hours at a time whenever he felt they needed correction. Sometimes they seemed disappointed that their father was rarely preaching at the high drama moments, when sinners fell on their knees and repented, but Martha thought this was exactly why she loved him so much, because he was such a quiet and compassionate man.

Henry believed it was important for the sinner to feel welcomed before he could open his heart. In the same way that he would invite a tramp home for a good dinner and a warm seat at the fire before he began speaking about his soul, Henry liked for camp meeting to be a place of welcome during the first day or two. Martha had known Henry to speak for three or four hours, speaking of the Lord's goodness, but also speaking directly to individuals in the crowd, thanking them for coming, mentioning any changes in the past year – a marriage, a new baby, the loss of a loved one – and reminding them that they were a community while they were there, and a community of believers when they returned to their homes, however distant. He always liked to speak to the children in the audience, telling them parables that they could understand but which also directed a lesson to their parents.

At some point, he would always tell a joke. "I'm not a man of great patience," he'd say, "and I often ask the Lord for help with that. I say 'Oh Lord, give me patience' when my mule refuses to pull the plow. And I say 'Oh, Lord, give me patience' when my horse throws a shoe twelve miles from home. And I say 'Oh, Lord, *please* give me patience' when I see my fields parched for rain, or my chicken coop raided by foxes, or my sweet potatoes developing the rot. And sometimes I cry out, O Lord, are You testing me? Are all these things happening just by chance, or are You trying to teach a lesson to a hard-headed man? I've tried to be good, I've tried not to swear when things go wrong, I've tried to be charitable and prayerful and I wonder why my life isn't easier. Why do things go wrong? Why is everything so much work? When will my prayers reach You? When are You going to ease my life? *When are You going to reward me, Lord*?'"

A brief pause then before he said, "And the good Lord looks down at me, shakes his head and sighs, and says, 'Oh Henry. Give me patience!'."

As the days went on, Martha could see Dovey falling under Reverend Edwards's spell. In fact, many women in the gathering became especially attentive when he was speaking. Some got the shakes, trembling with emotion until they could barely stay in their seat, their heads snapping from side to side, moaning and wailing. Others fainted, or cried, or kicked their feet and pulled at their hair. The men were not immune either. Several had already come down to the front and begged on their knees to be forgiven – for drinking, gambling, lusting, fornicating.

Dovey had remained quietly in her seat, but her eyes never left his face, and her hands kept turning one over the other while she rocked back and forth.

Camp meeting could pull forth some powerful emotions, and it was meant to be so, to break open a sinner's heart so that room could be made inside for the love of the Lord. Yet Martha was also aware that it could also create a love, or desire, for the preacher himself, as a man, not necessarily as the servant of God. She'd seen women who worshipped Henry, women who had made it clear that they would welcome a laying-on of hands in a completely different context than religious.

Henry had never strayed, she was sure, but then he was a middle-aged, mild-looking man – not unattractive, but not as magnetic as Reverend Edwards.

It could be a problem for a minister, being too good-looking. It could be a problem for his wife. Edwards had not paid Dovey any special attention, so far as she knew, but that didn't mean her worries could subside.

One afternoon, Reverend Edwards walked out to the area of the campground where the darkies were staying. Pretty soon, he was surrounded by a knot of them. He spoke, listened, and prayed over them. Negroes, free or slave, had always been welcomed at the Methodist church and at camp meeting, and Martha was glad to see him pay them some special attention.

However, when he returned, his face looked like a thundercloud, and he asked to speak with Henry. They walked a little way down the road, talking, and when Henry returned, he looked upset and asked where her brothers were.

"I'm not entirely sure. I saw John go toward the privies a few minutes ago. The rest are probably having lunch."

She watched as Henry and Reverend Edwards headed across the grassy area surrounding the arbor, over to the opposite side where Martha's brothers had taken two adjoining lots. After a moment, she decided to follow. By the time she caught up, the two preachers were deep in discussion with three of her four brothers.

As usual, Tom seemed to be speaking for them all. "I can't run my business without slaves," he was saying as she drew near. "They're needed, for helping with the wagons. I've got a darkie wheelwright and a cooper working full-time just keeping the wagons going and making barrels for shipping. I've put a lot of money into those darkies. Besides, it's against the law to free them."

"You could take them north to Ohio," Revered Edwards said.

"Oh, could I? Just like that! Give away some of my best men and then what? Maybe I should give them some of my best supplies too? A nice feather bed, or some china plates? Y'all don't understand business." Tom was getting red in the face. Martha wasn't surprised. He always was the bull-headed one. He squared up to the preacher, who stood a foot taller than him.

"We McLeods, going back two generations, have worked our tails off every day of our lives to build this business. We come down here on the Great Wagon road – and a mighty hard trip it was too – building up sales routes, to provide for our families, and yes, to support the church in all its need. We ain't just gonna give up our slaves and go back to grubbing in the dirt for an existence – "

"But you'd save your souls." Edwards reached out a hand to Tom's shoulder, but Tom pulled away. "I know it's not easy, what I'm saying, but you need to consider your immortal soul."

"The church allows slavery," Tom growled. "And the Bible is full of exhortations for slaves to bow to their masters, and for masters to treat fairly with their slaves. And I'll be da--. . . I defy you to find that I've mistreated my darkies. They're too expensive! I wouldn't beat them any more than I'd beat a good cow or horse!"

"But they're not cows or horses. They're men."

As Edwards again put forth his arguments, the men's voices rose and a small crowd began to gather. Out of the corner of her eye, Martha saw Dovey come up and work her way to the front. Edwards began praying loudly, asking the Lord to pour down His light and free Tom from the slavery of mistaken beliefs. Murmurs began to rise and some of the Negroes nearby began to back away uneasily. A few people exhorted Tom to give himself up to the Lord, others muttered that they didn't want their darkies to get any ideas.

Tom grew redder in the face, and his three brothers gathered shoulder to shoulder as if they were about to use their fists. Suddenly Dovey screamed and dropped to her knees. She wrapped her arms around Tom's legs and cried, "Please, Uncle, save your soul! Listen to Reverend Edwards! I don't want you to be condemned to Hell!"

She cried and wailed, falling to the ground. Tom, embarrassed, no doubt feeling stuck between a rock and a hard place, tried to help her up but she refused to stand until Edwards placed a gentle hand on her hair. She looked up then, with tears all over her face, and slowly got to her feet.

"Please, Uncle," she whispered one more time, and allowed herself to be led away by Martha and several other women.

That evening, Martha's brothers pulled out of their campsite and left, taking with them their slaves and their animals, and leaving behind some very uncomfortable feelings among many people there.

"It's getting to be a bigger and bigger problem," Henry said to Martha that night as they left the arbor. "I wouldn't be surprised if it split the Church in a few years. Almost everyone with a little money or land around here has at least a few slaves. And Tom's right. The law's against it even if they *wanted* to free them. I'll admit, I don't know the answer."

"What about Dovey? I can't say how shocked I was! She's put herself in a very bad position with her uncles.

And they've been so good to her, to all our children, over the years. Why, the very dress she's wearing was from cloth they brought all the way from Richmond."

"I was proud of her."

This brought Martha to a halt. Henry's eyes glowed and he gripped her arm. "That took courage! And conviction! And a sincere desire to stay right in the eyes of the Lord. Edwards was impressed, too. He asked about her afterward, wanted to make sure she was all right. I hope that tomorrow he'll speak with her. She's been too shy up until now, but maybe – "

"Henry, no! You have to give up that idea. She's too young, and I sure don't want a break in our family. If they married – what if she wants to go *his* way, and my brothers want to go theirs? I don't want to be pulled apart in the middle of all that."

Henry's voice took on a familiar stubborn tone. "I want my children to have Godly lives, Martha. And Edwards is a good man. If Dovey married him, and Peter and Matthew became preachers – "

"Matthew wants to be a merchant," she said flatly. "You know that."

"He's young."

So is Dovey!, she wanted to scream. Oh, how could it be possible that she and Henry were so far apart in their thinking on this? She blinked back the tears that wanted to fall, and simply said, "It's late. We need to get some sleep."

Henry helped her climb into the wagon where she and the girls and little Daniel had been sleeping each night, while the older boys and Henry slept underneath. It was lonely without Henry, but during the night it began to rain a little, so everyone crowded into the wagon together and she finally was able to rest when her husband curled against her.

As she feared, Reverend Edwards did make a point of seeking Dovey out the next day, and spoke with her for a long time. Dovey's face glowed as she looked up at him, and Martha knew she was falling in love. Martha had felt the same way when she first met Henry, entranced with him as a minister *and* as a man.

I should just put it in the good Lord's hands, she thought, and trust that all will end up as He intends. The trouble was, the Lord was a man, and Martha suspected He rarely saw things from a woman's point of view. But, she thought, I should have faith. I really should. I'm the minister's wife, for heaven's sake.

Little Daniel got a stomachache and then a fever, and she spent the next couple of days with him, dealing with chamber pot and bucket. She tried to get some ginger water into him, and bathed him with cool water from the spring. It was not unusual for people to pick up some illness when so many were crowded together, but after her experience with Mary, she took no chances and stayed close to her little one.

Every time the family returned to the tent for a meal, they were full of talk about the events in the arbor. It was better to them than the theatre, although for their father's sake, the children tried to reign in their laughter over some of the lamentations of the wicked.

"Mrs Ballard cried out that she was guilty of gluttony and sloth," Matthew whispered, "like it's a surprise to anyone."

Apparently, Reverend Edwards had not been scared off from speaking about slavery, and even held Dovey up as an example to them all. A few of the other preachers started to become uncomfortable about his remarks and on the day before camp meeting was to end, Henry and the others were called to a meeting with the trustees. For privacy's sake, the meeting was held at the church, a mile down the road. A couple of preachers from outside the district kept things rolling back at the arbor.

Daniel was finally feeling better, so Martha settled nearby in a shady spot out on a quilt, enjoying a bit of breeze and a few minute's respite while she listened to the preaching. From where she sat, she could keep an eye on the younger girls, playing cat's cradle, and Daniel, lying on his stomach, teasing ants with a blade of grass.

The older children were in the arbor, Peter and Dovey apparently listening intently, and Matthew drawing designs in the dirt with a stick. Although most everyone was aware of absence of the men central to the meeting, they still enjoyed the singing and Bible reading.

Late afternoon seemed to come too soon. With dinnertime approaching, she'd soon have to go back to the wagon and start cooking. She stood up to try to catch Peter's attention so he would go start a fire, but then she saw the trustees and preachers returning to the arbor, their faces grim. Reverend Edwards was not with them.

Bishop Poovey mounted the platform and held out his hands to ask for quiet. He announced that preaching would pause now so people could eat, and that they'd return for the evening session in about two hours. "Reverend Edwards will not be with us," he added, and let his gaze rove around the crowd. "We are sorry to lose him, but he has been called to another district and we must let him go. I'm sure you'll join me in prayers for his safe journey."

With that, he bowed his head and began to pray. From the corner of her eye, Martha spotted Dovey who got to her feet and stumbled out of the arbor. She hurried after her daughter and the two women made their way to the wagon. Dovey climbed up and hurled herself inside with a strangled sob and Martha, with one anxious glance at Henry, who had followed them, climbed in after her.

"They drove him off!" Dovey cried. She threw herself full-length on the pallet and buried her face in a pillow. "Pa and the others, they drove him off! I knew they would!" Martha crouched next to her, trying to raise her up, to push her hair back from her face and hold her close, but Dovey twisted away. "I hate them! They're just worried they might scare away the rich folk, like Mr Holland and Col. Graham, and all those folks who have slaves. How could they be so wicked?"

Martha tried again to hold her close, to hush her. She didn't want the whole campground to know their business.

Then Henry climbed in. He tried to reason with Dovey. "We're not saying he's wrong, daughter. We all agree that slavery can be a bad thing, in the wrong hands. But until we get direction from the Conference Charge, we're trying to hold off getting into deep discussions. Reverend Edwards understands that, but – "

"But you made him go anyway! You've *sent* him away – he wasn't called. You and the Bishop and all those other good, good men. Godly men! Holier than thou men. Y'all make me sick!" She threw herself back down and wailed loudly, kicking her feet.

"Now that's enough," Henry said, beginning to raise his voice, but Martha shook her head and asked him to let her handle it. He made a sour face but nodded and climbed out of the tent.

Martha sat next to Dovey and pulled her close. "Shhhh, shhhh," she whispered, rocking back and forth and smoothed her daughter's hair. "All will be well." Dovey shook her head and sobbed against her mother's throat. "I promise you, darling, all will be well."

"I love him, Mama."

"You don't even know him."

"I do! I do! He's a good man, a minister. We could be happy."

I don't want it for you, Martha thought fiercely, shocking herself to realize it. She felt disloyal to Henry in that moment, but it was true. She didn't want this life for Dovey. No privacy. Always being judged. She couldn't imagine it as worthwhile with any other minister than Henry – and at times, not even with him.

Sunday morning services drew the highest crowd yet, and the most converts. Multiple baptisms took place and christenings and even a few weddings. Henry was kept busy from early morning until late in the afternoon.

Martha did her best to get things organized so that they could leave before dark, but if they had to stay another night, it wouldn't matter. Dovey, wan and sad-eyed, did as she was asked, but maintained a mournful silence. She didn't speak to her father, nor respond when he attempted to speak to her, but otherwise she regulated her behavior in a manner that Martha couldn't help but admire. Her heart was broken, it was plain to see, but she was determined to be dignified about it. No doubt a sense of martyrdom was helping.

Martha's brother John, the youngest of the four and closest in age to her, came by with a small wagon and a couple of darkies, to help bring home her animals and anything else she wanted to send ahead.

"Maybe you could take the children," she suggested. "They'll be all right, one night by themselves." She didn't want to ask how Tom was holding up, but John volunteered that he'd calmed down once he heard that Reverend Edwards had moved on.

"I hope Henry ain't mad," John added. "We're real sorry if this has caused a ruckus. It never has before."

"I know. Don't worry. Everything works out for the best." She gave him a hug and told the children to go with their uncle, and to behave for Dovey and Peter. "They're in charge, now, so do what they say, and Papa and I will be back tomorrow."

After the children were gone, she was able to set things back in order inside their own wagon, to fold and pack and plan for the return home. Camp meeting was over. It was time to return to their lives.

That night, as she and Henry lay quietly beside each other in the wagon, he confessed his disappointment. "I thought this would be such a wonderful thing. A new start in our lives, a foundation for growth in our church, and a real time of closeness for our family. Nothing has turned out the way I'd hoped. The Bishop has had to go around putting out all sorts of fires within the community."

He sighed. "Everyone's riled up. Did you see those people today? About thirty of them came. You know who they were? Folks that heard of the commotion. And you know what they were hoping to see? A big dramatic showdown. I reckon they went back feeling mighty let down."

She waited, knowing he would continue.

"Preaching was flat as flapjacks today. I feel so . . . so . . . well, I guess Dovey's going to hate me all her life, now. She sees me as a fraud, a hypocrite. Maybe I am." He groaned and rolled on his back. "Maybe I am."

A surge of compassion ran through her. She spoke gently. "Don't take it so much to heart. These things happen. Dovey will get over it. She'll meet some other young man, and fall in love, and realize it was all for the best. All God's plan." She pulled her husband into her arms, the same way she'd pulled Dovey the day before, rubbed his back and smoothed his hair.

Look who's a hypocrite now, she thought. I never wanted Dovey to end up with that man, God's plan or not.

"Look," she said to Henry, pulling him closer into her arms, "you're disappointed right now in how things turned out, in the way that camp meeting ended. But try to take the long view. You and the other men have put something into place that might last a really long time. People will generally come away from this with some renewed faith, some little green shoots of trust and hope. Don't let this one thing drag you down. Think about the good you've done, and trust in that."

Gradually, she felt Henry relax and fall asleep. Tomorrow they'd go back home and soon the boys would go back to school and they'd all be busy with their usual activities. She'd be deep into preserving and pickling and keeping Dovey busy with housewifely chores. There was supposed to be a barn-raising next month, maybe Dovey would meet some other nice young fellow.

Martha had looked forward to the excitement of camp meeting, but she was glad it was over, and glad it could only come once a year. A person couldn't be caught up in spiritual rapture all the time. It was too exhausting and caused too much upheaval.

She took a deep sigh and stretched out, trying to relax enough to fall asleep. Just before she did, she had a vision of the years ahead, of all the camp meetings to come, and for a moment she wondered, how much could it really change things, after all?

The Small-Town Lawyer
1845

THE HAWK SAILED SILENTLY THROUGH THE SKY, *wings outstretched as he caught the air currents above the campground near Painter's Creek. The day was hot and humid, the air heavy, and the hawk glided in large, lazy circles above the wooden shacks and open grassy areas, above the animal pens and the path where people walked back and forth with buckets of fresh spring water. A smell of cooking food rose in the air as women stirred pots and children played games and babies slept in the sun. The hawk noted all this as he wheeled, intending to head for the river, but changing his mind at the sight of an infinitesimal movement down on the ground. He dove, snatched a squirrel off the field, and immediately rose again, to land on a lofty tree branch. With one claw wrapped around the squirrel's body, his powerful beak clamped down and ripped off the squirrel's head and most of its spine in one move. He tossed this aside and feasted on the still-warm guts and heart inside.*

For the hawk, this was a successful day. The squirrel, however, never knew what hit him.

Nathaniel Larkin looked out over the campground from the vantage point of his tent on the inner ring, facing the arbor. Morning prayer meeting had ended, and people were wandering back to their own tents or gathering in small clumps on the green, exchanging greetings and catching up with their neighbors. Several made their way over to his porch, knowing Nathaniel's history of hospitality, welcoming friends to try out his wife's cakes, pies, and biscuits with jam.

He always enjoyed the opportunity to hear what was on the minds of the good people of Painter's Creek and nearby Bennetton. It quickly became clear that the upcoming elections were stirring a lot of controversy.

Tate Humphreys argued mightily for improvements in roads, schools, and the railroad, while Old Man Loray insisted that there wasn't enough money, and that taxes should not be raised to cover those expenses. "I already work from can't-see to can't-see," he kept saying in his quavery old-man's voice. "And I hardly got a dollar to my name. I can't afford more taxes!" Several other men joined the argument.

"Now, now," Nathaniel said, gesturing for them to quiet down. "I know we each got our own worries. But this is camp meeting. You know Reverend Franklin discourages talk about politics here." He glanced around the dozen or so men gathered on his porch and, in a low voice, added, "He *discourages* it, but he don't forbid it. Especially not in the privacy of your own tents, one man to another."

The men shuffled their feet, eyes shifting from side to side, not entirely sure what Nathaniel was getting at. He pursed his lips and then said softly, "We each have our own views. I have clients among both the Whigs *and* the Democrats. So, I'm not gonna suggest how you should vote. But if you *want* to vote, I'm sending a wagon to Bennetton that day, and you're welcome to hitch a ride."

He turned to Tate Humphreys and asked about his prize heifer, Lilly. The men surrounding him gradually relaxed and got talking about other news – crops, the weather, recent events in that war down in Mexico.

Sometimes Nathaniel thought he'd have made a pretty fair judge. He had a gift for calming folks down and guiding them in the way they ought to go. In the meanwhile, he was just a small-town lawyer, handling wills and contracts and petty larceny. But even a small-town lawyer had a sphere of influence and he could initiate a chain of events if he wanted. And sometimes, as much could be accomplished with a wink, as with a handshake.

The men gradually wandered away, off to their own tents for dinner, and Nathaniel went for a walk. One of his neighbors fell into step alongside him. Retty Green was short, plump, and red-faced, and he always seemed slightly out of breath. Nathaniel quietly shortened his stride so the smaller man could catch up. "How's the farm doing?" he asked.

"Oh, fine, just fine," Retty replied, gasping slightly. "I wanted to thank you again for all your help with those trespassing charges. Lonnie never meant any trouble, you know. He was just having a lark."

"He killed Harrison's goat."

"But he didn't mean to! How was he to know that goat would fall off the barn roof? They're supposed to be such great climbers, goats are. I'm happy to pay for it."

Nathaniel stopped and peered down at Retty. Looming over and peering down were part of his lawyer's bag of tricks, skills that he could use in or out of the courtroom. "Harrison thinks your boy deserves to be taught a lesson. I can't say I disagree. This isn't his first time pulling such a prank; it's just the worst one so far. He's hanging with the wrong crowd."

Retty stood in front of Nathaniel, twisting and turning the hat he held in front of his chest. "I know. I know. But that talk you gave to him, that helped a lot. I truly believe he's changing for the better. Says he wants to go to the military institute in Lexington, and I'm working to get him in there."

"Lexington, huh?" Nathaniel pretended to reflect a moment, and then said, "Tell you what. I'll get my father to write a letter of recommendation. He's an old friend of the superintendent over there. But Lonnie has to keep his nose clean. Our little talk last month has convinced me he can do whatever he sets his mind to, that boy, if he'll just settle down. I'll take care of it."

"Thank you! Thank you! And tell your father, soon as slaughtering time comes, I'll send over a couple of hams. You know I'm famous for 'em around here. And I'll send one to your house too! Thanks a whole lot!"

The red-faced, sweating fat man scuttled away and Nathaniel chuckled softly as he continued on down toward the spring. Retty Green was about as insignificant as they came, but his boy Lonnie was surprisingly sharp, and Nathaniel did love a good ham.

Later that week, Nathaniel sat on the porch of the tent with his father and pondered the moon and the stars and the small rustling creatures of the night. "Nice clear night," his father said, rocking slowly, the end of his cigar glowing in the dark. Nathaniel nodded in agreement. There were a few things he and his father agreed upon. The value of a dutiful wife. The importance of choosing a son's path in life early. The maintenance of power. "Always know where your man lives," his father liked to say. "Where his gut really resides. That's the key. They say power flows from above, and the further downhill it flows, the more diluted and muddy it gets. I disagree. Power comes from one man, an individual, who exerts his will. *Exerts. His. Will.* Look at that fellow who's running the newspaper in Raleigh. He's done more for the Democratic party than ten congressmen. He'll go far."

Nathaniel just nodded, leaning back in his chair with his legs stretched out before him and his thumbs hooked into his vest pockets. His father's voice droned on and on, nothing that Nathaniel hadn't heard before. It was almost like hearing a bedtime lullaby. He and his brothers had grown up on it, and all had fallen in line with the old man's decisions, at least outwardly. Nathaniel had his own opinions here and there, and his own way of exerting his will. He'd made many a quiet visit to various tents over the past week, just reminding folks of favors done.

Friday would be Election Day. All the eligible taxpayers were able to vote for governor and members of the House of Commons, but only those men owning more than 50 acres of land could vote for state senators. Nathaniel and his brothers, thanks to their father's largesse, each owned farms of at least two hundred acres, while their father retained a hundred acres and the family homestead for himself. Nathaniel paid little attention to his land, having secured a reliable tenant who paid handsomely in produce, meat, and an annual rent. But he certainly valued his vote.

On Election Day, he and his father and his brother, Mark, rode together to the courthouse. Mark was eleven years the elder. Like their father had been, he was a justice on the state supreme court and spent most of the year in Raleigh, but he always came home for camp meeting and to vote.

Mark held the reins as the old carriage swayed and jiggled, going down the road. The senior Mr Larkin, too old nowadays to ride several miles horseback, talked in a careless way about the various candidates. When he mentioned Gordon Millbank, one of the men running for state senator and owner of one of the nearby iron foundries, Nathaniel couldn't stop himself. "That bastard," he spat.

"Whoa, Son," his father said, with a grin. "I don't like to hear that kind of talk. We know nothing about the gentleman's mother!"

"You've always hated him," Mark added, giving a touch of the whip to the horses. "Just because he beat you at everything in school and stole your girl, that's no reason to hate a man." But he, too, grinned.

Nathaniel glanced at Mark from under his brows. As oldest brother, Mark had always taken precedence at everything, even deciding – along with their father – that there was no purpose served by having Nathaniel go into politics. He should just keep his law practice going and watch out for the family interests in the county. They figured that was enough. Meanwhile, Mark loved being a bigwig and he made sure to remind Nat of it whenever they were together.

"Wish I had something on him," Nathaniel muttered. "I'd wipe that smug look off his face."

"Don't be a sulky child," his father replied. "If he serves our purpose in the state senate, that's all we need, and he's always been a loyal Democrat. He'll vote the party line."

Like I care? Nathaniel thought. But he only said, "Can you guarantee it? I don't trust him."

Mark gave a short bark of laughter. "Don't worry. He knows on which side his bread is buttered." He turned to give Nathaniel a long, evaluating look. "Millbank will be elected. He's an ass, but he'll be elected. Efforts have been made."

"You've done something? Paid someone off?"

"Let's just say everything moves better with a little grease."

Oh, yes, Nathaniel thought. He sat back in his seat and stared ahead. Just as he'd thought. Mark was bankrolling that scurvy son-of-a-bitch Millbank, propping up his iron foundry expansion, helping that jackass to succeed, damn it, and expecting plenty of benefits in return.

Things got lively as they neared the courthouse. Quite a few men were already liquored up, thanks to some of the candidates' welcome centers. There wasn't a woman to be seen anywhere about, all of them too aware of how rowdy the voting crowd could get. A few fistfights had already occurred, and a lot of shouting.

Nathaniel wondered where Millbank's wife was at that moment. Back home at the red-brick house near the foundry? Or here, behind the lace curtains of the local hotel? Or maybe with a clutch of other wives, drinking tea and sharing gossip at the home of the local banker or other leading citizen. His own wife, Louise, was alright. She did as she was told, but she was not Florinda Millbank, the true love of Nathaniel's life.

His gut twisted in knots. He absolutely hated Gordon Millbank.

Nathaniel and his father and brother did not stick around after voting. They had a long ride back to the camp meeting where their wives were waiting. It would be days before the results would be known for the local elections, and weeks before they'd get the state results.

Mark was in a good mood during the ride, his face ruddy from brandy. He joked and laughed most of the way, despite getting little or no response. Their father nodded off to sleep, made drowsy by the motion of the carriage. Nathaniel at last brought up the subject highest on his mind.

"So, you're sure you've got influence over Millbank, huh? I bet that cost you a pretty penny."

"He'll be in my debt a long, long while." Mark belched and seemed to recover a modicum of sobriety. "Don't worry about it. That's your trouble, little brother. You worry. You worry about what people think of you. Do they respect you? Do they think you're a good man? Do they *like* you? What a load of crap." He belched again and kept going. "No man got power by worrying. You've got to be ruthless in this business, my boy. Eat or be eaten – but you don't have the stomach for it. You're too soft. Too nice. You always were. So just keep happy being a big fish in a small pond, a nice small-town lawyer, and collect your fees and your hams." He turned to grin at Nathaniel. "Yeah, Pa told me. Seriously, Nat? A ham? That's all you got in return for a favor? You're a fool, Nat, a big soft booby. Millbank could chop you in half. No wonder pretty little Florinda married him instead of you."

The rest of the ride back to the campground was made in stone-cold silence. Mark left, and Nathaniel helped his father to bed, a simple pallet on a wide shelf of the tent. When that was done, he went out on the porch and settled in the rocking chair, there to contemplate the moon and stars and the unseen creatures of the night.

As expected, the vote count took weeks. Meanwhile, that newspaper fellow in Raleigh kept predicting the results, sure that the Democrats would trounce the Whigs. As it turned out, however, Governor Graham was re-elected on the Whig ticket, and several other Whigs got voted in too – including Gordon Millbank's opposition.

Yes, Millbank was out, although by a close margin. A few precincts reported voting irregularities, and it seemed that liquor had indeed flowed freely, but that was nothing unusual and no charges were filed.

On the evening that the news came out, Nathaniel and Mark joined their father in the parlor of the old homestead. Mark reread sections of the newspaper account out loud, with increasing bitterness. Their father puffed angrily at his cigar and occasionally pounded his fist on the arm of his chair.

"Can't say I'm sorry," Nathaniel remarked.

"Shut the hell up, Nat," Mark said, scowling. "You're not the one out all that money." He threw the newspaper into the fireplace, sending up a cloud of sparks.

Nathaniel quietly got to his feet and went out on the porch. This was the time of evening that he normally admired the moon and the stars, but the only creature of the night out there was Lonnie Green, stepping from behind the barn. "You got the money?" Lonnie asked, and Nathaniel handed him a packet, along with an envelope.

"Here's your money, and here's your letter to the Institute," he said. "With my father's compliments." Lonnie smirked, and took both items. Nathaniel added, "Come see me when you graduate. There's always work for a man like you."

Nathanial turned and went back into the house. For him, it had been a successful day. He returned to the parlor to sit quietly and rock, while his father and brother stared at the fire, stunned at the turn of events.

They just never knew what hit them.

The Young Lady of Fashion
1852

Saturday, July 31

Dear Lucy,

We have safely arrived at the spa hotel in Painter's Creek. Oh, my dear, it is so disappointing! Mama and Papa tell me it will look better in the light of day, but right now all I see is that my room is *tiny,* with no separate dressing room, and the washstand and commode just behind a small screen. *C'est terrible!*

You know how I have been dreaming of this spa all year, with visions that it would be like Bath in Jane Austen's *Persuasion,* but I have been terribly deceived. Maybe Papa will decide that it's not worth staying. I can only hope.

My pink skirt is terribly crushed by the long ride in the carriage. You were right.

With much love,
Evadena

Sunday, August 1

Dearest Lucy,

First thing, Papa marched us off to church services. But what a church! Apparently, our visit has coincided with some kind of annual revival meeting and we attended services at an outdoor arbor and sat on *log seats*! I could barely listen to the minister for fear of retaining splinters, or worse. You should see this place, surrounded by these crude *huts* where people live for two weeks while the revival is going on. Inside the arbor, the preachers stand on a raised platform, and the women sit to one side of the aisle and the men on the other, with the black house servants at the back and the field hands way out on the grass. I will say the singing is quite nice, even though they do not have an organ, just a man leading the singing one line at a time. Everyone sings with great gusto, not like our mincing little murmurs at church at home.

The preaching is forceful. I was quite terrified that the minister, a small man with a great booming voice, might suddenly point his finger at me and ask if I was saved. He actually did that to others there! He could probably have accused me of vanity, because I must say, I looked very well. Especially in that crowd where some of the women wore clothes five to ten years out of fashion. Truly, I do not lie. And the sad thing is, you could tell it was their best finery.

I was quite happy to get back to the spa, which consists of two large white buildings with verandas, a couple of smaller buildings, and numerous cabins and outbuildings. They are all clustered around the various springs, where the mineral water bubbles up and smells like *rotten eggs*. I do not think they will get *me* into that water, nor drink it neither. A lot of the other visitors are old, even older than Mama and Papa. There is one young man, Mr. Gates, who is not terribly good-looking, but he dresses well and is gentlemanly. Papa says he's looking to buy one of the iron foundries in the area. He's not much to write about, but at least it's someone to *practice* on.

The food is good.

Papa is calling, I will write more later.

Hastily,
Evadena

Wednesday, August 4

My dear Lucy,

Oh, how I miss you. If you were here, we could talk and laugh and make merry. As it is, I follow Mama around and think how bored I am, and reread Persuasion, and sigh with *ennui*. Papa has been in the mineral pond every day. All the gentlemen go in the morning, right down into the pond which has large rocks around the edges, and steam rising in the morning. Apparently, they just float around with servants to bring them cool drinks and light their cigars, which Papa says they do, right in the water. He likes it. He comes back quite jovial.

Mama has gone bathing once. The ladies do not go into the pond, they sit in a sort of large wooden tub or almost you could call it an extra-large cask, with benches around the inside of it, and the warm mineral water comes in through a trough. Mama says it's very refreshing and she warns me that she wants me to try it. She says you get used to the smell. I say, no thank you.

In the afternoon, we sit on the veranda, and a lady teaches us new ways to embroider or crochet or knit; anything you want. I am working on a new collar for my green silk. You will love it. The veranda is nice, there's shade and a good breeze most days. When there's no breeze, a servant operates a rather interesting arrangement of fans and pulleys. The older ladies gossip, but there's no younger ladies for me except one rather sour old maid of 23. Her name is *Tirzah*. Did you ever? She bats her eyes and flirts with Mr. Gates, who tries to be polite in return. It is quite disgusting to watch her.

Dinner is always quite good. When the ladies retire, we go down to a sort of summer house, called a gazebo, and have lemonade and watch the fireflies. They burn citronella candles to keep away the skeeters, but it is very boring. But after the men come down, a small colored orchestra plays music and that is pleasant. I wish they had a ballroom, but they don't, and I must fight to hide my yawns.

The girl who cleans my room is a very pretty mulatto. Her name is Rosa and she has much better manners than Zia. I'm quite weary with Zia these days. I believe she has picked up an admirer from among the servants here and keeps finding excuses to go down to the kitchens. It would be just my luck for her to fall in love again, as she does every time we travel, and then I have to put up with her sulks when we return home. Last time, she kept sniffling until finally I had to slap her. You know how I hate having to resort to such a thing. Why does she drive me to it?

More soon,
Your Evadena

Sunday, August 8

Lucy, *mon cher,*

I'm sorry I haven't written more. I expect you'll probably get all these letters at one time anyway – they only pick up and deliver mail here EVERY OTHER DAY.

We went to church service at that amazing arbor again this morning. Oh, you wouldn't believe the uprorius behavior – I was quite shocked. Women screaming and crying and pulling their hair loose, men getting down on their knees and vowing to give up liquor, not to mention babies crying and even dogs fighting in the aisles. It was as good as a minstrel show. I believe I shall be quite prayerfully devout in church when I return home to *civilization.*

I did finally try the mineral bath and, my goodness, it was surprisingly pleasant. They give us these old chemises to wear (the water stains them an orange-ish color, so I certainly don't want to wear one of my own nice chemises) and the water is warm, which you'd think wouldn't be nice because the weather is *hot,* but when you get out, you feel quite refreshed. They have a canopy over it for shade, and screens all around for privacy. While we are in the water, we drink cool ginger lemonade and just relax and sort of *float.* I've never been in water up to my neck before (when seated) and it makes you feel weightless. After, we rinse off with fresh spring water which washes away the egg smell, and have our hair dressed by this woman who comes to the hotel every day and introduces us to all kinds of fancy *coiffures.* We are quite elegant the rest of the day and play card games and all types of parlor games. When I return home, I'll teach them to you.

I must tell you – I almost decided on selling Zia. She was getting so impertinent, it couldn't be overlooked, and quite jealous of Rosa, who is so sweet and really *understands* how to be helpful without being familiar. I asked Papa to see if the hotel would let me do a trade, but he said no, he was sure Rosa would be too expensive. But I *threatened* Zia with being sold and she cried and begged me (on her knees, to be sure!) not to, so I decided to be gracious about the whole thing and told her I'd forgive her one more time. I gave her a new kerchief and we have entirely made up. I'm sure she will be much more obedient now – *for a while.*

Tomorrow we leave for Bennetton, about ten miles away over some more of these horrible rutted roads. I hope they have better stores there. Painter's Creek only boasts three stores and, I can tell you, they are pretty sad excuses. The only thing I bought was that kerchief for Zia and a new pair of garters. They are blue. After Bennetton, we are headed for Asheville, and I hope to Heaven after that we will return home. I miss you and all my dear friends.

With all my love,
Evie

PS Would you ever believe it? Mr Gates and old Tirzah are *engaged! Quel dsastre!*

The Amputee
1866

GIDEON JOHNSON AND LITTLE GORDY regarded the rather skinny chicken looking back at them. "She won't lay still," Gordy said, frustrated and angry. As if to confirm his statement, the chicken again tried to get up off the chopping block, kicking her feet, working her wings to get free, twisting her head into an upright position and staring at them with one eye then the other. She looked indignant about the whole situation.

"Think it through, son," Gideon advised.

The boy thought it through. He gripped the hatchet in his right hand more tightly and with his other arm held the chicken firmly in place. He thought a bit more, and then said, "I gotta wring her neck first."

"That's it. Now remember what I told you. Hard and quick. Don't make her suffer."

Gordy set the hatchet down, put a hand to the chicken's neck and quick as he could gave it one hard twisting pull, then dropped her to the ground. She flapped about for a bit and then went limp.

"Good boy! Now finish up—your Ma's waiting." With that Gideon turned away, knowing his son needed to recover his dignity after making his mistake. At nine years he might be a little young for slaughtering a chicken, but these days boys didn't get to be young for very long.

He headed into the house, unconsciously rubbing the stump of his right arm. It often ached just above the missing elbow and for the millionth time he said to himself, *if only*. If only I still had an elbow with a little stump below, enough so's I could carry things in the crook of it.

But there was no use in thinking it. Might as well, while he was at it, wish for his right hand back. Might as well wish for those missing toes on his left foot...or his old job, his dead brother, his infant daughter he'd never got a chance to see. He sighed heavily.

All those years lost to the war. But *if only* didn't get the chores done.

As he entered the kitchen his wife paused in her sweeping and turned a smile his way. "You better get shaved," Milly said. "You want Preacher to see you looking like that?" The sunshine from the window behind her outlined the high round belly under her apron where the new baby was growing. "What do you think he wants with you?"

"You know as much as I do," Gideon replied, although he had a pretty good idea. It just wasn't something he wanted to think about.

As it turned out, he was right. Almost as soon as he arrived, Preacher said, "I want to get camp meeting up and running for this summer. And I'd like you to join the Trustees. It's a big responsibility, but everyone respects you, and you'd add a good level head to the mix."

"I don't know, Preacher. I'd have thought the days for camp meeting were over. People are lucky if they can make it to church service once every couple of months when you come through on circuit. I doubt there's anybody round has time to spend a whole week just praying – "

"*Just praying?!* Why, listen to yourself! Right now is when we *need* camp meeting more than ever!" Preacher leaned forward, thrusting his face toward Gideon's, the scar across his forehead and right eyelid suddenly vivid. He'd been a stocky man before the war, and now loose jowls hung down like a hound dog's. "People have lost hope. More'n a year's gone by since the war ended, and where are we? Some's worse 'n ever. Broken down. Fed up. Maybe turning to hard liquor and whoring and gambling when they don't even have the wherewithal to feed their kids."

He stared at Gideon with that one good eye and little flecks of spittle gathered in the corners of his mouth. "It's time to shake 'em up," he continued. "Time for 'em to bring the Lord back into their hearts and minds so they can get back to doing the things they need to do. By God, I'd like to take 'em all by the scruff of their necks and shake some sense into 'em. Don't you see, Gideon? We *need* camp meeting. *Amen to that*! So now I ask you – take on this calling, help get this thing a-goin'."

"I'm just a farmer, these days," Gideon said. "And a pretty poor one at that. Who am I to tell folks to drop what they're doing and leave their farms to spend a week at camp meeting? Half the folks round here don't even have shoes to bring them that far."

"Then by heaven, we'll find a way to bring 'em. Send out wagons and mules, carry in the sick and the old ones, and the widowed and orphaned. *We'll bring 'em in.*"

"I'll go." The words, spoken softly, came from behind Gideon. He turned to see Milly, standing there in the doorway. Out of modesty, she had made herself scarce once Preacher arrived, but now she ignored the niceties. "I want to go. I want to see my friends. And your ma and pa, Gideon, they'll want to go. Might be their last chance, you never know. I want Gordy to experience something outside of this farm. You can do what you want, stay here at home if you feel you must. But the rest of us are going."

After all that, Gideon felt he had no choice, so during the next few months he met with other trustees and set dates. He found folks willing to help. Some scythed the tall grass in the passways, others fixed up a couple of tents damaged by storms, and a few more cleared the mess left behind when stragglers from Stoneman's Raid spent the night at the campground in April of '65. The Yankees had tried to set the place afire when they left, but fortunately a light rainfall the night before left everything too damp to burn very much. Still, there was charred wood to clear away and boards to remove where the Yankees had carved nasty words and pictures.

Word passed quickly about the plans for camp meeting and nearly every man in the area managed to put in at least a little work toward getting things ready. Gideon was astonished at the generosity of those who had so little for themselves, offering to help procure such things as straw for the tent floors and grain for the animals and kindling for cook fires.

Everyone pitched in. People were starved for the company of old friends and far-flung relatives. They longed for something from 'before' that would remind them of the good old days and were willing to move heaven and earth to get there.

They began arriving the first Saturday in August. They came in farm wagons and buggies, on mules and on foot, families helping families and an organized group of men fanning out in every direction to bring those who couldn't find a means of getting there on their own. The folks brought along cows and chickens, fresh produce from their gardens, and baked goods and preserves. They brought along quilts and rocking chairs and porch swings, beloved things that had been passed down through generations.

On move-in day, Gideon watched as people arrived from near and far. There was old lady Barker, 85 if she was a day, and right close by, his own daughter, Lacie, a bit more than a month old. Every soul arriving was ragged and underfed, and some sickly – but they had come. A good many of the men had either a pinned-up sleeve like his own or an empty trouser leg or were on crutches. Some had eye patches or bad scars. Even so, they all acted cheerful and excited, hurrying to greet each other with open arms.

There were a lot of missing faces, too, but these were acknowledged with respectful voices and warm embraces for those remaining. Gideon's Ma and Pa were there, excited to see their old friends, sloughing off the weight of the war years with every move they made to get their tent cleaned up and ready to occupy.

Milly happily showed off the new baby, and as for little Gordy, he was in heaven, having other little boys to run with. They swarmed over the campground and down to the spring like a pack of puppies, wrestling and laughing and falling all over themselves. Gideon saw the joy on his son's face and thought, well, at least he's happy, for now.

As for himself, he just felt isolated from all the enthusiasm, as though he were watching something from far away.

Their family tent was in the first row, west side. His grandfather had leased the lot in the first round of sales, back in 1830. And in '33, put up a two-room wooden shack with open-slatted sides, a shingled roof, and a sleeping loft. Nothing fancy, but a heap better than the canvas tent they'd used before, when camp meeting was held at various locations.

That evening when his Ma had settled in her rocker on the freshly swept, hard-packed dirt floor of the 'porch' in front of their tent, she got to remembering. "First camp meeting I ever went to was 1828, when they used to hold it at the grove by Tuttle's Church. We brought the canvas from Grandpa's covered wagon to use as a tent and slept on pallets on the ground. But that ol' canvas was so old it had tiny pinholes all through it, and when it rained – oh my, did we get wet! I wadn't more'n 16 or 17 then. Had a new dress with purple flowers. Lordy, I was proud of that dress."

For a moment Gideon could see her as a girl, shy and tremulous, unaware of all the ways life had of waiting in her path to stomp her down. She brushed at her apron and continued. "But when the preaching commenced, and the preacher said we should throw away all vanity, why I got right down on my knees and called the Lord to save me from the Devil's hold. Ma said I spoke in tongues and got the shakes. But all I could remember afterward was having to wash the mud out of that dress!" She smiled at the memory. "And later on, I met Jacob here, when camp meeting moved here to Painter's Creek. Didn't do no shouting nor shaking that time – just prayed with all my soul that he'd like me too. And I reckon he did. We married that Christmas, in 1830."

On Sunday, the preaching got underway, three ministers taking turns with a heck of a lot of singing between times. Gideon didn't approach the arbor at all. He had designated himself and several other men to keep an eye out for rowdies. A group this size tended to attract the kind of folk that showed up with their own kind of purpose. Maybe wanted to sell spirits or get a dice game going at the fringes of the property. And throughout the county there were some men who had taken to relying on a snort of whiskey to help them face postwar life.

With this in mind, he had organized a rotating order of men for keeping guard in the east field, where their livestock was held. The county had largely been spared the ravages of a Union troop marching through, since the fighting had come no closer than Bentonville, well over a hundred miles away. Even so, nearly every farm thereabout had suffered some kind of thievery from deserters, or wanderers, or the just plain desperate.

He took his turn in the rotation of guard. He couldn't hold a shotgun but he could sure raise a hue and a cry should anything happen. Between times, he roamed the campground to keep an eye on things, unable to sit still. Seemed like no matter where he went, he could still hear the singing and exhortations to repent.

In the evening, some of the men gathered to talk. They smoked their sad corncob pipes stuffed with rabbit tobacco, though the stuff wasn't good for much except keeping the midges away. No one wanted to talk about the war, and by common consent most even avoided speaking about politics. Too many of their womenfolk and children were within earshot, and nowadays a man couldn't talk politics without commencing to cuss. So instead, they talked about the good old days when they'd been kids running around the campground, like little

Gordy and his friends, catching minnows in the creek, chasing fireflies, and competing to see who could run the fastest or jump the farthest.

"I remember the time we found that ol' barrel," Joe Nixon said. "Remember how we took turns rolling down the hill in it? Till we all got sick." Gideon remembered that year. He'd been eight or nine and had mastered the art of barrel-walking out behind the north side tents until one of the ladies jerked the barrel away and began chasing them all with a switch in hand. She kept after them till they got themselves back to the arbor. He could still see that woman in his mind's eye. Could even hear her screeching. "*Y'all s'posed to be at the preaching!*"

They'd all laughed and snuck away again. Back then, attending preaching was the last thing on his mind.

And it was still the last thing he wanted to do, even now, but it was certainly foremost in his mind. As a trustee, he was supposed to set a good example. His Milly's sorrowful gaze didn't help any. She wanted him at the arbor, though the women sat in one section and the men in another.

But he just couldn't do it. Since the war, he just couldn't feel like any kind of Christian. Not after the things he'd seen and done.

As the week went on, the weather grew warmer and steamier. Even when it rained, things didn't cool off. Steam rose off the roofs of the shacks and left a weight in the air like a wet sheet over his face. In the arbor, folks were constantly fanning themselves with whatever came to hand – a fancy lady's fan carefully preserved since before the war, a spray of magnolia leaves, or small leafy branches, or maybe just a folded paper. He had spotted one fella with a fan made from a forked stick and a handkerchief.

Gideon still avoided going into the arbor, but he prowled round the edges, keeping an eye on things. Not everyone stayed in the arbor all day. Even preachers sometimes needed a break. And just about always you could spot a group of ladies sitting with their sewing on their laps and gossiping in the shade with their babies and younger children, while the bigger children gathered in gangs to play games in the passways.

Between the sermons, the men moved in and out of the arbor according to their urges. Maybe played horseshoes, or a game of mumblety-peg on the benches between the tents. They talked and laughed, enjoying the rare break from their chores. It was in the evenings that their talk turned serious – farming problems, the shortage of supplies, the shortage of cash, the shortage of manpower. Isaac Lester said, "If'n I could just get a couple of farmhands, I could manage. All I've got's me and little Luke. And him only twelve." The short supply of working men was an acute problem, affecting them all. Not enough able-bodied men, and although few of the farmers in the area had ever kept a large number of slaves, having one or two field hands would have made all the difference.

"Well, I have my brothers, 'cept for Grady of course," Frank Jenkins said, "but I ain't got a mule, my plow's busted and my well's gone dry. We're hauling water from the creek." One by one, other men spoke of the hurdles they were facing, some of them shame-faced that they hadn't been able to solve their problems on their own, and others resentful because they thought other folk had a much easier time of it.

A few joked about their problems. Hiram Morris said since his foot had been shot off, he'd given up his dream of being the end man in a minstrel show. And Ira

Dugger, known before the war for his high-stepping bays and fancy carriage, claimed he still had the best trotters in the county. "You should see them," he said. "Two grasshoppers and a bay leaf. I challenge any of you to put up a finer matched pair."

The men all laughed, and Gideon felt emboldened to joke about his arm. "There're so many rabbits and deer taking over my place I'd be in fresh meat forever – if I could shoot'em!" He pantomimed taking a shot with a rifle, his empty sleeve making the point for him. "Now if the blamed things would just *stand still*!"

Roddy Tucker, in the midst of the chuckles that followed, turned serious and suggested putting down a salt lick for deer and setting himself up behind a fallen log to steady the end of the rifle. "Lord knows we shot a lot of Yankees that way, even when we was wounded ourselves. From behind a fallen tree or the bottom of a ditch."

From the bottom of a ditch. Gideon closed his eyes, fighting the memories. Two Yankees just swimming in the pond – not looking for any trouble, just laughing and splashing in the water. Their clothes and rifles on the grassy bank. Then the bright red blood on their pale skin as he shot them both dead.

He jumped to his feet, murmured an excuse, and headed toward the privies. Inside one of those dark smelly upright coffins he waited till the trembling stopped. Waited for his head to clear. Better to suffocate in the foul air of the privy than let anyone see this sweat running down his face or his hand shaking, or to hear the moaning he could not keep back, no matter how tightly he clamped his good hand over his mouth. Shooting an enemy soldier on a battlefield was one thing. A man could harden his mind to that. It was the other times, the times he had to kill a man who meant him no harm but was simply in his way that kept coming back to haunt him. That sentry, asleep at his post. The almost grown boy in the cornfield...not even a soldier, just a kid on a farm. But in the wrong place at the wrong time, and about to raise a hue and cry.

And his friend Jeffries, moaning in pain with a bullet in his guts. He could still feel what it was like, holding Jeffries when a patrol went through. Holding him down, muffling his groans, and then when the danger had passed, looking down and seeing his buddy's agonized death stare. These things and all the others...things you couldn't do and still call yourself a Christian.

He heard voices outside the privy and knew that people were getting ready to call it a day. He mopped his face with his sleeve and stepped out, walking quickly with his head down, gulping in fresh air.

Back at his tent, he found Milly had Gordy out back, washing his face and hands and feet from a bucket of water. The boy looked to be already half asleep. Gideon carried him to the straw-stuffed mattress tick and covered him with a sheet, then kissed Milly goodnight before she climbed up to the loft with their baby, alongside his mother.

He washed himself then, and after changing into an oft-mended nightshirt, stretched out on the pallet next to his father. The old man seemed to be asleep, but after a bit he spoke into the quiet and calm of the darkness.

"Son, you missed some powerful preaching this evening."

"Sorry," Gideon said. After a pause, he added, "I had other things to do."

"Not as important as this. How can the Lord help you if you turn away? Think it through."

Think it through. Seemed like he'd been hearing those words from Pa all his life. Words of wisdom. But right now, the last thing he wanted was to think things through. The more thinking he did, the worse the future looked.

He had no cash money. His father was growing older, while Gordy was still so young. His farm needed many things he could not get. And the state legislature. It was in chaos – such chaos there was no way of telling where it was headed. Was there any way forward? If so, he wasn't able to see it. Maybe he could have made it all work if he still had his right arm. If *only* he still had an elbow with at least a bit of a stump below…

Saturday dawned red and humid. "Red sky in the morning, sailors take warning," Milly murmured as she fried eggs over the cookfire behind the tent. "Better see what you can do for the animals, in case it rains hard later."

Gideon agreed and poured himself a cup of bitter chicory coffee. It tasted foul but at least it gave him something to do so he didn't have to talk. Milly sensed his mood and kept chattering idly about folks she'd seen this week, noting who had babies, who'd married, who'd moved away or moved back from some wartime refuge.

The baby woke before they finished eating. Milly began nursing her, humming quietly, an apron thrown over her shoulder for modesty. She said, "Good preaching yesterday. I felt so moved…felt strong again, Gideon. Strong enough for anything! I know things are going to get better."

"No, they won't."

"But if you'd just come to the arbor, listen to Preacher – "

"Stop, Milly. I can't do it. To sit there and listen, knowing all the time – " He choked off the words, but inside he continued: *Knowing all the time that God has turned His face away. And why wouldn't He? Surely by now the Lord could see how disgusting people are. I disgust myself.*

Milly might guess what he was thinking, but he felt it better not to say it. And since there was nothing to say, he got to his feet and headed for the east field. The men had rigged up chicken pens and a brush shelter for the cows back before camp meeting began, but with a storm maybe coming through, they'd best be battening things down a bit.

A few were already there, including Huck Findlay, who before the war had made saddles and harnesses. And there was Josiah Gates, owner of the small iron foundry. Unlike Gideon, these two had been able to go back to their trades, though it meant some business dealings with Yankees. But no one around needed a one-armed wrong-handed bookkeeper. He was just plain out of luck. If it weren't for his folks, who still had their farm and could offer Gideon and his family a home, where would they be right now?

The men worked together and soon rigged a tarp over the chicken pens. And Huck provided some old leather strapping for firming up the brush shelter. As they continued with the tasks, Gideon became aware that Huck was staring at his pinned-up sleeve and the way he hitched up his shoulder to balance a large branch until it was strapped into place. Gideon flashed him a bitter look and Huck's face flushed a dull red.

"Sorry," he muttered. "Listen, I been meaning to talk with you 'bout something me and Harold Beam have come up with." He broke off then, watching as

Josiah finished the rigging, and Gideon moved away, not acknowledging Huck's words.

Last thing he wanted was to get involved with any other projects. All week long, the men had been talking on and on about the needs of the county, or ways they could help the widows and orphans, maybe get the school going again, maybe set up some kind of roster so they could trade labor and goods and skills.

The way Gideon saw it, all that preaching gave them incentive, and now they wanted to be Good Samaritans. But he'd had enough. All week, and indeed these last few months, he'd been helping the community. And he'd had enough. He was ready to get back to the farm and do his own chores. He didn't want to help anyone, talk to anyone, think about anyone. He just plain wanted to put his head down and work.

All through the week, more people arrived every day. Every tent was put to use, and some folks camped out in the grounds beyond the tents. The preachers had to work in shifts, taking a break when their voices gave out. Now Gideon found himself directing traffic, indicating where people should leave their mules and wagons, trying to convince those who were anxious about missing everything going on, urging them to take at least a few moments to water their animals and make arrangements for straw and kindling.

It was hot sweaty work and the day miserably warm. The air was filled with noises and smells, and the dust that got kicked up made his eyes sting. Meanwhile, the sky was looking worse and worse, almost green. He headed to the arbor, intent on getting his family back to the tent before the storm broke.

Inside the arbor, under its old shingled roof with wide overhangs, the crowd was singing *And Are We Yet Alive?*

And are we yet alive,
and see each other's face?
Glory and thanks to Jesus give
for his almighty grace!

He searched the sea of faces. About halfway back on the women's side he spotted his mother and Milly with the baby, but didn't find his father and Gordy until he stepped a bit further inside the arbor and worked his way up the side aisle. With everyone standing to sing, shoulder to shoulder, their voices loud – whether tuneful or not – he had to pause at the end of each row, scanning faces for his father's curly white whiskers. When at last he spotted him, he had to ask the man at the end of the row to nudge his neighbor, and for that man to nudge *his* neighbor, to get his father's attention.

His father motioned for him to come join the singing, but Gideon shook his head and Pa just grinned a little and kept on singing.

Preserved by power divine
to full salvation here,
again in Jesus' praise we join,
and in his sight appear.

Finally, apologizing and stepping carefully over everyone's feet, Gideon made his way to his father's side. Little Gordy immediately climbed up on the seat so he could put his arm around his father's neck.

Gideon leaned close to his father and spoke into his ear. "We got to get out of here. Storm a-coming. Help me get Ma and Milly." The old man shook his head and sang on, louder than ever, a smug look on his face. "I'm not joking! It looks like we're going to get some hail."

Just then a sudden billowing of wind swept through the arbor and folks clutched their hats and bonnets. With the wind came a few drops of rain, then a mighty crash of thunder, and the storm broke. Rain poured down in a sweeping torrent with a cold chill before it. Women squealed and folks crowded in closer to the center, filling the middle aisle and gathering around the platform. Preacher motioned with his hands, inviting people to come up on the platform with him, and kept on singing.

> *What troubles have we seen,*
> *what mighty conflicts past,*
> *fightings without, and fears within,*
> *since we assembled last!*

Gideon held tight to little Gordy and twisted his head, trying to see if Milly was alright. "You think this is funny, don't you?" he whispered furiously to his father, whose shoulders were shaking with suppressed laughter.

"Isn't it? The Lord decided to get you in here one way or another. You may as well stop fighting and start singing!"

Finally, Gideon caught sight of Milly, safe in the middle aisle not far away. He caught her eye and she smiled, still singing her head off, the same as everyone else. She held the baby wrapped tight in a shawl while Ma stood next to them, her arms around them both.

All those fools singing.

> *Yet out of all the Lord*
> *hath brought us by his love;*
> *and still he doth his help afford,*
> *and hides our life above.*

Well, he was cornered and trapped. Little Gordy's arm was wrapped so tight around his neck he couldn't have broken free if he wanted. The threatened hail began to fall, raising the noise level almost to the breaking point and threatening the security of the arbor's double-shingled roof. Hail bounced off the roofs of the tents and hit the ground like a volley of minie balls.

He began to sweat and turned to his pa, wanting him take Gordy, but Gordy wasn't letting go and Pa wasn't offering to take him. *I have to get out of here,* he thought. *I can't stay, can't take this.* His body began to shake and he dropped down onto a seat, his son against his shoulder.

He buried his face in the boy's hair. His shaking grew worse and the men around him began reaching out to touch his shoulders or back, laying on their hands and singing more robustly in the mistaken belief that Gideon was seeing the Light.

But he wasn't. He saw only the Dark. The black nights when even the faintest noise warned of possible danger. The black water they waded through in creeks oozing with blood. The black hours he spent after finding bodies in an old cabin, bodies of a woman and a baby, probably starved to death. Tears prickled his eyes and he rocked back and forth, clutching Gordy and drowning in his nightmares.

No, he managed to say to himself. Think it through. You're not there…you're not there, you're in the arbor, holding your son, and Pa by your side. *You are not there.* He blew out hard and breathed in huge gulps of air. He forced the words to sound in his mind. You're not there, you're here. All around you, people singing. Listen, the voices are real. The hail is real. The straw on the ground beneath your feet – it's real. Smell the straw. Feel your son's arm around your neck. Think it through. Listen to the singing.

Then let us make our boast
of his redeeming power,
which saves us to the uttermost,
till we can sin no more

Let us take up the cross
till we the crown obtain,
and gladly reckon all things loss
so we may Jesus gain.

The song ended. All around him people were raising their hands and shouting. "Amen!" "Praise the Lord!"

The hail slowed and dwindled into rain. He got to his feet, still shaking, but now from relief. It was over. Gently he pried Gordy loose and mopped his face with his sleeve. It was over, he could breathe again. The men around him gave a final pat to his back as Preacher motioned to everyone to sit down. His words calmed the crowd and they gradually returned to their seats. The rain subsided to a mere pattering, and soon thereafter to a steady dripping from trees and roofs. The folks sat silent, listening to Preacher's words, ready to accept his message.

Gideon felt almost deaf, isolated from everything around him, but it didn't matter. He continued to sit silently, eyes closed, absorbing the quiet surrounding him. When at last people began to stir, to stand and move out of the arbor, he left Gordy with his father and made his way down to the spring, to where clear water ran out from between the rocks. He cupped his hand and poured the cold water over his head, again and again, until his shirt was soaked through and his teeth began to chatter. Exhausted, he pulled his shirt off and wrung it out one-handed, using his stump to hold one end tight against his ribs.

"So, you have *some* use of your right arm," a voice said behind him. Gideon turned to see who spoke. Huck Findlay stared back. "Some men don't. Their shoulder muscles have shrunk." Huck came closer, picking his way carefully down the slick slope. He reached to touch the end of Gideon's stump. "Does it hurt?"

Gideon, stunned, just stared for a minute. Then, "No. Not too bad. Aches now and then in wet weather."

"I've been making wooden legs," Huck said. "Me and Harold Beam. He makes the legs, I make the leather stirrups to hold them in place. We're wanting to try some arms, but haven't been able to figure out how to do a joint that will hold in place. When you said that thing about if only you had an elbow with a little stump below, you gave me an idea."

Gideon shook his head. "I didn't say that. I've thought it a million times, but I never said it out loud."

"Yeah you did." Huck's gaze concentrated on Gideon's shoulder. "I'm thinking maybe you're right, a permanently bent elbow. We could put a lower arm, maybe six or seven inches long, and stick a hook in the end. It wouldn't look like a regular arm or hand, but it'd be useful for some jobs at least. Carrying a bucket, or maybe even guiding the end of a rifle barrel. We could buckle the wooden arm onto your stump, maybe make a kind of harness across your shoulders. I'd like to give it a try."

Gideon just stared at Huck. Then stared at his stump, trying to imagine it. At last he muttered, "I don't know if I could pay you."

Huck nodded thoughtfully. "That's alright. If you let me work out my design on you, I'm pretty sure I'll find plenty of other customers to pay the bills. We've been thinking it might open up a whole new line of work. And right now there's a bill in the state government. They're fixin' to help veterans get fake limbs."

He helped Gideon pull on his wet shirt and patted his shoulder. "I'll come out to the farm in a few days. We'll see how it goes."

Sunday. Last full day of services at the arbor. Everyone would be packing up to leave the next morning and head back home. Gideon made his rounds, reminding folks to bury their slops, clear away debris, and rake out the straw before leaving. There was always a risk of a fire at the campground, so no need to provide extra kindling.

The midday meal, on this last day, was a shared meal. Folks brought food to the trestle tables, filled their plates and settled on the ground on quilts and blankets. Times as they were, the spread might not be as bountiful or varied as in previous years, but it was nevertheless heartily praised and eaten. Gideon settled on a stump, balancing a plate piled with cornbread, baked yams and fried catfish. He thought he'd never tasted anything so good.

Milly spread a blanket beside him and settled down with a plate of her own, for the baby was sound asleep on a folded quilt. After a few mouthfuls she said, "Good, isn't it?"

"Yep."

"All of it, I mean – not just the food." She let her gaze wander over the crowd, close on a thousand people enjoying good food, fellowship, and revitalized faith. When she turned back to him, she smiled. "I'm so glad we came."

"Me too."

She stared at him, obviously a bit surprised at his reply. He told her about Huck's proposal. She took his hand in hers and tears welled in her eyes.

"All this time," he said, "I've been thinking *if only, if only*. Looks now like my 'if only' maybe will come true, but I'm not sure what comes next. Can I really move ahead? And if I can, I've got to start thinking farther than the next chore. Or next season, even next year. I've been scared to do that." His wife's eyes glowed. How he wished they were alone together so he could hold her close and kiss her sweet face. "I was stuck on *if only*. But now I feel hope, at last. Oh Milly, I have so much to think through."

The Prince of Painter's Creek
1879

I'M GOOD WITH NUMBERS. ALWAYS HAVE BEEN. Ma says I was born counting. Well, when you're the youngest son in a family of twelve, that's how it is. You start counting to see if there's going to be enough potatoes or pancakes, or slices of apple pie, and most of the time you can figure there's not. So, I ended up good with numbers. I can total a column of figures and be right every time. I can look at an inventory and see the mistakes, figure out the profit margin on a wagonload of goods, and understand the odds of drawing an inside straight. I know when things don't add up.

My youngest son Hubie lives right next door, and every morning I get a little ray of sunshine in the form of my youngest granddaughter, eight-year-old Gaynelle, when she brings me my breakfast. I suppose an old coot like myself could manage to fry a couple of eggs, but why go to the trouble? Especially when I can get a better breakfast by having my daughter-in-law cook it, and have some company to boot? Gaynelle's a noticing little thing, and right away that morning, she told me a big bird had left droppings in the yard. "Biggest I ever seen, PawPaw. Like maybe a buzzard did it. Or a coupla buzzards. Or a whole flock." I looked out to see and, sure enough, a big pile of spatterings covered the bushes between my yard and Hubie's. It wasn't bird crap, though. It was puke. Foamy beer puke. A lot of it.

Well, I told her not to worry, and later I threw a couple buckets of water over it and washed it away. Her older brother Loy is running around with a bad crowd these days and if things don't pick up, I'll have to take a hand in it. Hubie's too mild with the boy, and that just don't work with a boy as restless as Loy.

These are the times when I miss my Thelma. Well, tarnation, I miss her all the time, but especially when it comes to problems with people. She understood folks, like I understand numbers. She's the one who said we should get Hubie to build a house right next door to us. "We're not getting any younger," she said. "One day we'll want one of them living nearby. I think Hubie's the one." So, we did, and I never regretted it. Their house is nicer'n ours. Plenty big, nice clapboard on the outside, wide front porch. Ours is still just an old log house, but it's good enough for me. Most of their kids are grown and off on their own now, 'cept for little Gaynelle who came along when they thought they was all through. And eighteen-year-old Loy, who drives the wagon from here to Bennetton during the day and hangs out with his rowdy friends at night.

Anyway, I hitched up my suspenders and carried my worries with me over to the store. I still keep the books. It makes me feel useful and Hubie never liked that side of things. He's good with the customers; he likes wearing his clean shirt and tie and he launders his beard every day. I like to be more comfortable, and I stay in the back office with my ledgers and bills of lading and the money box. I fixed myself a cup of joe and planned to work on the books and think over the situation with Loy, but I was interrupted by a passel of trustees from the camp meeting.

"We need a word, Johnny," S.D. Hoyle said. I've never been sure what the S.D. stands for, but I think of him as Sour Dough. The old skinflint never smiles. "It's about your store hours during camp meeting coming up. We'd like you to close every afternoon."

Well, I try mighty hard not to swear. My Thelma never liked it. So instead I took up my knife and a piece of kindling. I enjoy a bit of whittling now and then. "Continue," I said.

"We're setting up a rule that there be no selling of watermelons or lemonade or candy or ice cream on or near the campground. Of course, no liquor. No one should set up a barbering tent or anything that's commercial. We're trying to keep the campground pure of vendors and such. Distractions. You understand."

"I do. Very sound reasoning, I'm sure." I brushed the small pile of shavings off my desk to the floor.

"Your store's only a quarter mile from camp meeting," he pointed out, starting to grow a little red in the face. I surely enjoyed that.

"Yes, indeed it is."

"It's a distraction." He glanced from side to side at the other trustees. They shifted a little, tried to present a united front.

Now here's the thing. The trustees included Clark Thompson, who always makes some money at camp meeting time with his sawmill, providing new boards for tents that need repairs. Ivey Church hauls away the horse droppings and sells 'em as fertilizer. John Brothers rents the fields around camp meeting for his dairy herd the rest of the year, so while he doesn't actually make money during camp meeting, he still profits by its existence.

"Why don't you just spit it out, S.D.?" I asked. "What do you want me to do?"

S.D. ran a finger around the inside of his collar, and kinda hemmed and hawed. Finally, he said, "Close up early. Open the store from morning till noon, so folks can get what they *need*, but close it after that so they're not distracted by things they just *want*. Like them baseballs and such."

The baseballs had been Loy's idea. I thought it was kinda stupid myself, carrying a supply of these newfangled baseballs and bats. What's wrong with a rock and a sawmill slat, if they want to waste time with some dern-fool Yankee game? But Loy insisted the young men at the new seminary would take right to them, and he was right. And what the seminary fellas had, the farm boys soon wanted. I've seen boys come in here with no shoes, and holes in their trousers, but Lordy, they'll fork over what little money they have on a shiny wooden bat. Makes no sense, but there it is. My Thelma woulda understood it.

"What if they buy what they *want* in the morning and come back for what they *need* in the afternoon? I don't control what folks buy." I slid a long curl of wood from the piece of kindling. It was shaping up nicely.

"If you put a notice out ahead of time that you're only going to stay open until noon, they'll figure it out quickly enough." The other trustees muttered 'yeah', and Ivey added, "And besides, it'll give you more time to come over to camp meeting yourself, enjoy the preaching." I shot him a glance and Ivey subsided into silence and a shrug.

I finished my whittling. I had a nice sharp stick there. No real plans for its use, but a sharp stick always comes in handy one way or another. I could use it, for example, to draw a line. "Well, fellers," I said, getting to my feet, sorta absent-mindedly tossing my stick in the air and catching it again, "I appreciate your concern, and how you've brung yourselves out here to speak to me, but I'm afraid my answer is no." S.D. spluttered a little, and I continued. "As you know, I've had a few financial setbacks this year, and I just can't see my way to closing down early. A lotta these folks live way out of town, and they don't get to any stores very often. It takes them a while to decide what they're gonna spend their money on. They might *need* to visit a coupla times before they decide what they *want*, and I aim to allow them that time. So, if you'll excuse me, I got work to do."

I gently herded them out my office door, through the store and out the front entrance way to the street. There I casually jabbed my sharp stick into a burlap sack of chicken feed. "Y'all have a pleasant day," I said, and they turned, mumbling amongst themselves, and headed down the road back toward the campgrounds. Now, I wasn't trying to threaten anyone with my sharp stick, of course. I just wanted to make a point.

After they left, I stood on the porch a while, just looking around. Besides the store, I own most of the property along the road here. As the youngest son, I pretty much got the rottenest bit of land that my daddy owned. All my brothers got the good bits before I came along. They had cotton farms spreading further'n I could see, all the way from Keith Crossroad down to the Howard's Ferry road, and all through late September, their wagons piled high with cotton would drive right past my store on the way to the mills in Catesville.

I got the piece of land nobody wanted, on account of it was rocky and uneven and had the campground right up alongside it. But I'm a man willing to bet on myself, and over time I bought my brothers out of McLeod Brothers Hauling and Trading and ran it myself. So, when it looked like the railroads was gonna come through there, I thought 'at last! I finally got the best piece of the pie!' and I divied it right up into commercial and residential lots, put up a coupla houses for my kids, built the store and a gristmill, and thought I was about to be a man of means. I could just *see* the depot and warehouses that would be built on my lands. But the railroads didn't come through after all, thanks to some kind of piss-pot politics I didn't know how to play, and here I am, the Prince of Painter's Creek, you might say, lord of all I survey.

At the moment, all I can survey is one rattle-trap wagon pulling up to the gristmill, Old Man Robinson coming up the road to buy his one little pouch of chewing tobaccy, two dogs lying in a patch of sunlight, and a one-eyed cat. Like I said, I've had a few financial setbacks this year, but I've done the numbers and I believe it will all come out fine in the end.

I went back to thinking on the situation with Loy but hadn't come up with anything by the time camp meeting started the following week. Those two weeks are hectic for us, so I just put my head down and worked. So did Loy, as far as I could tell. I didn't see no more beer-puke on the bushes, and his father kept him so busy loading and unloading wagons, I don't believe he had any energy left for gallivanting.

So, it came as a surprise when I found out what he'd been up to.

Every day during camp meeting time, except Sunday, I was busy at the store all day. In the evening, after Hubie's wife Dora gave me my supper, I wandered on down to the campground to visit. Preaching usually commenced again in the evenings in the arbor, but I mostly wandered the passways, stopping at this tent or that to greet old friends. My family owned two of the tents. I bought them myself when the Rawlings family died out, but there are so many of us now that only the ones who live farthest away stay overnight in them. The rest of us just visit. It's nice to get together though.

I have to say we're a bully lot! Always lots of talk and fun and babies being passed around. Great-grandbabies now, sitting on our laps or crawling on the grass. My Thelma and I had eight young'uns, five boys and three girls, and they all growed up pretty well. My oldest, John Jr., he owns one of the mills in Catesville now, and his brother Earl works for him. Hector, my second boy, runs the gristmill for me. Hubie, of course, runs the store. Joe died in the war. He'll always be 22 years old to me, while the rest of the fellas have moved into middle age. My girls all married pretty well, honest men who do a day's work, but only Stella still lives in the area. Still, can't complain. Nobody wants to listen to some old fool complaining.

Ol' S.D. stopped by the tent while I was sitting on the swing with little Billy on my lap. He crooked a finger and indicated he wanted to speak privately, the old fart. I handed Billy off to his mother and walked down the passway a spell with S.D.

"Johnny, we got a problem," S.D. said, his voice low but his eyes just a'gleaming. "Your grandson, Loy, he's causing a disturbance."

"How so?" I asked, my own voice just as low but my ears suddenly burning.

"You heard how someone rolled a big wasp's nest down the aisle at preachin' this morning?"

"Yeah. Caused quite a ruckus, I believe."

"You bet. Anyway, we heard it was Loy and some of them Pike boys from down Loweville way. And they been hanging around the arbor after dark, drinkin' and whoopin' it up. Impersonatin' the preachers and pretending to baptize each other. It ain't right."

"You got proof of that?"

"Ezra Leeper saw 'em."

"Well, talk to Hubie then. He's Loy's father, not me."

"It's a fifty-dollar fine, you know, if he's found drunk on camp meeting grounds."

And you'd just love that, wouldn't you, I thought. *Practically peeing yourself with glee.* But all I said was, "I'll check into it," and I walked away. Give a little man a little power and it goes right to his head.

Not that I took it lightly. It sounded exactly like the kind of thing Loy would do. I stumped around the passways for a while, looking to see if I could find him, but he was nowhere in sight. Talked to Hubie, too, who admitted he just didn't know what to do with the boy anymore. All his other sons had been easy. Train 'em up in some trade and they were set for life. His oldest, Hubie Jr, worked at the store, with William in Salisbury at that end of things, and Alan in Bennetton. For them, continuing the McLeod Brothers into another generation was right where they wanted to be, but Loy was a restless fellow. Always had been. I understood that, all right. I'd been a restless fella myself.

Things kept boiling. Loy was late for work the next day, and clearly hung over. I grabbed him before his pa could see him and poured some coffee down his gullet. "What are you being such a blamed fool for?" I asked. "You think anyone will respect you for acting like this? Don't be an ass."

He jerked away, all sullen-like, and slid down in his chair. "I hate it here," he said. "I'm thinking of going west. Tennessee, maybe."

"What for? What's there that you can't have here?"

"A life." He glanced up at me and looked down again. "What am I gonna do here, PawPaw? Just drive a wagon all my life? You know Hubie Jr's, gonna get the store. There's never gonna be nothin' left for the youngest son."

"Well, ain't you just a poor old thing!" Oh, I was angry. Those same derned words I'd said myself, about the same derned age. But they sure sounded different coming from someone else's mouth. "You want something better, you gotta work for it. You can't go around proving yourself a dad-blamed fool and expect a reward. You think I got this far by being a fool? I made mistakes, sure, but I learned from them and didn't expect a handout. I bet on myself to win. Now, get out of here and get that wagon loaded, and think about what you're doing and where you're headed."

He slouched off and I wondered briefly if he'd be coming back again, but I had other things to think about now. I tried to head them thoughts off by working on the books, but it kept coming back to me. That youngest son thing. It's hard being the youngest son. You're always trying to catch up. The other fellas are always going to be older, stronger, more able. They'll be shaving their chins while you're still wetting your britches. They'll be riding horses while you're still learning to walk. And if, by chance, you ever manage to do anything that none of them have done before, you'll be praised with a sneer of condescension. *Oh, look at him, the baby, finally able to blow his own nose.* For a long time, being the youngest always made me feel left behind and left out. Later, it made me bitter when Pa's will was read and they got all the good stuff. I was only nine when he died. He probably didn't think that much about how uneven the division of his land was. But I thought about it. And by *golly*, I did something about it.

And now, here was Loy, complaining about the same thing, and he could think he was in even a worse spot, because he was the youngest son of a youngest son of a youngest son. His older brothers probably *would* get the best parts of the family business. They were already settled married men while he was still running around with a gang. And if he ever straightened up, they'd still look at him with that same sneer of condescension.

I hauled myself down to the camp meeting again that evening, sat on the swing again with little Billy, and looked around. Camp meeting's been going on for almost fifty years now, right in this spot. My Pa had bought a couple of lots back in 1830, but as my brothers' families grew, we all had to buy more spaces. From twelve siblings, the next generation had grown into almost sixty cousins, and the third generation was now spreading even further, and that's just the blood-relatives. Some have moved away, and we don't all have tents here but clearly, what had been enough for one generation just wasn't going to cover the next. It's true in camp meeting and in houses and in businesses. If you're successful, you got to expand and find a way to keep everyone productive and contributing. And when one generation begins to step down, the next one has to be ready to step up.

As I was settin' there, a rise in voices made me look up. People were gathering in little knots, passing some kind of news. I could see it ripple through the passway, from one tent to the next, filling people with awe and excitement. "They put someone in the hoose-gow," I heard. "For rockin' a tent."

Rockin' a tent was the latest thing the trustees had seen fit to ban. Trouble-makers liked to throw rocks on the tin roof of a tent of someone they disliked. It was just mischief but, of course, the trustees would want to put an end to it. They were some of the tenters who got rocked the most.

I handed little Billy over again and made my way through the crowd to the grassy area surrounding the arbor. The hoose-gow was a small shed where they put trouble-makers – usually drunks – until they calmed down or sobered up. I dreaded what I might find, but when I got there, it was the Pike boys, and *only* the Pike boys. Clearly drunk, they were yelling from between the wood slats; pretty foul-mouthed they were, too, a real spectacle. Loy was nowhere in sight. I scanned the crowd as best I could and then headed away from the campground, back home. When I got there, Loy was on the back porch. Sober.

I sat down next to him and pulled out my tobaccy pouch. Offered him some but he shook his head. He looked pretty downtrodden, just a pitiful spectacle, so I stuffed my chaw into my cheek and tried to conjure up my Thelma. I needed some advice.

"Pretty night, tonight," I said after a while, gazing up at the moon, nearly full. It *was* a pretty night, not too hot for once, and the crickets chirped away like mad. "Might rain before morning. By the way, your friends are in the hoose-gow."

Loy shrugged.

I thought a bit, and then I said, "Boy, you ever play cards much?"

He looked at me, as well he should. It was as if I had proposed robbing a bank. Around here, no one admitted to playing cards. After a minute, he said, "I've played whist."

"Whist is for sissies. I'm talking about poker. Five-card draw." I already knew the answer, but I wanted to see what he'd say. "You can tell me. I played plenty in the old days." Finally, he nodded. I chewed and spit. "What's say you and me play a coupla hands. Let me see if you're any good."

Still hesitant, he followed me into the house, and I lit the lamp and pulled a pack of well-used cards out of a drawer. I use 'em for solitaire these days, but he wouldn't know that. We sat down and I shuffled and went through the rules for a stripped deck, since there were only two of us. Then I dealt the cards.

It was a beautiful game. We played several hands and I could see he was taking my measure at first, and then playing more boldly as we went along. Boldly, but with control. The boy understood the odds. As I shuffled the cards for yet another hand, I mentioned I was thinking about retiring from the business. He said nothing. "Trouble is," I added, "your Pa doesn't like keeping the books. He'll need someone good in my place."

Loy said nothing, but he sat up a little straighter. He's young, I thought, only eighteen. Too young for this kind of responsibility? But I was good for a couple more years; I could show him the ropes and take his measure. This hand got us going. We kept drawing a card at a time and added to the pile of peanuts we were playing for instead of cash, just to keep score and not call the Devil down on our sorry selves. But I was ready for bigger stakes.

"I got a good hand here," I said. "And no poker-player should go around bragging on that while the game's still on, but I'm thinkin' we should make this hand count for something. What do you say?"

He examined his cards. "What you want to bet?"

I leaned forward, careful to cover my hand. "A little horse-trade," I said. "I win, you come to work for me. I teach you all about keeping the books, and you take over when I retire. You've shown you have a head for business when you want to; them baseballs are flying off the shelf. But you gotta give up drinkin' and runnin' around."

His eyes met mine. Lord, he reminded me of my Thelma just then, same blue-greeny eyes. "I'll take you up on that," he said. "And if I win, you give me a hunnert dollars, so I can maybe head to Tennessee."

Well, hell. I mean, heck. *Sorry, Thelma.*

Final draw. Loy drew one card and sat up a little straighter still. I was drawing an inside straight. I had the seven-nine-ten-jack. All I needed was an eight and the odds were good. I slowly pulled the card from the deck and turned it over. Succotash! Another nine. Not what I expected.

Loy smiled a little and laid down his cards. Full house, fives over jacks. He'd won. I cursed my stupid self inwardly and went to the dresser where I hide my cash. Two twenty-dollar bills, five tens and the rest in singles. "Here you go," I said, my voice sounding heavy even to me. "One hundred dollars."

"Thank you," he said, taking the money and getting to his feet. He *counted* the derned bills, squared them off, and handed them back to me. "Consider this a down payment. I want that dinky little lot over by the campground, south of the spring. It ain't good for nothin', but I got an idea about it. Meanwhile, if that offer still holds to come work for you, I'll do it. Hubie, Jr's boy is old enough to start driving the wagon." He clapped my stunned self on the shoulder and reached out to shake my hand. I didn't say nothing, afraid I'd start a-blubbering. "I better get some sleep," he said and headed for the back door. "Got to work in the morning." And he was gone.

Well, like I say, I understand numbers. I know how to count and add and subtract and I do know the odds of drawing to an inside straight. And although it might seem I messed up here and it turned out well only because of Luck, I gotta say I had a feeling that in the long run, everything was always gonna add up just fine.

Then again, I mighta got played. Maybe Loy had something like this in mind all along. You know what? I hope so. I surely do hope so. I like a fellow who's not afraid to bet on himself.

Lady Jane and the Mill Girl
1886

Lady Jane

WE REACHED THE CLEARING AT THE TOP of the ridge on Sawyer Mountain Road and for a moment Papa reined in the horses so we could see the view, a long valley below with nothing visible but the tops of trees. Not a single building, not even the road ahead was visible. I knew that down below were at least a dozen farmhouses and the crossroad with Dillon's Mercantile. Somewhere at the bottom was the campground, but for now, all we could see was a crazy quilt of all kinds of greens. Even my brothers were quiet for once, looking at that.

It was my favorite part of the ride to camp meeting, that moment of peace and quiet before we got to the campground. Anything or everything could lay ahead.

Papa clucked to the horses and our wagon moved on. Soon we were shut in on both sides by so many trees that we had no view at all. Finally, we came through the slot between Sawyer Mountain and Macklin Rise and the trees fell back so we could see houses and barns, and shimmering white cotton fields on the long gradual downhill to Painter's Creek.

And then we were there. Camp meeting.

It was all busy, busy, busy, getting settled in. I helped Vida Mae sweep out our tent and put down straw. Helped Mama make up the pallets in the sleeping loft. I thought I would starve to death before Mama finally broke out the ham biscuits and pickles and peaches and we could eat. Everywhere around us, in all the tents, people were doing the same, settling in for yet another week of camp meeting and singing and preaching. Mama and Papa walked off to greet their friends and catch up on the latest news. My brothers tore off to play with the other boys. And I went to Heaven.

That's what I called it. Heaven. My special place, a little way into the woods that surround the campground. Near to the colored folks' own small white chapel with the pretty carving on the roof. It was my special place that I discovered all by myself when I was seven. That was four years ago, and I still haven't tired of it. Someday, I would like to live there. It was my quiet place to read and think and ride Black Beauty. Some people might've just seen an old tree with a limb that grew out sideways, but I saw Black Beauty, my beautiful black stallion. Every year, I read the book all over again. For me, camp meeting was a magic time of quiet afternoons in the shade, sitting sidesaddle on Beauty, gently jogging up and down. Or stretched out on a quilt in the shade, rereading the book for the eleventieth time, and reliving his story all over again. This was my Heaven.

The Mill Girl

I seen her when I was sweepin' out Miz Clark's tent. Up on the sleeping platform I was, and through the open slats I saw the girl walk away from the campground, across a field and into the woods behind that white chapel. She carried a basket and a quilt, and I wondered what she was up to. A girl like that, in a fancy dress and stockin's and even shoes in this hot weather don't belong walkin' off by herself. Anyone would know that. Even me, who ain't been to camp meetin' before.

It sure do seem strange, a buncha fancy folks livin' in these shacks. They ain't no tents, just shacks. Our mill house is better'n these. But eve'body seems all excited to be there. And I'm excited too. When Ma told me I was goin', to help Miz Clark with fetchin' water and taking out the slop bucket and carryin' wood for the cookfire, I was so surprised I stopped right there on the road and nearly busted out bawlin'. I'm gonna get paid a whole dollar for the week! That's twice what I'd make at the mill.

Miz Clark made it all set with Mr Hutchinson, the supervisor, so I won't get in trouble. Miz Clark's husband was a important man at the mill afore he died, so I guess that's why she was able to swing it. Ma says to be sure to tell Miz Clark how grateful I am, but I'm so grateful I could bust out singin' every minute. And I'm even gonna sleep in the same tent as Miz Clark, but just not on the sleeping platform. And she already gave me one of her sweet biscuits, made with real sugar, and I ate every single little crumb, it was so good – and licked my fingers too.

So, when Miz Clark tol' me I could take a little time to myself before supper, and walk around the campground a bit, I did just that. These tents go round and round and round, three times, and in the middle is the church benches and lotsa people already settin' there, a-talkin' and a-prayin', and a coupla folks practicin' singin'. But the other girls looked at me and looked at my bare feet and my old dress, and begun whispering and giggling. So, I decided to go out back, across that field, and see just what that girl in the fancy dress was doin'.

Well, that silly thing, she was just settin' on a big ol' tree limb, bouncin' it up and down, and goin', "Whoa, my Beauty! Steady now!" I watched from behind a bush a while, and then crawled closer, and finally I stood up and just watched. She was havin' herself a real time of it, actin' like that ol' limb was a real horse or somethin'. It was just plain silly, and her all dressed up in that fancy dress. Then she saw me and she stopped bouncin' and got off that limb. "Who are you?" she said, "Come here."

So, I came there. She said, "What's your name. I'm Jane."

She was mighty stuck-up, way she said it, like I had to answer. Huh! She ain't no mill supervisor.

So I said, "What you doin', ridin' that ol' tree limb? It ain't no horse."

"Yes, it is!" she said, and tossed her fancy little curls. "This is Black Beauty, and he's my beautiful horse. And this is my special place, so you can just go away."

"Oh, you own these woods?" I glanced around. "I don't see no fence. I don't see no signs."

"Yes, well, this is my special place anyway. Now go away!"

Well, that just made me sore. I sat right down on the grass, and stared at that little white chapel, and just waited. After a while, I pulled up a fat blade of grass and whistled through it. She stood and watched me a while, and then said, "How do you do that? Show me."

So, I showed her. Ain't nothin' to it, once you seen how. But I'da thought a girl like that would know how already. We blowed our whistles a while, and then she said, "I'm hot. Want to go down to the creek?"

I'd already been to the spring, to haul water for Miz Clark, but the creek was a little farther away. So I went with her and I was so hot, I jumped right in. It was only up to my knees anyway, and I scooped some of the water onto my face and neck. Sure felt good. Then I looked back and there was that fool girl, kneeling at the edge of the creek, trying to cup water in her hand and spilling most of it before it got to her mouth. She said, "I'm not supposed to get my shoes wet."

"Well, take 'em off, Silly."

After a moment, she did. Took off her stockin's too and shoved them in the shoes and tied the shoelaces together and hung them around her neck. Her feet was the whitest feet I ever seen. Whiter'n babies' feet. Like they was brand new and never been used. But pretty soon the both of us was splashin' in the creek and pouring water on our hair and havin' a fine old time. In fact, we was pretty much wet from head to foot, and suddenly she said, "Oh! I have to go! Mama won't like I got so wet."

She started to take off a-runnin', her shoes still slung around her neck, but stopped short and said, "Hey, what's your name, anyway?" I said, "Sairy." And she said "Sairy? You mean Sarah?" I just shrugged, and off she went. I splashed a little longer, but finally decided I should go see if Miz Clark wanted anything. When I got to the tent, she was noddin' off in her rockin' chair on the porch, so I just picked up her little straw fan, and fanned her with it, and then fanned myself some too. It was nice.

Lady Jane

Surprisingly, Mama did not scold me about my dress, just told me to change clothes and hang it out in the sun to dry. Mama has been distracted lately, seems like. At home, she looks out the window a lot, and here at camp meeting, she goes off by herself. Papa is busy most of the time. As one of the trustees, he has to keep an eye on things and spends a lot of time meeting with the other trustees. They're not happy with how things are going at camp meeting this year. It seems the new minister isn't drawing the kind of crowds they're used to.

In the morning, as I packed my basket for a day with Black Beauty, Papa said, "Well, Lady Jane, what are you doing today?" I thought quickly and said I was meeting Sarah and then going to the children's program. I knew he'd think I meant Sarah Davidson, a girl from our church, and that was fine with me. Papa patted me on the head and went his way. I felt a little guilty about that, but I hurried off to Black Beauty anyway.

Sairy didn't show up for quite a while. I got tired of riding Black Beauty, so I spread my quilt in the shade and began reading my book instead. When she did arrive, I was so glad to see her. She was wearing the same faded dress as yesterday, and barefoot again, too. I envied her. Mama had given me a little speech that morning about keeping my clothes tidy, and today's dress has dozens of pleats that can get so wrinkled.

Sairy stared down at my book and I explained what I was reading. I offered to share it with her, but she suggested I read aloud instead, so I started over at the beginning, and read about Beauty's life as a colt, with his mother in the barn. After a while, I stopped and looked at Sairy. She was lying on the quilt with her eyes shut. "Are you asleep?" I asked.

"No, just thinkin'." She rolled over on her stomach and looked up at me. "Is this what you do all day when you're at home? Just read books?"

"No!" I felt a little irritated. "What's wrong with books? I like stories."

"Oh, I like the story just fine. But I'm just tryin' to figure your life at home. No one I know reads as good as you. Most of 'em don't have anythin' to read anyway."

"Why not?"

"Cause we're mill folks, Silly! Don't you know what that means?" She sat up, looking cross. "We work all day in the mill, or all night. I work days. I'm a spinner. I run four sides. My Ma, she's a warper. The twins are helpers, one for me and one for Ma."

"You have twins in your family?" I was enraptured. "I've only seen twins once in my life. They were just little babies, and you couldn't tell them apart, but babies all look alike anyway. How old are your twins?"

"Seven." Sairy looked at me like I was a creature in a zoo. "Margie and Suzy."

"And can you tell them apart?"

"Not when they're sleepin'. But when they wake up, Suzy's always frownin' and Margie's always smilin'." She turned away for a minute, and I thought maybe I had offended her, but when she turned back, she was smiling and suggested we go over to the creek again.

All day long, thoughts about those twins danced in my head. I couldn't stop myself from asking more. She didn't seem eager to answer my questions, but she always did, eventually. After a while, I could just *see* those twins. They both had long, dark hair, Sairy said, and I pictured two matching little girls with long ringlets and ruffled pinafores, their heads bent together over a picture book or baby dolls. So sweet. When Sairy said she used to 'mind' them while her Mama went to work, I told her about helping with my youngest brother when he was a baby. "I used to push his carriage all around the garden, and sometimes I gave him his bottle. I love babies."

Again, Sairy looked at me as if I were some strange creature, but she did talk a little then 'bout when the twins first started to smile or crawl or walk. We sat by the creek with our feet in the water for a while, then she said she had to go help Miss Clark. She was gone the rest of the day, but I was quite happy . . . walking around the campground, imagining the twins were walking with me, each holding one of my hands.

Sairy

I didn't end up playin' with that ol' Jane as much as I thought I would. She's such a stupid. All excited about the twins, goin' on and on about baby-mindin', when it's plain as plain she ain't never really done such a thing. Ain't changed a diaper, ain't dealt with runny noses and squallin' and tryin' to keep two babies from fallin' into the fireplace or drownin' in a ditch. I minded those twins for three years while Mama worked, until I was ten years old and she told the mill supervisor I was twelve, so I could get some work.

We got ol' Granny Heavner to watch 'em then, since she needed somewheres to live, and when she died, the twins came to the mill with us as helpers. I remember how hard it was to take care of them, their bottoms all chapped from wet diapers, always squallin' for food, always climbin' on things and gettin' in trouble. But I didn't tell Jane about that stuff. I pulled my few good memories out of my head, but tellin' them made me sad. Was like once I pulled 'em out, I couldn't stuff 'em back in again.

I surely enjoyed her readin' to me about that horse, but even that made me sad. I could see things was goin' bad for Beauty so I said, "Why'd you read me such a sad book?"

Jane looked surprised. "It ends happy," she said. "I like sad books if they have happy endings."

Well, shucks. Why read sad books? Ain't life is sad enough? If I could read and had lots of books to choose from, I'd only read happy ones. I did go to school once, for a coupla months 'fore the twins was born. I can read a little and write my name, but that's about all. And here's this Jane that's got all these books at home, and clean dresses, and a Papa, and those fine white feet.

I started feeling mad about the whole thing. And I 'spect my face looked just like Suzy's frown.

But overnight, I lay there in Miz Clark's tent, listenin' to her snore, and hearin' the crickets, and lookin' out at the stars. I thought to myself, Miz Clark was a mill girl herself. But she married a mill supervisor and just look at her now. She has a nice house, and her daughter's family livin' with her, and maybe she lives rough at camp meeting but that's because she likes it. It makes her think about when she was young. But she has plenty to eat and a soft bed now. Maybe my life won't be just workin' at the mill all my days. Maybe I won't be like Ma, with a dead husband and three live children. Maybe the book about my life will have a happy endin'.

So, the next day, I went over to find Jane at the Black Beauty tree again. I took along a bit of rope I found, and we managed to tie it to the end of the limb. Jane got on, setting 'sidesaddle', she calls it, and I pulled on the rope like the bell ringer at the mill. That limb went up and down, faster and higher than before. Jane said she felt like Beauty was almost flyin'. I had fun too, jerkin' on that ol' rope, and getting' pulled up into the air 'long with it. We took turns till we was both dizzy. Then we laid on the quilt and watched the sky go round and round. Jane read some more of the book, and things just kept gettin' worse and worse for Beauty. Finally, I said I didn't want to hear any more. I thought, don't make me feel so sad over some silly horse story.

Just to get even, I told her 'bout watchin' Mama have the twins. Jane thought I was gonna tell her this nice sweet story, but when I got to all the blood and mess, her face turned red and she wouldn't look at me. So just to finish it off, I told her about how women and girls bleed, and what they have to do to get a baby. I don't think she believed me. I wouldn't'a believed it myself if I hadn't seen the twins get borned. I think she was crying some, but I felt so hot inside my chest, I couldn't look at her neither. I don't know why I wanted to hurt her. It felt good when I was doin' it, like I was pushin' her down in the mud, but after, I felt ashamed of myself.

She got up and walked away and I let her.

That night I kinda hinted to Miz Clark that I'd be happy to keep workin' for her after camp meetin' was done. But she said she didn't need no helper back home. She was nice about it, and her eyes was kind and she give me one of them little sugared biscuits, but I could see there was no chance. Her daughter's family took care of her every need back home, and I woulda just been in the way. I'm just a mill girl. Always will be a mill girl. Won't never have nothin'. But at least I know what's what. And don't have no fool notions 'bout stories with happy endin's.

Lady Jane

I didn't want to be with Sairy after that, but I didn't know what to do with myself. I didn't feel like reading and I didn't feel like riding Black Beauty. Camp meeting was spoiled for me. Vida Mae finally got tired of me mooching around, so she put me to work shelling peas and washing butterbeans, and I spent a couple days doing that and going to the children's services. One afternoon, Mama got all dressed up in her new dress with the fringe and the braid and the fancy buttons and went out walking with her new parasol with the lace trim. She looked all happy and excited and I wondered if she was planning some kind of surprise, like on Papa's birthday last year. I started to follow her when she went out, but she turned around, and said, "Jane! I don't want you right now. Go see what your brothers are up to, and make sure they get to the children's service. Scoot now!"

Well, I knew what my brothers were up to. What they'd been up to all week, catching minnows down by the creek, or collecting rocks to throw at people's tents at night. I don't think they've been to children's service even once, and Mama and Papa haven't even noticed. Papa's still unhappy about how camp meeting is going. Hardly any sinners have come up to be saved.

I decided to follow Mama anyway. Stayed a ways behind, so she wouldn't notice me, and followed her right out of the campground. It was hard to find hiding places once she got to the open meadow, but it didn't look like there was going to be any surprise anyway. She just dawdled along, twirling her parasol. Mr. Dillard, who owns the Mercantile, walked up and lifted his hat to her, and then they walked on together.

Mama smiled up at him. And something in the way she did, made me a little sick to my stomach.

I crouched down behind an azalea bush and watched. They were just talking and walking along slowly, but Mama smiled and sort of swayed like a flower in the breeze, and when Mr. Dillard smiled back, he seemed to be saying things she liked. Then her parasol went up and the two of them leaned close. I couldn't see their faces, but it seemed to me like maybe they kissed. Mr. Dillard put his arms around Mama's waist and held her close.

I started to stand up, to run over there, but suddenly a hot, sweaty hand clamped down on my arm. I jumped and turned to see Sairy's face close up to mine. She whispered, "Don't go over there. Your Mama won't like it."

I turned again and this time I could see for myself they were kissing. Fancy kissing, not like when Mama kissed Papa in the morning when he went to work. It was kissing that made me feel hot and cold, and like I was going to throw up.

"Come on," Sairy whispered. She pulled me away from where we were crouched, to back behind some trees. "Let's get out of here."

I stumbled along behind her, too upset to object. What was Mama doing? *Why* was she doing it? I thought about those nasty things Sairy had told me about what grown-ups did, and right then I had to bend over and throw up, right on the grass. Then I started crying.

Sairy held my hair back, and when I was done, she offered me a small jug with cold water in it. "I got a biscuit, too," she said, holding it out to me, but I shook my head. I had to get out of there.

All I could think of was Black Beauty, how I could rest there. I couldn't go back to the tent, that much was for sure. What if Mama came back? Or Papa came in? But as we got close to my Heaven spot, we saw several boys playing on Black Beauty. Riding my horse! Two were my brothers, and there were three other boys, all sitting on the limb, and one more boy pulling on the rope, making Beauty jump up and down.

Too hard! Too hard! I heard the wood crack. It split down the trunk and the limb fell to the ground. They'd killed him!

The boys all scrambled off and jumped on the limb, cracking it further until it split open all its length, and then they started tearing smaller branches off and beating it. I just stood there, frozen in shock. Sairy was screaming and yelling. She grabbed rocks and clods of dirt off the ground and began throwing them at the boys.

"Leave it alone!" she screamed. "Damn yez, leave it alone!"

The boys jeered at her until a couple of them got hit by the rocks, then they began running toward us, sticks in hand. That's when I stepped forward and my brothers recognized me. I screamed at them, and I guess my brothers decided an old tree wasn't worth me telling Papa, so they called their friends off and ran away.

Sairy and I ran toward Beauty. He was *dead*. He lay splintered on the ground, ripped open, the dry old wood exposed. He'd probably been sick a long time already, but this was so pitiful. Sairy dropped to her knees and picked up some of the pieces like she could maybe put him back together, but I threw myself on top of him, crying "No, no, no, no!"

All Sairy could do was pat my back. Soon we were both crying then, tears streaming down our cheeks. Finally, we found some light leafy branches and laid them over him, covering him up, putting him to rest.

We sat there a long time, arms around each other, check against cheek, mingling our tears and sobs. It was silly, I knew. He wasn't a real horse. But oh, he felt real to me.

Finally, sniffling and wiping our faces with our skirts, we headed back to the campground. I still didn't want to go to the tent, so I suggested we both go to the children's service. I thought it would soothe me to sit in the arbor, think about God, and just rest my weary heart. Sairy shook her head. "It ain't no place for me," she said. "I'll go check on Miz Clark."

She gave me a fierce hug then and turned and ran away.

That evening was a strange one. Papa showed up at the tent, irritable that things were still not the way he expected. "People just aren't the same as they used to be," he fretted, walking around and around the room. "And where's your mother?" I jumped at his angry tone, but just shrugged my shoulders. Vida Mae also sensed his mood and was extra quiet setting out the evening meal.

Mama came in late. She didn't look happy and excited any more. She looked – I don't know – tired and nervous. She jumped when my brother knocked over his cup of water and put her fingers to her forehead like she had a headache. Somehow, we got through that meal, and Papa said we were all to go to the evening service and *set an example*. I didn't want to, I just wanted to go to bed and pull the sheet over my face. I couldn't bear to think of Beauty, lying out there in the darkness, all shattered and killed.

The service went on and on. The ministers took turns, each one trying to work the crowd up, but sinners just didn't respond. One of the preachers took his turn and called down the wrath of heaven. He begged the Lord to rile these folks up, to make them realize they needed to change their ways. "Shake them up, O Lord!" he called up to the rafters.

Then out of nowhere, the earth began to tremble. Old Mr. Parker, who used to live out West, shouted "Stampede!" But everybody else either screamed "Earthquake" or "O Lord, forgive me!". The arbor shook and swayed, the whole thing kind of popped and rattled. One big tremor, then another and a few minutes later, the worst tremor of all. Everyone sort of froze in place while it went on and on. Mama clung to Papa and I clung to my little brothers.

Then the tremor stopped, and the spell was broken.

All around, everywhere, people began screaming all over the place, dropping to their knees, crawling fast as they could to get out of there. We all streamed out of the arbor, out into the open grassy area between the arbor and the tents. The tremors stopped but folks were still shouting and screaming, calling on the Lord, calling each other. The reverend climbed up on a stump and held out his hands, calling for quiet, and said, "Let us sing." Our voices rose, quavering and breathless at first, in *How Firm a Foundation*, which I could never thereafter sing without remembering that moment when our foundation, my foundation, was shaken to its core.

Eventually, we all went back to our tents. Nobody slept for a while, we all just stayed out on our porches or in the passways. I saw Miss Clark waddling down the way, checking on her friends, but I didn't see Sairy.

The next morning, we packed up our things to leave. I couldn't go without saying good-bye to Sairy and went running over to Miss Clark's tent, but it was too late. The tent was empty and forlorn, firmly shut until next year's camp meeting.

I never learned what happened to Sairy, whether she stayed at the mill, or found another fate. Miss Clark became ill and couldn't attend camp meeting the following year. Life pretty much went back to normal, except that before Christmas that year, Mama had a miscarriage.

When I was thirteen, Papa bought me a gentle mare of my own and I learned to ride. I thought of Sairy often, and with love – but I never read *Black Beauty* again.

The Freedman
1895

GRADY TOMPKINS WALKED ALONG Gilead Church Road between fields of cornstalks that rose higher than his head. Weeks of hot, sunny days had baked the dirt road hard as iron beneath his feet, and birdsong filled the air. Grady hummed as he walked, pulling behind him a low-built wagon piled with fresh vegetables, and eggs packed in straw. Then he broke into song, old spirituals sung in a deep bass voice that was known throughout the county.

It was a beautiful morning. The camp meeting near Painter's Creek was nearly over, and that meant it would soon be time for the Sawyer's Grove camp meeting to begin. Hundreds of colored folks from miles around would meet for prayer, music, and renewal, and Grady's son, James, would lead the preaching.

How Grady loved to hear his son preach! His heart absolutely swelled with pride at James's words, his educated voice speaking of Scripture, and the deep bass tones lifting the people from underneath. James was in his fifties now, a well-established minister in Raleigh, leading one of the larger colored congregations in the state. His wife, Beulah, was educated too, a teacher trained at one of the first Normal schools in the state after the war. Both were pillars in their community. Grady filled with joy every time he thought of them, both come up through slavery into positions where they could help other former slaves, and the children of slaves, to rise into their own free will.

Grady turned his thoughts to the day ahead. He'd deliver his load to McLeod's store, and then go back home to make sure everything was ready at the house for his son's arrival. He'd help his wife Zona dress and eat breakfast. These days, it took all her strength – and all his – to accomplish the simplest of things. She fell over so easily. Even with a cane and his arm around her, Zona could barely make it from the bed to a chair, or from one room to another. He had to tie a belt around her and hang onto it to keep her from crashing to one side or sliding to the floor. Soon, she'd be completely bed-ridden. He hated for James to see her like that.

Grady's song faded away as he thought about the problem, but he was fast approaching McLeod's store anyway.

Young Mister Loy McLeod ran the store started by his grandpa, and also kept a small food stand at the corner directly across from the campground. During camp meeting time, he got extra deliveries in from the local farmers for those folks attending who no longer brought their own cows or chickens. All through the ten days of camp meeting, Grady never got to taste an egg or have an ear of corn for himself, but that was alright. The extra cash money came in handy.

"How you doin', Mist' Loy?" he asked as he approached the hearty-looking man. Loy McLeod had married the previous winter, and now he looked keyed-up and jaunty all the time. "Been keepin' well?"

"Sure have, Grady. How 'bout yourself?" As Grady brought the wagon alongside the back porch of the store, Loy reached down and began helping to unload it. "I guess your boy is coming home any day now, huh?"

"Sho' nuff! He'll be preachin' up a storm, that's for sure!" Grady laughed and slapped his old straw hat against his leg.

Loy counted out the money due and handed it over to Grady. "I sure am glad to see all these eggs. Can't keep enough on hand. This year, the Veteran's Association is pulling out all the stops, and we have a lot of extra folks at the campground."

"Veteran's Association?"

"Yep. Veterans of camp meeting – those folks who've been coming to the campground every year who are more than sixty years old. We've got 89 of them this year!"

Grady chuckled. "Well, suh, you reckon I could join? I come every year until the War. And I'm for sho' over sixty!"

Loy stopped to look at the old man. "Did you now? Well, yes, I guess you did. I remember when the slaves used to come along to camp meeting. I was just a boy, but…"

"Yes, suh! Yes, suh! I was 'bout 14 years old the first year there. I b'longed to old Colonel Paterson, by then, what had the iron foundry. Used to cut wood for the forge. Lordy, that was hot work!"

Loy moved up a step and hefted the basket of corn. "Better days now, I guess." He nodded at Grady and headed inside. Grady finished emptying his wagon, tipped his hat to Loy's back, and turned to go.

Even all these years later, some things never changed. Slavery was still an issue to most folks, he thought, as he headed back to the farm. Some wished it was back again, and others acted like it never happened. Like they'd nothing to do with it. Loy's family had owned slaves. Grady remembered several of them. They mostly worked in the family's earlier business, repairing and driving the wagons that delivered goods across the central part of the state. Loy would have grown up with some of them, but he was the kind who liked to act as if he'd forgot all about it – so long as the coloreds stayed separate and remained quietly in 'their place'.

Better than the kind what hates us, I guess, Grady thought. As for himself, he didn't dwell on his years of slavery. Didn't pay to remember. Way he counted it, his life began when he was freed.

He had only one regret – that he'd never been able to find his Mama after the war. She got sold right after he was sent to Colonel Paterson's, and nobody knew where. Just that she'd got a whipping 'fore she went. All those years, he tried to find some clue, but he never did. What he'd give, to see that slender woman with the soft voice.

Back home, he helped Zona dress and eat, and saw her settled on the front porch where she could watch for James. She hardly said anything anymore, but she wasn't confused in her head yet, and she was excited at the prospect of seeing their eldest son and his wife. Grady did some totting up in his books, keeping track of the farm's production. He was a tenant farmer, and had to pay rent to the owner, Mr. Moore, twice a year. Over the years, he'd built up a good farm and never once been late with his rent, even in '91 when a late snow killed a lot of his crops.

He raised a little cotton, a lot of corn, and cane for molasses. He kept chickens and caught fish and grew enough vegetables for his own kitchen and to trade for apples, lard, tobacco, and the like. Thinking about his farm made him swell with pride again. Young Eustis Cook helped out – well, nowadays it was more the other way around, he helped Eustis – and he hoped Mr. Moore would let Eustis buy the tenancy when he was dead and gone.

It was close to supper time when James and Beulah arrived. Zona was sure glad to see them. She held their hands and beamed up at their faces, till they teared up a little through their smiles. Grady had fried a chicken and cooked up a mess of greens, and Beulah brung a beautiful white-flour cake, real city food, that slid down the throat as sweet as you please. But he saw how they watched as he helped Zona go out back, and the way she didn't say much, and could barely find her mouth with her spoon. Once he'd tucked her away in bed, he joined James and Beulah out on the porch to sit and watch the moon.

After a bit, James said, "Daddy, you need some help. Mama gets more puny every day. And I can see your back is acting up."

Grady waved the words away. "I'm 79 years old, son. Just takes a little longer to straighten up these days. You'll see. Happens to us all." He took his time lighting his pipe. "Zona and me, we just fine."

"No, Mr. Tompkins, you're not." After all these years, Beulah still called him Mr. Tompkins. She loved everything very formal and proper. "One of these days, she's going to fall over, and you're going to fall over, and no one will find you until next morning, when Eustis comes to milk the cows. And maybe not then! Eustis never sticks his nose in the house."

"You seen a doctor?" James asked. "I worry 'bout your heart."

Just because a man got dizzy out once in a while, it didn't mean he was on his last legs, Grady thought. "Son, they's just one doctor who'll see colored folks and he's all the way over to Bennetton. He don't come out here, and I don't got the time or money to waste on hearin' him say I'm gettin' old."

"But what if something happens to you, and Mama is all alone in the house? Do you ever think about that?"

Grady looked straight at his son. *What do you think*, he wanted to say. *What in tarnation do you think?* But all he said was, "No, son. I don't think about nuthin', all day long."

James and Beulah looked at one another. She said, "You could come and live with us. You know we would make you welcome. And we have the room, now that the children are grown." She reached out and touched his hand. "Wouldn't you like to lay your burden down?"

Grady struggled to stay calm. After a moment, he said "God will tell me when it's time to lay my burden down." He swatted at some gnats and got wearily to his feet. "Till then, I needs my rest." He shuffled slowly into the house, leaving James and Beulah on the porch.

As he walked away, he heard her murmur something, and James' deep voice in reply. "What else can I do? If he doesn't want to come with us, I can't make him."

Took a long time before sleep came. Zona lay next to him, curled on her side, her soft snores coming unevenly as they did these days. Sometimes she stopped breathing for long seconds, until he had to nudge her into drawing the next breath. He knew they was getting old. He knew they didn't have many years left. He just couldn't afford to dwell on it.

The next morning dawned bright and hot, with the promise of a day that would be hotter still. Humidity lay heavy in the air, the kind that usually led to an afternoon shower. He dressed, gathered eggs, fed the animals, and made his daily trek to Painter's Creek, silent for once as he walked, no song in his heart. Mr. Loy was sitting on the edge of the store's back porch, smoking a pipe. He offered Grady some of his tobacco.

Grady paused a moment. Never before had he been invited to stuff his pipe in Mr. Loy's presence, let alone help himself to the other man's tobacco. Slowly, he accepted, and they smoked in companionable silence for a few minutes.

"Guess what?" Loy said after a while.

"What?"

"I'm going to be a father." A grin started up on Loy's face and Grady laughed out loud.

"Well, I'll be! A father! Ain't that good news! Yes, suh!"

Loy's grin ran all over his face. "Yep. Folks 'round here thought I'd never amount to a hill of beans, and now look at me. A married man and soon to be a father. Before you know it, I'll be downright respectable."

"Well, your granddaddy sho' would be proud. He thought a lot of you. I'm right happy for you."

"Well, you be sure to tell Zona, would you? And bring her to see us when the baby's born. Should be before Christmas."

"I will sho'ly do that. Yes, suh!" Still chuckling, Grady unloaded his wagon, collected his pay and walked away, tugging the wagon behind him. As he walked along Gilead Church Road, between the tall rows of corn on each side, Grady felt his spirits rise. A new life. That was always a good thing. He raised his voice in praise.

There is a balm in Gilead
To make the wounded whole
There is a balm in Gilead
To heal the sin-sick soul

Sometimes I feel discouraged
And think my work's in vain
But then the Holy Spirit
Revives my soul again

The sun on the back of his shoulder blades and neck grew hotter as he trudged. No breeze could sweep down between the rows of corn. He thought about camp meeting to come, when he would lend his powerful voice to praise the Lord in music. He'd been leading the singing many a year, since the Sawyer's Grove camp meeting got started.

The sun seemed to grow even hotter, as though it was coming right down to earth, and Grady broke out in a sweat. He raised his hand to mop his forehead and suddenly felt a crushing pain in his head. He fell like a stone, landing halfway across his wagon. *What happened?*

For a moment, he was a boy again, reeling from a crack of Colonel Paterson's cane. "I don't whip my slaves," the Colonel liked to say. No, but he'd swing that sharp malacca cane across the side of their heads or the back of their legs if he was displeased. He'd been known to break a cane across some slave's head or back, but he always had a spare tucked away somewhere.

Grady couldn't move. He lay face-down on the wagon, his cheek against its dusty surface. He knew it had to be some kind of stroke. He could smell the metallic tang of the red dust, rich with iron, the same iron that led to so many forges and foundries in the area, like Colonel Paterson's. He'd been sold to the Colonel when he was twelve. Forced to leave his mama and everyone he knew. He worked at the forge all through the war, when it was going night and day, trying to replace miles of track that had been torn up by the Yankees. He and the other slaves had fed the fires, even after word had come that Lincoln freed them. No one dared run off at first, afraid it was a lie, afraid the patterollers would get them.

The sun shone relentlessly. He was caught in a patch of sunlight, fierce as any fire. A cloud of gnats buzzed around his face, mercilessly torturing him, and he could not raise a hand to swat them away. His hat had fallen off – he could see it lying inches away. He tried to speak, but only a deep, guttural moan escaped, and he felt saliva running from his mouth onto the dusty wooden slats of the wagon.

Get up, he told himself. *Shake this off and get up! You got to get home to Zona!* He did manage to shift one foot a little, the toe of his old shoe sliding to one side. The effort wore him out. Grady closed his eyes, trying to draw on all his strength.

He seemed to be wandering. He could smell eggs, rotten eggs, the smell of the old mineral springs at the spa, in the terrible days after the war. There seemed nowhere for the freed slaves to go. The northern army deserted them, and the southern whites hated them, and absolutely no one would help them. Even the Freedmans' Bureau couldn't do much. Overwhelmed with requests for help, they just mainly focused on finding indentures for orphaned children.

He and Zona and some of the others from the foundry had squatted at the old deserted buildings of the spa, looking for shelter, trying to provide for themselves.

For a few hopeful months, they thought they had a plan. Put in vegetable gardens, hunted and fished. But soon they were chased off by the militia, spurred on by the surrounding white community. Some went west, some went east. Many of them died of starvation and disease. He and Zona lost their younger children. James survived, and their daughter Caroline, but the younger ones sickened and died.

Why was he back at the spa, Grady wondered. How did he get there?

Slowly, so slowly, he drew one leg up and tried to get to his feet, but his strength gave away again. His head pounded as though someone had cleaved it with an ax. An axe. He pictured himself swinging an axe, chopping wood. Young and strong and able. He'd first become a sharecropper, working the fields for Mr. Moore, grateful for a place to live and a shelter for Zona. Mr. Moore was a good man, he consented to Grady's joining the Sawyer's Grove church, started by missionaries for the colored folks, and center of their community. Grady's powerful singing voice had carved the way, made him a pillar of the church. He had a good memory for songs, and made sure to teach them to younger folks, so they could be carried on.

The church started a school for the freed slaves, and he made sure James went, even though by then he was a grown man of twenty-seven. Grown-ups sat alongside the children to learn their letters and numbers, and although the school could only meet on Sundays, after church service, at least some of the Negroes learned to read. James's son John, seven years old, learned fast. He helped teach his father, who helped teach Grady. That's the way it was. The day came when Grady could read and write and cipher, and that was a proud day. He'd become an *educated* man.

The buzzing of insects grew louder, and Grady could hear the ragged sound of his own breathing. Seemed like he'd almost forgot how. In, out, in, out, choking on dust from the straw and the road. A long road through the corn fields. His corn fields. They might be owned by Mr. Moore, but it was him what broke the ground, plowed the fields, and worried over his budding plants. During his tenancy, he'd fixed up the house and outbuildings, bought his own mule and plow, and devoted his life to the farm. He wasn't about to leave it all now.

With a deep groan, he managed to turn on one side. His legs were still dragging over the side of the wagon. He reached out and grabbed the low side rail. Inch by inch, over what seemed an eternity, he shifted himself further onto the wagon and flopped belly-down on the straw that had cushioned this morning's eggs. Slowly, he propelled himself down the road, drawing the wagon along by gripping the corn stalks at the edge of the field and forcing the wheels to turn a little at a time.

Sweat poured down his face, dripping into his eyes, but he hadn't the strength to wipe his forehead. His left arm and leg hung useless, dragging in the dust, but he was able to push and pull a little with his right arm. The corner of his mouth slobbered, and gnats crawled over him, flying into his eyes and nearly driving him crazy.

It felt like weeks and months went by. Every so often, he'd pass out, and come to when the sun shifted in the sky and blazed down on him again. He prayed for rain. Just a gentle rain, just those blessed drops on his face, his tongue. How many times had he laughed, just for pleasure, when a long-awaited rain finally arrived, to nurture the parched fields and bring the hope of tomorrow. The wagon rumbled along, cornstalk by cornstalk, the toe of his left shoe dragging in the road, and scratchy straw under his belly, working its way into his shirt, making him sneeze. Each sneeze seemed about to separate his skull from his neck. *Oh Lord*, he thought, *don't let me die from sneezing*.

Was this how the Lord felt, carrying His cross on the way to Calvary? Staggering under its weight, already in pain from his lashings, and knowing – worst of all – *knowing* what was ahead? Yet the Lord had the courage to go on.

Grady didn't know what was ahead for himself. He closed his mind to all his own bodily pains and just watched his hand reach for another cornstalk, pulling on one after another. The strength of his right arm seemed to grow, indeed his right arm seemed to become all he had; a pull of muscle from shoulder to forearm, from wrist to gripping fingers. That was all he could count on.

He *had to* keep trying. He had to get to Zona.

He could tell when he was nearly at the end of the field. The corn on this northern edge never grew as well – the ground was higher and water ran off more quickly, so the stalks were thinner and less mature. They bent and gave as he pulled them and tore loose from the soil. Oh, please Lord, he thought. *I can almost see the house.* He panted, drawing on the last of his strength, and then he saw a woman he knew, wavering against the sunlight. A woman he'd lost, so long ago, when he was just a boy and sold to Colonel Paterson. That slender woman with the soft voice. He watched as she approached, and as she came close, he said, "Mama."

Them Caswell Cousins
1900

NELLIE CASWELL SIGHED AS SHE LOOKED out over the front yard, where her entire family was going berserk as they always did when packing for camp meeting. Honestly, they could never do anything in a normal way. Running around like chickens with their heads chopped off. And Mama cracking the whip, shouting, "Put those blankets there! Watch out for my pies! Have you lost what little sense the good Lord gave you?"

Pa, above the fray, sat on the porch in his old rocker, grinning and occasionally puffing on his pipe. Every now and then, he'd say, "Gently, Virge. Gently. Don't scare the livestock." He glanced over at Nellie. "Good as a show, ain't it? Your Mama's a firecracker."

Yeah, thought Nellie. A real firecracker. About to explode. Her five brothers ran around, trying to follow Mama's commands. Problem was, she kept changing her mind.

Nellie dragged the old humpback trunk down the porch steps and lugged it out to the wagon. "Took you long enough," Mama grumbled.

"Well, it wasn't easy to pack! You got so much starch in those shirts, it's like breaking boards to fold 'em."

"Never you mind, Missy. You'll thank me some day, after I'm cold and dead in my grave."

Yeah, right, Nellie thought. Lord knows, it'll take a week to wrestle Mama into the ground after she dies. *Not till I finish sweeping*, she'll say, and *don't forget to pack the good cornbread pan in with me*.

Nellie's older sister, Hazel, watched from the safe distance of her own yard. Now that she was married and lived across the road, she only joined the family when it was to her advantage. *Traitor*, Nellie thought. Hazel grinned as if she could read Nellie's mind.

"Don't be a pouty puss," she called.

Nellie turned her back. Hazel's mother-in-law was no picnic either, but she lived way over to Catesville. Lucky pup.

Uncle Orry and Aunt Ally's family were due to arrive soon, so they could all ride as a group to the campground. 'Them Caswell Cousins', as they were known to all in Painter's Creek, would be together for the first time since Hazel's wedding in April. Eight boys, all with the Caswell cowlicks and snub noses, a regular mix of terrors and sober-sides. And then there were the three girls – cousin Deb, the Pretty One. Hazel, the Talented One. And herself. Just Nellie.

Honestly, she knew she wasn't 'just' Nellie, but nobody else seemed to – yet. Deb was so obviously the Pretty One that it couldn't be disputed, and Nellie loved her enough not to mind. And Hazel, she could sing like a bird and play the piano better than anybody. But the best that could be said for Nellie was that she was still finding her way. Someday, though, she knew she would do something special, and people would really sit up and take notice.

But honestly, most folks were dumb as rocks. They couldn't see what was right in front of them. According to Hazel, who liked high-falutin' words, they were *obtuse*. Someday, they'd be surprised. Come hell or high water, someday she'd make a real name for herself.

Now Mama was yelling, "Get your head out of the clouds, Nellie! Shake a leg!" She pointed to the kitchen chairs lined up on the driveway. "You and Victor, stand 'em upside down 'round the edge of the wagon so they won't take up room. There's plenty enough inside the wagon to hold 'em in place." Victor made the mistake of rolling his eyes and Mama slapped him upside the head. "Don't you get uppity with me! You're not too big to put over my knee!"

Pa laughed. Victor didn't.

Finally, the wagon was packed to Mama's exacting standards and Uncle Orry's family arrived in their own wagon. As promised, Deb wore her blue-and-white checked dress, to match Nellie's green-and-white and, of course, she looked pretty as paint. Victor helped her down from the wagon and Nellie ran over to grab her hands and whisper, "This year is going to be such a heap of fun!"

Deb nodded and glanced around. "Seems like an eternity since April!"

Just thinking of the week ahead put Nellie in a tizzy. With Hazel staying at her husband's family tent, there'd be room for Deb up in the sleeping loft, so all night long they'd be able to whisper and giggle. Deb was more than just a cousin. She was Nellie's best friend. The *best* kind of best friend, who could share everything – every secret, every thought. No matter what happened as the years went by, they'd always have each other.

Mama was still ranting up a storm over things she was just sure hadn't been packed, or things she didn't think she would need, but maybe she should bring them anyway, and other things that were just things. Nellie wanted to yell, *For cryin' out loud, the campground is only a mile away!* They could nip right back to the house if they needed something.

Why couldn't Mama be more calm? Like Pa? Nellie noticed her older brother, Victor, turning red in the face as Mama hectored him about harnessing their mule, Bluebell. He knew how to do it! He was twenty years old, for heaven's sake, not twelve. She didn't need to embarrass him in front of Deb and the rest of Uncle Orry's family – but when Mama got herself all het up, was best just to stay out of her way.

Nellie often felt sorry for Victor. He was the calm, silent type and hated to be the center of attention. He would inherit the farm someday and she planned to live with him – the two of them unwed, sharing a companionable silence and a similarly lax attitude toward housework.

Finally, both families got underway. The wagons creaked slowly down the road. They were packed so full, no one could ride in them 'cept little Gerry, only four years old. He was perched on top of Bluebell with Victor alongside to hang onto him.

Hazel temporarily deserted her husband and in-laws to join the girls. "This is your year, Deb," she told their cousin. "Time to make a conquest. Everyone knows camp meeting is the best place to meet and court. I met Boolie when I was sixteen. We spent a year getting to know each other, and a year engaged, and look at me now, a married woman with my own home!"

Nellie liked Boolie, but she saw nothing exciting about being a married woman with her own home. It only meant a lot of work for very little reward, the best part of which was getting out from under Mama's thumb. But then there'd be that husband to deal with – so not worth it at all.

She said, "Thanks for the advice, but no thanks. We've got plans of our own."

Deb whispered, "We do?"

"We sure do." She turned to Hazel. "And we don't need to waste the final fleeting days of our youth primping and preening. We're fixin' to have fun!"

"Well, excuse me for living!" Hazel replied and walked off in a huff. Didn't matter. Nellie knew she'd be back. Some things just couldn't exist in the universe, and a bottled-up Hazel was one of them.

Later, when they'd finished supper at the tent and the dishes were washed and packed away, Nellie begged to wander the passways with Deb. Mama pushed back her hair and glanced around as though looking for some housework to do. Finally, she sighed and said, "Well, just be sure you come back when you see fireflies. And take Gerry with you."

"Oh, Mama! We can't have any fun with him along!"

"Take him or stay here. Makes no nevermind to me."

Augh! That's the way it had been her whole life, always had to drag one of her younger brothers along with her. As far as she was concerned, five brothers were four too many.

Deb didn't mind. She held little Gerry's hand and encouraged him to prattle away about his marbles and his top and the ragged old cloth cow he called Budgie. Deb liked little kids, probably because she only had three brothers.

As they meandered, Nellie shook off her crabbiness and suggested they go down to the Bog. The southeast corner of the campground, just slightly downslope, tended to perpetual muddiness, hence its name. The girls ended up at the family tent of Lynette Paterson, one of their fellow students at the Female Academy.

Lynette's mama always had lemonade and gingersnaps at hand. She was one of those jolly, well-upholstered mothers. And Lynette had no younger brothers, the lucky duck.

The three girls soon settled on the swing, talking and laughing. Gerry sat on the edge of the porch, murmuring to Budgie.

Lynette began filling them in on the latest. "Munson Kemp has finally gotten taller. Skinny as a rail, but taller." She stared as a few boys sauntered by. As soon as they were out of earshot, she said, "What is it about boys from *out of town*, that makes them so much more interesting than the boys from round here?"

"We haven't known them our whole lives, that's why," Nellie replied. "It's hard to get excited about a boy that you can remember picking boogers."

"Picking boogers," Gerry repeated softly. "Boogers."

They watched as another lanky boy walked by, his gaze sliding from girl to girl. "Don't know that fella," Lynette said, "but he's got a bicycle. I saw him riding it out on Shandy Creek Road."

"I wish I had a bicycle," Nellie said. "And bloomers to wear while riding it. But Mama would have a cow."

"Have a cow," Gerry murmured. "Budgie!"

Nellie turned a frown toward her little brother. He could be an awful tattle-tale. Nevertheless, she continued, "*Not ladylike*, that's what Mama would say.

And *frivolous*. Her idea of fun is cleaning the pantry and finding a jar of preserves she forgot about."

When the fireflies began to show, the girls headed back to their tent. Gerry walked between them, holding their hands, and Deb carried Budgie. As they headed up the slope, Victor passed by, gravely tipping his hat to them.

Deb asked, "Where's he going?"

"Home. He'll stay at the house every night so he can feed and water the animals and bring us fresh eggs and milk in the morning."

"That's too bad. He'll miss out on all the fun." She turned to look after him as he walked away.

"Who cares? It's the beginning of camp meeting, and we have eight whole days to have fun!" And she made Gerry and Deb run all the way back to the tent.

Little Sunday turned up hot and sunny, and the arbor filled with people who were smiling and happy in anticipation of the week to come. Mama went loco as usual, making sure her brood was shining clean, their clothes up to snuff, and the boys' hair slicked to their heads. Nellie suffered in her first corset, sweating to death. Hazel sat with Boolie's family, looking unusually pale. And Deb, beautiful as always, managed to sidle in between Nellie and Victor. A faint sweet scent of lavender came off her dress.

The preacher was Reverend Benjamin Ames, a general favorite. Nellie tried to pay attention, but she couldn't keep from staring at the bicycle boy, two rows ahead. He had wide shoulders and a tall, straight, suntanned neck above his white shirt. She imagined him riding that bicycle, his hands on the handlebars, his legs pumping the pedals. She could almost see him lunging down Shandy Creek Road, in and out of patches of sunlight, bicycle spokes whirring. She wondered, *What would it be like to ride with him*?

The congregation rose to sing, interrupting her daydreams. She lurched to her feet, a few seconds behind everyone else. Deb didn't seem to notice. She sang out with her sweet voice and a smile on her face. Of course, she didn't always notice what was right in front of her. Nellie loved her to death, but there was no denying that Deb could be a bit obtuse.

Just last night, when they were whispering in bed, Nellie enumerated all the things she wanted to do while at camp meeting – visit McLeod's store, play tennis with her brothers' rackets, practice archery with the bows and arrows Deb's brothers had brought along, go berrying, and walk over to the old cemetery next to the Methodist church, to collect honeysuckle.

"I don't know," Deb said, her voice low. "I kinda want to stay around the tent and the arbor."

"Good golly, *why*?"

Deb had shrugged. "I like the music and seeing everyone. I like to be able to just walk and talk, and not get all hot and sweaty. I'm sixteen now, and . . . "

"Oh Lordy," Nellie responded, throwing herself back on her pillow. "Don't tell me you're all ga-ga over some *boy*."

"No! Not really. I mean, there's not really anyone I have my eye on, but . . ." She stopped and snuggled further under the sheet. "Just . . . I just want to hang around here."

Nellie couldn't understand it. Stick around the tent? What fun was that? The best part of camp meeting was having a little freedom and getting out from under Mama's eagle eye. Couldn't Deb see that?

Oh, it was so frustrating! First Hazel, now Deb! Why did they want to rush into marriage? Didn't they want to have any *fun* first? Well, they were crazy, just plain crazy. She, Nellie, was not going to fall in love anytime soon. *To heck with that!*

On Monday, the weather was just boiling. Even Nellie had to admit it was too hot for tennis. The girls settled for taking a quilt out beyond the ring of tents, to sit under an oak tree, eat strawberries and allow the breeze to caress their bare feet and lower legs. At least, Nellie, Deb and Lynette did. Hazel was all prim and proper, like usual. Her dress came down to her ankles, and so that was all she would expose.

Nellie, watching, knew she was in no hurry to reach the age of putting up her hair and letting down her hems. Entrance into young womanhood would 'commence with Commencement' so she had plenty of time. As she idly teased an ant with a blade of grass, a group of boys came into view, talking and laughing. They shoved each other in playfulness, and they all had wet hair which probably meant they'd been bathing in the creek. That boy was with them, and he had his bicycle.

At the boys' appearance, all the girls sat up and demurely spread their skirts, even while pretending to be unaware of the boys' presence. Lynette began chatting animatedly, winding the long curl that hung over her shoulder, and arching her back slightly.

Nellie stared frankly at the boy. He was never going to notice her, not with Deb and Lynette nearby, so she felt free to watch as though she were invisible. He wasn't like some of the other fellas. Their clowning became even more boisterous once they noticed the girls, but he just watched the girls, his hands in his pockets. His eyes roved over them almost as though he were speculating which would run the best in a race. Nellie had seen that look in Pa's eyes when he went to the livestock auction, before he decided which calf or mule to buy.

"Nellie, don't stare!" Hazel whispered. "It makes you look fast."

She didn't care. She stared at him until finally his gaze crossed her face. Crossed it and returned. She stared at him as hard as she could till her eyes felt like they were going to burst into flames. He grinned at her and a chill ran right down her back.

The spell broke when the boys began showing off – shoving and wrestling each other – and Hazel got to her feet and made the rest of the girls get up, gather the quilts, and head back to the tent. Nellie followed dutifully, but glanced back once, thoughts of Lot's wife in her head. The boy was still watching her and grinning. "Nell, come *on*," Hazel barked, and Nellie came on.

Tuesday, she didn't see him. Victor arrived at the tent with the morning milk and eggs and suggested taking a wagonload of cousins down to the river to do some fishing. This was a big treat for the girls for they were rarely allowed to go so far. They put some straw and quilts on the floor of the wagon, packed a picnic lunch and jugs of spring water, and rode down the dusty, bumpy road past the church and five miles beyond to the river.

Of course, Mama insisted that Nellie take Gerry with her. *Augh!*

Nellie loved the river. She didn't get there often, but she surely loved to watch the water flow past, rippling over rocks and eddying in pools where tree roots crisscrossed and interrupted the flow. She liked seeing herons stalk through the shallows and hawks wheeling overhead. In her mind, she pictured herself floating down the river – maybe in a canoe, maybe on a big riverboat paddle-wheeler – and exploring strange new places. Why, all the world lay out there waiting! So much to explore and discover!

As soon as they arrived, the boys immediately rolled up their britches and took their fishing poles out into the water. Victor volunteered to keep an eye on Gerry, who had his own pint-sized bamboo rod. It was such a hot day that even the girls went wading, with the back hem of their dresses pulled between their legs and tucked into their belts.

"Look – bloomers!" Nellie joked, pulling at the sides of her dress to create puffs. "Shocking! Send for the sheriff!" Of course, it didn't matter in front of brothers and cousins if her bare knees and calves were exposed. Besides the water covered most of that. It was delicious to feel the cool mud beneath the river squishing up between her toes, and fun to try to catch tiny frogs and minnows with her bare hands.

After lunch, most of the girls took a little nap in the shade. Nellie didn't feel a bit sleepy. She made Gerry lie down next to Hazel – *don't wanna*, he insisted, even as he yawned – and the rest of the boys went beyond the riverbend to do some skinny-dipping. She headed in the other direction, climbed a tree, and watched clouds go by.

Deb and Victor walked off on their own, gathering wildflowers and sweet grasses to bring back to the tent. Deb was about the only girl Victor ever talked to, Nellie thought. Her gentle ways got past his shyness. It was good of Deb to take the trouble. Most of the time, because he was so silent, people got in the habit of ignoring him.

Sometimes Nellie wished Deb could marry Victor, even though she knew it was impossible. First cousins couldn't marry. It was too bad, because if they got married, Deb would live close by the rest of their lives. She dreaded the thought of Deb marrying some stranger from far away where they might never see each other again.

By late afternoon, the boys had caught a fine mess of fish, so it was time to head back to the campground. Cleaning fish was not Nellie's favorite task, but everyone pitched in, and oh, that fried fish was so delicious!

On Wednesday, Nellie saw the boy again, this time at the late-afternoon prayer meeting for young folk. This was Nellie's first year being included in this group, instead of the children's prayer meeting, and of course, Hazel had to give advice about it.

"Wear your pink striped dress – it's pretty without being too dressy, and Deb can wear her blue striped. And the white ribbons. And I'll lend you my tortoise-shell comb."

Nellie endured all this by picturing the advice marching in one ear and dripping out the other. Hazel jerked and pulled her dress into place and sighed over it. "You picked up an awful lot of freckles yesterday. Should've stayed in the shade." She smoothed a little pomade on Nellie's hair and finally, stood back to get the overall effect. "Well," she sighed again, "I guess you'll do."

"Praise indeed," Nellie responded. "Don't break your neck over it."

"Well, just behave yourself. No more staring at boys – you're getting worse than Lynette! Mama will wear you out with a switch if she learns you were staring."

Hazel finished with several other admonitions which Nellie withstood by mentally humming the *Star-Spangled Banner*. She wondered if the boy would be at the arbor.

And he was – sitting with Tucker Grisham and completely ignoring the prayer service. His bold gaze traveled up and down the benches, pausing at any face that caught his interest. Just before it got to Nellie, she glanced away, feigning indifference. When she figured it was safe to glance back at him, she found him still watching. He grinned and a flush rose in her cheeks. She couldn't look again until service was over.

Once they rose from their seats, she saw him begin to head in her direction. But then, just when life was about to get interesting, Victor came over and took herself and Deb under his wing, saying "Mama said to bring you both right back, no dawdling on the way."

Honestly, how was a girl ever supposed to have any adventures when she was only allowed to be around brothers, cousins, and dip-doodles she'd known as puppies? And when they got back to the tent, and it might have been possible to get permission to walk the passways, Deb up and declared she wanted to stay at the tent and listen to Uncle Gerald play his fiddle. She plunked herself down on the swing and Nellie had no choice but to join her. Girls weren't allowed to go walking alone on the passways.

A crowd of friends and relatives gathered round as the evening turned musical, with Hazel leading the singing, and everyone joining in on the choruses. Even Victor, who couldn't sing a lick, added a tuneful whistle. Nellie felt bored right out of her mind. So, she sang flat and slightly behind, on purpose. *Lord a'mighty!* Her family gave her the pea-doodles.

But Thursday – oh, Thursday would live in her mind forever. She'd been sent to the spring for a bucket of water, to wash the lunch dishes. Mama had instructed her not to linger, but then went on down the passway to visit old Mrs. McLeod, so no one really noticed when Nellie walked as slowly as she dared to the spring.

And there he was, standing with some other boys in the field between the spring and the tents. They were taking turns riding his bike down the slope to the spring. He saw her and immediately walked over, taking her bucket in his hand and filling it for her. A real gentleman. "Well, hello there, Nellie Caswell," he said softly.

He'd asked someone for her name! She flushed and looked down at the ground. "I like your bicycle," she said. "Sure is a nice one."

"It's a Stearn's Yellow Fellow. Came all the way from New York." By one accord, they turned and headed back toward the tents, but slowly, walking close enough to each other that her hand brushed once against his.

Nellie couldn't even remember later what they said. Something about his classes at the high school in Bennetton and her brothers and his sister, and other nonsense like that. It didn't matter, they just walked along and took quick glances at each other's faces. She saw he had freckles too, and a patch of sunburn on his nose, and nice teeth and long eyelashes. His name was Gil Anderson and he was sixteen, two years older than her. When she bashfully admitted to being only fourteen, he said, "That's okay. I think it's alright for a fellow to like girls from one year older to two years younger. They don't have to be the same age." He would be graduating in a year and then he thought he might go to college. "Either that or out West. They're still looking for good men to serve with the Texas Rangers, and I'm a crackerjack at riding and shooting. Or maybe I'll work for the railroad." He flexed a muscle for her.

Eventually, sadly, they arrived back at the tents. Nellie didn't want any of her family to see her walking with a boy, so she turned to him and said she had to go. He gave her the bucket but took hold of her hand for a second first. "I sure hope I see you out walking later," he whispered. "I'll watch for you."

She managed to carry the bucket to the cooking shed without spilling it, but heaven knew how. Her mind was awhirl, and her heart kept thumping unevenly, leaving her dizzy and kneed. "So, this is when my real life starts," she thought. "I'll be dipped."

But that evening it rained and rained and rained. A hard, steady downpour that meant everyone had to stay inside. There was almost always at least one evening like this during camp meeting, but sometimes it ended early and Nellie set her hopes on that. She helped clean up after supper, and volunteered to read to Gerry, and even put on a waterproof and took the slop bucket out to the privy in the rain after Hazel threw up into it. By the time she got back, though, it was clear that the rain was going to continue for a while. She half-heartedly listened to Pa talking about how he was maybe going to 'raise the roof' next year, and put in a second floor on the tent, instead of just having the loft.

"The McLeods have done that on all four of their tents," he said, "and it just works a treat. Two bedrooms upstairs, and plenty of space downstairs for a bigger table and more chairs." He gave Mama some kind of mysterious smile, and said, "We're going to need more space, I'm thinking. Who knows what the future will bring?" Nellie hoped it wasn't going to bring another brother. Five was more than plenty.

She climbed up to the loft to find Deb, but she was lying down, face to the wall and her back to Nellie. Nell touched her shoulder and caught a glimpse of her face. She was weeping. Silently, barely moving, but Nellie clearly saw the gleam of tears on her cheeks.

"What's wrong?" she whispered.

"Nothing. Nothing. I'm being silly." Deb wiped her face with her hands and shook her head. "I'm just tired. Please, leave me be." She turned again to the wall, pulling a corner of the sheet over her shoulder and face.

W*hat the heck was that about?* Nellie thought about the day just past, when she'd been so happy talking to Gil. What had Deb been doing? She'd just been hanging around the tent all day, not doing much of anything that Nellie could see, just sitting on the swing with Victor. Could he have said something to upset Deb? It didn't seem likely, he hardly ever said anything at all, and almost never lost his temper or said rude things like some other brothers Nellie could mention. Why wasn't Deb talking to her? They could talk about anything!

A few minutes later, Mama came up to the loft to go to bed. There went any chance of getting Deb to speak up. And truth was, Nellie discovered she didn't particularly want to say anything about her own thoughts, either. She fell asleep, to dream of riding double with Gil, swooping down the path to the creek.

On Friday, she was bustin' to break loose all day. She kept trying to make excuses to leave the tent. "Don't you need a bucket of water?" she asked Mama.

"Yes. Take Gerry with you." *Augh!*

"Want me to go get some blackberries?"

"Yes. Take Gerry with you." *Criminentlies!*

"I need to go to the privy."

"Okay. Take Gerry to go, too." Oh, mercy Maud, she was going to lose her cotton-pickin' mind!

Finally, she just slipped away, like a cat in the night. Disregarding any of Mama's preachings or Hazel's nagging, she went out onto the passways and found Gil over near Bachelor's Corner, where all the single young men hung out. He immediately came over when he saw her, and they went off to the field between the campground and woods.

He brought his bicycle. "I'm going to teach you how to ride," he said, smiling. "I teach all my girlfriends how to ride."

Nellie thrilled at his words. Yes! Let Mama have a conniption fit. She didn't care. Her face flamed at the boldness, when he set her on the crossbar of his bike, and his arms went around to her to reach for the handlebar. She gripped the center of the handlebar and balanced herself carefully – and off they went, across the field on the narrow path to the creek, jouncing over rocks and picking up speed. She squealed a little as they rode downhill. He chuckled and tightened his arms. His legs kept bouncing against hers as he pedaled, so she held herself in more tightly, and learned to anticipate bumps and turns. The movements of the bicycle began to feel more familiar, more natural.

Once they got to the bottom, they walked the bike back up, talking and laughing. He explained about balancing the bike by keeping it moving forward all the time, and how to use the handbrake. "Of course, you need to watch out for your skirt," he said. "Can't let it get twisted up in the spokes. You have to hitch it up a bit." He glanced at her ankles. "Tuck it in around the crossbar." He smiled again.

When they got to the top of the slope, he suggested she try a solo ride. She positioned herself on the bicycle as he gave detailed instructions. "You'll be fine," he murmured, as he finished. "Here – this is for good luck." Suddenly he leaned in close and kissed her cheek.

Nellie gasped. She took a good grip on the handlebar, settled her feet on the pedals, and took off. Oh, it was like *flying*! She pedaled madly, weaving a little at first and then she got the knack of it. The bike soared down the path, moving like the wind, and she felt a surge of freedom she'd never experienced before. Now, this was something! This was adventure! She could go anywhere on a bicycle – across the state, across the country! She came to the creek and instead of stopping, she rode right through it, splashing and jolting over the stones at the creek bottom, then up the other side. Here she had to lean harder into the bike, standing slightly on the pedals the way she'd seen others do, up the path toward the woods. From far behind, she could hear Gil shouting for her to return. *Ha! In a pig's ear!*

Reckless with success, she kept riding. The path leveled out and came even with Gilead Church Road. She swerved onto the road, watching for ruts, and finally pulled up with a flourish at MacLeod's store. Old Mr. Loy sat out on the bench at the front, watching as she approached.

"What you up to there, Nellie Caswell?" he called, grinning around his pipe. "You gallivantin'?"

"I'm riding a bike!" she panted. Two women came out of the store, staring at her. She realized too late how she looked – her hair coming loose from her braids, her face and dress covered in a fine red dust. Without another word, she wheeled around and set off the way she'd come.

Gil didn't look any too happy when she returned. He held the bike while she climbed off, brushing at her skirt and face. "I didn't say you could ride that far," he snapped. "You coulda busted a spoke or somethin'." He bent to examine the wheels. "You're lucky you didn't wreck the tires. Who said you could ride off like that?"

"I just wanted to try it!" she said. "I didn't hurt it."

He glared at her and then calmed himself. "You want to ride again?"

"Oh, yes! Please!"

"Oh, you like it that much, huh?" Gil grinned lazily at her. "Okay. The price is one kiss. A real kiss."

Nellie stared at him. He wanted to kiss her? *Lawsy!* Without giving herself any time to think about it, she leaned toward him across the bike, her lips puckered.

"Not like that," he whispered, and drew her into his arms.

The bicycle seat pressed painfully into her belly, and Nellie pushed back, just as Gil's lips met hers and his tongue probed strangely into her mouth.

"Hey!" She pushed against him harder and broke free. For a moment she just stood there, catching her breath, shaken, a bit confused. Then, "Can I ride it now?"

Gil's brows came together in a frown, and the corners of his mouth went down. "Oh, I get it. You were just interested in my bike, all along." He gave her a disgusted look. "You're a tease. Girls like you give other girls a bad name." He jerked his bike around and mounted it. Just before he rode away, he said with a nasty grin, "Ain't that your brother over there?"

She glanced up to see Gerry, standing a few feet away, dragging Budgie by the tail. Of course. Just her luck. Gerry stared at her as Gil rode off. "You kiss a boy," he said.

"No, I didn't! You never mind!"

"You kiss a boy!" Gerry took off running back toward the tent. "Mama! Mama! Nellie kiss a boy!"

Nellie ran after him, but he could duck through the crowded passway faster than she could. Holy Moses butter'n'beans! If he got to Mama before she did, she'd be knocked into the middle of next week. Nellie put on a burst of speed, but she could see ol' big-mouth Gerry ahead, pulling on Mama's apron to get her attention. Mama bent down and listened, then turned and gave her the most awful look, and it was all Nellie could do to totter those last few steps. She got a sharp pinch on the arm, and instructions to *get up in that loft and stay there. Wait until your Pa hears!*

Nellie climbed up into the loft. There were hours to go before bedtime, and little chance that Mama would calm down by then. The loft bedding smelled musty and damp, but she mushed her face against one of the pillows. Oh, she was in a mess of trouble now, but all she wanted to do was dream of her ride, over and over. In only five days, her whole world had changed. She never imagined it could be like this. In all her life, she'd never forget it.

Of course, it was all hell in a handbasket when Pa got back to the tent. He gave her that long look that was worse than any whupping, and Mama pitched a variety of hissy fits, preaching about *more ladylike behavior* and *not getting a reputation* and *upholding the family honor*, until Nellie thought she might as well just dig a hole and climb into it, because Mama was never going to let her leave the house till Judgment Day.

Deb prudently wandered off elsewhere with Victor, so she wouldn't have to be witness to Nell's shame. For the rest of the day and all day Saturday, Nellie had to stay with Mama and the old ladies and babies in the arbor, and park herself at the tent the rest of the time. Her chance at adventure was over, and she couldn't stand it. Earthbound, after flying so high.

Of course, Hazel had to crow. "Told you so! Next time, you should listen to me."

"Go choke on a peach pit," Nellie replied.

On Big Sunday, after the preaching, after all the eating, when people were sitting around relaxed and happy and content to rest before packing up to go, some kind of flap blew up at Deb's family's tent. Nellie never knew what it was, something that got hushed up and smoothed over. All she knew was that Deb wasn't allowed to come over and spend the night anymore. Nellie managed to get one chance to talk to her, by waiting at the privy for her to come out. "Was it because of me?" Nellie asked. "Do they think I'm a bad girl and don't want you to have anything to do with me anymore?" She felt like crying. Deb was her *best friend.*

"It wasn't you," Deb gently replied. She'd clearly already been crying herself. "It wasn't you at all. It was me. I wanted something I just can't have." She gave Nellie a hug. "I'm going away for a while. Papa's sending me to Charlotte, to stay with Aunt Frances. I'll finish school there. They think it's best. They think I'll learn to forget."

Nellie didn't understand, and Deb wouldn't say anything further. Packing up when leaving camp meeting was always a little sad, and a lot less exciting than packing to come, but this time it felt even more depressing – and *strange*. Victor had brought the mule and wagon, but he looked just furious about something and left right away, walking back home all by himself. Strange thing number one.

Hazel didn't help pack at all, just sat on the bench with a cold wet cloth pressed to her face, moaning. Strange thing number two.

Boolie and Mama kept grinning at each other, for no reason at all. Strange thing number three. *Mama, grinning?*

And Gil never appeared, not even from afar. Nellie kept glancing around, watching for that yellow bicycle, sure that she'd seen it from the corner of her eye, but no beans.

At last the wagon was full – even to Mama's expectations – and they headed down the road toward home. Hazel sat in a rocking chair in the wagon, fanning herself, with the slop bucket handy. She sure was making a big deal out of a little indigestion, Nellie thought.

She walked alone, trying to detach herself from the family hubbub, and turned over her thoughts. So many strange things this week, but it didn't matter. Nellie might be chained to the farm for the rest of her natural-born life, but at least she had her precious memories. She would never forget. Not in a hundred years, a hundred camp meetings. Not in a hundred thousand million camp meetings, would she forget the Yellow Fellow and her first bicycle ride. She was an adventuress now! Not that anyone in her family would notice. They never noticed anything happening right in front of them. They were just so obtuse.

To Julia, with Love
1916

THERE ARE THOSE – MORE, PROBABLY THAN WE KNOW – who believe in ghosts. Who accept as true that there are spirits who haunt the places where they lived and died, and phantoms who have not yet settled in Heaven or Hell. Such folks are sure those presences are drawn particularly to old houses or structures. The older and shabbier, the better, with few visitors to bother them.

Camp meeting certainly fits that bill. Many of the tents are nearly a hundred years old. Their timbers have had time to absorb all kinds of shadows and traces, emotions and prayers. It's possible that ghosts linger in the rafters of the arbor, watch from the oak trees, and glide along passways after dark.

You surely have felt their presence. You know you have.

Maybe you'll say it's nothing. Just memories taking hold of your imagination. And why not? Inside the tent, you're surrounded by the loved ones of your past. Aunt Violet's table and chairs. Grandma's Bible. Your mother's hymn book and her recipes for chicken slip-downs and red velvet cake.

Your tent is steeped in recollections of camp meetings past . . . memories of running barefoot on the grass around the arbor, sleepy hours resting against your mother's shoulder during preaching. That day you got caught trying to play the organ, and good Lord, all the food! Wonderful meals eaten at the old table with the flowered cloth, or watermelon consumed on the bench outside as juice dribbled down your chin.

How could you *not* experience the shades of your ancestors? They were all around you. You grew up encircled by relatives, inundated with family – your grandparents, cousins, uncles. And when they left, they left too soon. You were never ready, and they were surely surprised. The mystery revealed. And then . . . yes, what then?

Is it reassuring to think that your long-dead family is still by your side, watching over you? Or is it terrifying – to think you're never alone. You surely wouldn't enjoy your Papa's presence every minute of your life – his stern expression of disapproval, his narrow view of morality. What if he'd been there with you, two years ago, when some folks wanted to close camp meeting down? Saying it had become too worldly, a place of hilarity rather than holiness.

But you spoke up, telling the Truth as you saw it: that not everything God gives us takes place during preaching. Some of it comes in the middle of the quiet night, to the sound of crickets and light from the stars. You said you felt the Lord's hand on you during meals shared with family, more family than could usually be together. You felt His love spreading around the table. You were eloquent. You spoke with determination and meant what you said. But could you have said it if you knew Papa looked on?

And your brother, Russell. Oh, you might not want to believe he was nearby all the time, especially if you made a mistake. He was so good at catching you out, so quick to pounce on an error or slipup. His scorn made you writhe.   Or maybe it would be good to finally tell him how you felt, once he was not able to talk back. Lord, how you longed to love him, to look up to him as a younger sister should. You were ready to nearly worship your big brother – so clever, so gifted – but instead he liked to shut you down and walk right over you. Just once you'd have liked to tell him so. *Shame on you.* And if you could, how satisfying would it be?

More likely, you would want to see your little boy. To hold him, stroke his dark curls, and press his soft cheek to your own. But he never came. Of all of them, he was the one you'd have welcomed. Instead, only nightmares, where once again you could not save him. His tiny soul flickered and was out, and the empty place inside you will last forever.

Why? Why didn't he come? There've been times when you knew the spirits were there. Your grandmother's voice, your mother's soft touch, the weight of another body on the mattress, or the sight of quick movement just at the corner of your eye.

Have they really been there, or was it just the terrible longing of a mournful mind? So many things unsaid, so much time wasted. No wonder we can never quite let go.

And the spirits themselves – what are *their* regrets? Do they linger out of choice or are they caught in some kind of limbo, unable to free themselves from whatever it is holding them to the Earth? What would they say if they could? What would they think of the changes? Electricity, telephones, automobiles and plank roads. Even ragtime music and women demanding to get the vote.

Would they warn us of troubles ahead? What about the flood last spring? Did they know it would wipe out every bridge on the river? That it would leave behind destroyed crops and toppled buildings and dismantled train tracks? If you listened more carefully, would you have been able to save those people who drowned, or do ghosts only know what's passed, and not what's ahead?

So many questions, and no answers. You might wish to ask them about the state of the world, about this war in Europe, about so many soldiers and civilians dying over in France and Belgium. Are you safe? Will your loved ones be called to fight? Will the President keep his promises?

Memories, imagination, faint traces or real presence . . . you don't know the truth, you can only guess. And I, your late husband, can only watch and wait, until some far future date when you are with me again. Yes, I can only watch and wait, and once in a great while, reach out to stroke your shoulders or run a finger down your spine.

The Bennetton Bugle
1924

DEAR READERS, I preface this week's Painter's Creek column with an apology for its absence in last week's paper. I was sick with tonsillitis. However, nothing much happened, so you haven't missed a thing.

This week, I am visiting camp meeting near Painter's Creek, which has been an annual tradition for almost 100 years. I interviewed Reverend Joseph Calley, of the Bennetton circuit, who is lead pastor for this event and who will be preaching alongside Reverend Crowell of Asheboro, Reverend McCarthy of High Point, and Reverend Thompson of Charlotte.

"We expect around ten thousand visitors on Big Sunday," he said. "We'll have worship in the arbor and in the outer fields, if we overflow, which we expect to. Please let your readers know that no food or beverages will be sold that day, and that they should bring sandwiches or other food for themselves. There will, of course, be fresh spring water. We have decided to ban sales of lemonade, watermelon and ice cream, which in recent years have produced a carnival-like atmosphere. Everyone is welcome to attend, but we hope the rowdy elements will stay away. Also, everyone is asked to bring a box to take home their trash. Thank you."

This reporter can remember the war years, and especially after the Armistice in 1919, when over twenty thousand people attended the Sunday preaching, to give thanks for peace. At the time, there was much discussion that these numbers might give rise to growth for Painter's Creek, an influx of new businesses and residents, maybe even a rail line. However, as the numbers returned to their pre-war levels beginning in 1920, such talk was abandoned. "It's the radio I blame," says Reverend Calley. "Nobody cares about the Lord anymore. They just want jazz."

I visited among the many people who had moved into their family 'tents' for the week of camp meeting. Quite a few hold family reunions during this time, including the Johnson-Boswell family with over fifty members in attendance. Mr. Gideon Johnson, patriarch of the family, when asked his age, announced "I am 89 years, four months, and seventeen days old." This reporter remembers being quite frightened as a young child by Mr. Johnson's wooden arm, a memento of the hot action at Sutherland Station in 1865. However, I soon learned he was a kindly man, a successful farmer and was for more than ten years the postmaster for Painter's Creek.

TAKE CALOTABS FOR THE LIVER
BEWARE OF IMITATIONS
SUTTON DRUG STORE, BENNETTON

Both the arbor and many of the tents are highly regarded as original and authentic to the campground, dating from the 1830's. One of the most interesting structures, though, is the hoosegow, or Jail, located on the campground. Every year, due to the size of the crowds, camp meeting is legally entitled to select a mayor and police officers to control disorderly behavior, such as disruptive activities and breaking Prohibition laws.

Two of the more famous, or infamous, frequenters of the hoosegow were the Pike 'boys', Gable, now 64, and 'Ten-Mile', 66. I asked the two brothers about some of their more notorious escapades.

"Oh, we was just trying to have some fun," Gable replied. "Just messing. We put some old chicken gizzards behind the pulpit once. They drew a pack of dogs right in the middle of preaching. Another time, we moved the preachers' outhouse down to the crossroads. And there was the year we added our own padlocks to people's privies, so's we could watch them go crazy when they couldn't get in there. Just little stuff like that."

I asked them what they remembered most from camp meetings past. "All the pretty girls," 'Ten-Mile' replied.

"And he do mean ALL the pretty girls," added Gable, and those two old gentlemen commenced to giggling at each other.

"Be sure to mention I said hello to Miss Gaynelle McLeod," Ten-Mile said. "She was the prettiest of 'em all. Still is."

Speaking of pretty girls, Miss June Almyre was the hostess for a bridal shower given for Miss Jessamine Howard, right there at camp meeting, at Miss Almyre's parents' tent. A profusion of roses and crape myrtle blossoms decorated the main room and front porch, and a selection of cakes, tea sandwiches, and pickles were offered the female guests.

Miss June Almyre is a typist at the Bennetton Bugle, and an ornament to the office. It is her job to type up all my notes before they go to the editor, Mr. Nash, and considering the state of my hen-scratching, it's lucky for me she has good peepers. Very pretty blue peepers.

IS YOUR STATIONERY ALL IT SHOULD BE?
DO THE RECIPIENTS OF YOUR LETTERS RECEIVE
THE KIND OF QUALITY THEY EXPECT?
COME SEE THE VARIETY OF STYLES AT
TALBOT & TALBOT DEPARTMENT STORE

As always, quite a few small-fry can be found at camp meeting. The boys and girls tend to congregate in groups on their parents' tent porches or run wild through the passways. I witnessed an altercation between several small females, hotly debating whether more than one of their dollies could be named Annabelle, and which girl had named her doll Annabelle first.

Similarly, I saw three small boys, brothers, playing mumblety-peg on their porch. The youngest watched intently but did not play, and his older brother said, "Ma won't let Ernie play anymore. He keeps missing the board and stabbing his big toe." Ernie mournfully showed me his bandaged toe. "Does it hurt?" I asked. "Nope," he said with tears in his eyes. "But they're using *my knife*."

While at camp meeting, discussion came up regarding the increasing numbers of automobiles in the area. "This is the first year," one man said, "that autos have outnumbered buggies and wagons." Talk then turned to the rash of automobile accidents this year, and particularly the big accident two weeks ago right in front of the new high school, in which four men were injured. "They all drive too fast, especially on these roads, and usually they're lickered up," was the consensus. Certainly, the concerns about illegal liquor have grown in the county, especially after the discovery of 250 gallons of peach beer in Morley Rudisill's cellar.

The discussion then turned to the need for better roads, and the astounding fact that the state highway department has decided not to improve the old stagecoach road, which runs right past the campground, and instead develop the road that runs through Keith Crossroad, nearly three miles north. It is considered a more direct route to Bennetton from the bridge at the river, and mainly runs through farmland at this time. Once again, Painter's Creek gets passed up by progress.

A STUBBORN FACT

If we cut the price of tires, we'd have to cut
the quality too. That would not do you any
good. We would rather sell, and we believe
you would rather buy, good tires at fair prices.
The Diamond Cord we offer is a tire of
remarkable value at a very reasonable price.
DIXIE GROCERY COMPANY
SOLE DISTRIBUTOR IN BENNETTON

On the subject of Progress, Reverend Calley asked me to state specifically that the campground now has electric lights for the arbor and passways. The individual tents are not hooked up to electrical power yet, so that means everyone is still going to have to use their hand-held fans, instead of electric oscillating fans such as are popular in many homes and offices.

Indeed, at the Bennetton Bugle, we are constantly under the necessity of putting paperweights on any loose papers sitting on our desks. Just last week, it was necessary for myself and Miss June Almyre to retrieve nearly a week's worth of obituaries before they flew out of the room. I will add, Miss Almyre was a good sport about the need to crawl around on the floor grabbing papers. She has a delightful smile.

One thing that has certainly not changed at Camp Meeting is the prevalence of skeeters and no see'ums. Not only is it necessary to burn citronella candles, but many campers also swear by the use of lavender oil. "I remember there used to be a patent medicine that people bought for bug bites," said Mrs. William (Nellie) Howard, our well-known local aviatrix. "Mama always bought a big bottle of it at the beginning of the summer. Boy howdy, did she have a conniption fit when she found out it was only baking soda and water. It worked swell but cost about four times what she would have spent on just plain old baking soda, which she already had on her kitchen shelf."

THIS WEEK'S HUMOR

Husband: I just opened this checking account for you
last week,
and the bank says it's almost empty already.
Wife: That can't be true, I still have nearly half the
checks left!

If a man's face is his fortune, some of us are
stuck with small change.

Be sure to check this column next week for a full
description of the final Sunday at camp meeting, as
well as any other Painter's Creek news. Some weeks
it's difficult to find enough to fill this column, but camp
meeting is always useful for producing stories. For nearly
one hundred years, this event and place have been the
source of religious renewal, family reunions, and indeed,
many a courtship has begun here. So if you're reading
this, Miss June Almyre, which you have to, being the
typist, I respectfully suggest we meet at camp meeting
this evening, where I will treat you to a Cheerwine and
a pleasant chat while we stroll the time-hallowed circuit
of the passways.

Submitted by reporter, J. Thomas Broadwell,
August 5, 1924

The Mother-in-Law
1936

IN LATE AFTERNOON, THE SUN DIPPED BELOW the outspread branches of oak trees beyond the campground, and blessed shade crept toward the rows of tents. It would be hours yet before the heat broke, but at least now there was a sense of relief and a small stirring of activity among the campers who had spent the hottest hours of the day languidly chatting and fanning themselves. Now, women rose to begin preparations for supper, children settled down to quieter games than their morning energy allowed, and men slid imperceptibly into naps over their newspapers.

Alveena Sycamore stirred too, wrapping her knitting around the needles and placing it in the tote bag she brought everywhere. "Time to go fix supper," she announced to her friend, Gladys Puge. She groaned slightly as she stood up. "Joe and Caroline will be here."

"How's she doing?" Gladys asked, wrapping up her own needlework. "Any better?"

Alveena thought for a moment about her daughter-in-law, then said, "I don't know, Glad, I really don't. Sometimes she seems right cheered up, but it's not a normal cheerfulness, you know? Kinda bright and brittle, like china 'bout to shatter. Other times, she's quiet and peaceful." Alveena took her seat again and faced her friend. "Better than last year. But dreamy…like she's livin' in her own head. I sure don't understand that girl."

Caroline's behavior, ever since the death of her little girl Daisy, had been a big concern. She'd taken it hard. Any mother would, of course. Daisy was a bright, beautiful little girl, whose death from heart disease had been almost beyond understanding. One moment, she was a healthy little five-year-old, and the next, a wasted, pale wraith who looked like a wax doll in her coffin. It had been one of the most heartbreaking experiences of Alveena's life, let alone Caroline's and Joe's. But Joe had regained his balance enough to force himself back to work, the way men do. Caroline, however, stayed home and spent most days in a rocking chair staring out the window. She spoke little, and it seemed like she just refused to step back into her own life. Grief was something Alveena understood, but this was something more, a sickness that fed on itself.

She said to Gladys, "I told you about their bird, didn't I? They have this little parakeet, Petey. It talks a bit, says things they taught him, and things he just picked up. Like *pretty bird* and *Petey wants a cracker*, and *Rise and shine*. I was over there 'bout a month ago, and the bird began making this awful noise, this kind of shuddery, heaving sound. Joe jumped up and threw the cloth over the cage to shut him up. I just froze. Couldn't say a thing. Lordy, Glad, that bird sounded just like a woman sobbing. He musta heard Caroline."

"Oh mercy!"

"Caroline didn't even seem to notice. But holy smoke – it sure gave me the heebie-jeebies. Little Daisy's been gone for two years, now. And Caroline has yet to come back to normal."

She rose to her feet again, groaning a little from stiffness. Gladys did the same, and they giggled at how pitiful they sounded. "It's getting so's I can't sit more'n half an hour at a time," Gladys said. "I'm afraid one of these days, I'm just gonna rust in place, like an old tractor out in the field."

"I know. I wonder how long I'll be able to keep going. I'll be 63 in September. Mama died when she was 60."

"Now, don't get all morbid on me. My mama died at 45, and I'm still going strong. Mean as ever." She grinned and for a moment, Alveena could see past the steel-rimmed eyeglasses and the grey hair to the 12-year-old 'Glad' who had the best ideas and got into the most mischief, and who was her best friend in the world. They'd gone through school and weddings, childbirth and motherhood together. They'd commiserated through the 'change', and held each other's hand when death visited.

Nowadays, they didn't see each other nearly enough. Gladys lived with her husband in Bennetton, where he was superintendent at the bottling plant, and Alveena was out at the farm where she and her husband Walter raised their four boys. Walter was gone now, and Walt Junior, nicknamed Juney, ran the place. One of the best parts of camp meeting was the opportunity to spend time with Gladys and other women her own age.

Alveena went on down to her own tent and set about fixing supper. She had a mess of okra, some fatback and some leftover cornbread, so she fried it all up, even the cornbread, slicing it thin so it got nice and crisp. She made coleslaw to go alongside and sliced strawberries for dessert. Joe and Caroline arrived in Joe's Model T, and Caroline did seem fairly cheerful, for once, wearing a flowery print dress and a bow in her fluffy blond hair.

She'd even baked a chocolate cake, which certainly knocked Alveena for a loop, and made her wish she'd gone to more trouble with the meal. True, the cake was a bit lopsided, but it was the effort that counted.

Caroline helped with the dishes. She was still not very talkative, but she smiled and was bright-eyed. Afterward, they all went out to sit on the porch, and Joe and Caroline sat together on the swing, holding hands. Alveena didn't say anything about it, she just hoped this break from grief would last. Maybe Caroline was pregnant again? Alveena had hoped and prayed that they'd have another baby to fill their hearts. Maybe it had finally happened.

She began to think that her suspicion was true, when she saw how Caroline watched all the children playing in the passways, especially any little girls that went by. Alveena had seen her watching children before, but then it was with a sad and hungry expression, now she seemed almost ready to laugh. Oh, how Alveena hoped it was true.

The last couple of years had been tough. Walter had died only a few months after Daisy, and it took so much effort to go through the motions each day. She'd done it, so as not to grieve her children still further, but she knew it was hard just to force oneself to get out of bed. Walter's life, though, had been long and full. And on his deathbed, he said "I got nothing to kick about." So she had known she shouldn't either, and had gone out of her way to reach out to her daughter-in-law. But Caroline turned away.

Since then, much to her shame, Alveena had distanced herself. When someone is drowning, you have to be careful, else they'll pull you in too. She did, though, feel sorry for Joe. Caroline had never exactly been the kind of wife a man could lean on. A silly little flapper she was, in many ways, always up for dancing and happy times, but darn near hopeless for life's struggles.

And life had sure been a struggle, these past few years. Nobody had any money. She was lucky to have the farm, and Juney to run it. They'd never raised much cotton, so all the boll weevil damage hadn't hit them personally, but it sure affected the South in general. Especially mill workers. Two of her boys had to find other lines of work, but turned out they were adaptable and strong. The country's finances, following the crash, had been bad, but not as bad as damage from the boll weevils.

She had always prided herself on being strong. All the time they were raising the children, she and Walter had worked side-by-side to build their farm and their dairy herd, and grow crops so they could put clothes on everyone's backs. Later, when things got a mite easier, she'd expanded her skills in growing vegetables and flowers, baking all sorts of good things, preserving, canning, and quilting. In 1928, she was awarded the Homemaker of the Year prize by the county Women's League. When hard times hit, she used her creativity to stretch a meal, or make old clothes look new again. That was a woman's first job – to help her family. She pitied Caroline, but she couldn't help getting a bit impatient, too. She wasn't the first woman to lose a child. It was surely time for her to rouse herself.

That night, when the campground settled down and people tried to sleep, Alveena lay on the cot in the upstairs room with an electric fan sending cool air back and forth, and she made a new vow. She would try again to be a friend to her daughter-in-law. She prayed to the good Lord that if He did choose to send them another baby, it would be healthy and have a long, fruitful life.

Lying there, with every little noise keeping her awake, she imagined a time, perhaps a year from now, when a small child might be sleeping in the corner of the bedroom where they had always put the crib.

The sound of cicadas filled the air, along with the hum of the fan, and a low, even snore from Joe in the next room. There was no door between the two rooms, just a sheet hung in the doorway, and she could hear every little sound. Of course, she could also hear noises from the adjoining tents, since only a few thin boards separated them. She could distinctly hear somebody coughing, the drop of a boot on the wooden floor, even a small child whining.

She was almost asleep when she heard footsteps leading from Joe and Caroline's room, the sound moving down the stairs and out the back door. She figured it was Caroline going to the privy, and then realized, no, the footsteps stopped on the back porch. Then a different sound, the creak-creak of the porch swing. The sounds settled into a rhythm and lulled her to sleep, and in the morning she wondered just how long Caroline had stayed out there, in the dark by herself.

At any rate, Caroline seemed fine in the morning, humming some sort of catchy tune as she fried eggs and toasted bread. Alveena made coffee, and they all sat around the table in a sort of friendly fog, slowly coming awake.

Soon after breakfast, Alveena trotted off to morning prayer meeting. She'd long ago given up trying to persuade her family to join her. Not one of her four sons bothered. They were willing enough to send their young'ns to the children's and youth services, but they seemed to feel that attendance on Sunday was good enough for adults. Her two middle boys, Bud and Rowan, didn't even show up at camp meeting at all. She herself didn't believe in missing a single preaching. And while she was at it, she had a little heart-to-heart talk with God. "Please, dear Lord," she thought, "Help me *like* Caroline a little more. Help me to love her. I know I'm always seeing her shortcomings, and I shouldn't."

When she returned, Joe and Caroline were gone, and so was their auto. So she took her knitting back over to Gladys' tent, where they laughed themselves silly over old stories of misadventures. "Oh, don't make me laugh anymore," Gladys moaned. "I can barely hold my water these days!" This, of course, made them laugh even more, especially when Gladys began a tight, jerking little run, trying to hold her knees together as she scurried to the privy. And Alveena herself had to hop a bit and pray, waiting for her turn. Getting old, she thought, was no laughing matter. Literally!

She went back to her own tent for lunch and found Joe making a meal of hard cheese, pickles, peanuts, and a Pepsi Cola. "Where's Caroline?" she asked, noticing that the car was gone again.

Joe shrugged. "She went to town. It's a long day for her here, she gets restless."

Alveena didn't like the sound of that. In her day, a woman didn't just go driving off by herself. Not that they had automobiles back then, but she wouldn't have driven off in the buggy, either. It was all part of this new generation, always on the move. "She seems to be doing better," she said, tentatively trying Joe out. If he wanted to share any news, she was surely ready. "More cheerful."

Joe just sort of grunted and let out a long belch.

"Joe! Shame on you!"

He grinned, looking like a kid again, and she smiled back at him. He announced he was going out for a smoke, so she cleared his plate and rinsed the soda bottle, still smiling. Well, he did seem in a good mood. That was promising. Maybe they knew Caroline was pregnant but weren't ready to announce it yet. Maybe they were planning to announce it on Big Sunday, when Juney's family would be there too. Maybe they had really turned the corner. The thought gladdened her heart. A new baby in the family would lift her own spirits, as well. "Please, Lord, let it be true," she whispered.

A little shade fell on her sunny day, though, when Caroline returned late in the afternoon, all flushed and happy, looking prettier than she had in years. There was something about her, something Alveena couldn't quite put her finger on. Her daughter-in-law was smiling, but almost too fiercely. And she seemed distracted, humming little snatches of music and fidgety in her movements.

Alveena felt a familiar sense of annoyance, and then felt ashamed for feeling it. Just as people dealt with grief in different ways, they dealt with joy differently too. Another woman might act quietly serene in such a situation; certainly if Caroline felt a bit nervous about a new pregnancy, that was understandable. What was not so understandable was how she continued to creep out of the tent every night and sit in the swing until the wee hours. And every day, she drove off, with Joe's acceptance and a complete lack of explanation. Surely, there was something just not right about her continued bright smile but dreamy absent-mindedness. And that constant humming!

Finally, Alveena couldn't stand it any longer. She insisted Joe tell her what Caroline was up to with this driving to town so often.

All he said was, "Aw, leave her alone, Ma. She's happy for once. Ain't that enough?" But she noticed that he, too, was watching Caroline closely. Maybe even concernedly. He spoke gently to her and often sat close, holding her hand. Caroline seemed to appreciate his attentiveness, and yet…and yet, she didn't *need* it. She was completely content to abide in some kind of bright-colored daydream.

On the fourth morning, Alveena said to Gladys, "I love camp meeting. I love being with you and all our other friends. I love the preaching. But I have to say, one thing I don't love is all this time spent with Caroline and Joe. I'm 'shamed to say it – but I swannee, they're makin' me crazy! I'm seeing too closely into their marriage – a heck of a lot more than I want to know. Caroline's up to something. She surely is. She's off gadding about in her own little world. Joe's worried too, but he won't *do* anything. I think – "

She broke off her words, unsure whether she wanted to tell Gladys. Maybe she didn't have the right to do so. And if she said the words, might that make them come true? But then it came rushing out. "I think she's . . . having an affair."

"No! No, she wouldn't! Joe's a good man."

"Makes no nevermind. I hate to think it of her, I surely do, but what else can it be? She keeps running off in the car and coming back all in a tizzy. I don't like it, Glad! I want to know the truth."

"Well, then, do something about it! Follow her into town. See what she's up to. We can take the DeSoto."

Gladys's little runabout was a sore subject between them. Gladys had learned to drive back in the early twenties, while Alveena had been content to let Walter do all the driving. "You're a fool," Gladys told her at the time. "Stop living in the Dark Ages. Lots of women drive."

"Lots of women smoke cigarettes and cut their hair, too," Alveena had said, "but you won't catch me doing it." It was one of their worst arguments ever and caused bad feelings between them for months. They'd finally agreed to disagree, but now that Walter was gone and she had no way to get around, Alveena sometimes felt that Gladys had a strong desire to come out with, "I told you so…"

At last she said, "If Caroline takes off today, we'll just follow and see where she goes. Better to know the worst, than just fret myself to death."

From then on, though she felt a bit ridiculous about it, Alveena kept a close eye on her daughter-in-law. When she saw Caroline primping a bit and putting on a hat, she hustled over to Gladys's. With a prayer on her lips and her heart in her mouth, she rode on the worst ride of her life

"My stars, Glad, do you need to find every pothole and rut in the road? You're driving too fast. *Watch out for those chickens!*" The weather had been dry and they ate a lot of dust, but it wasn't hard to follow Caroline, even with other vehicles in-between. There was only one road to town. They'd have seen if she turned off.

Finally, praise the Lord, they made it into Bennetton without killing anyone. They found Joe's car parked on Main Street, just outside the movie theatre, and caught sight of Caroline's yellow dress as she entered. Gladys and Alveena stared at each other for a second, shrugged, bought tickets and went in. There were a lot of people in the lobby, buying candy and sodas and popcorn, but Caroline must have gone directly into the darkened theatre, and with a great many misgivings, and a lot of whispering, shushing, and trodding on peoples' toes, they finally settled in seats a few rows behind her.

A newsreel played, then a cartoon and a short comedy, then a Shirley Temple movie, called *Poor Little Rich Girl*. Alveena could hardly follow the story line for watching Caroline. The light from the screen was enough for Alveena to see that she was intent on the film, sometimes moving her lips, and once, reaching her hand forward, as if she wanted to touch the little girl.

Was *this* what was going on? Some kind of fixation on Shirley Temple movies? The movie had been playing all week. Did Caroline come to watch it over and over? Or was this simply a place for a sleazy get-together with some man? When the movie ended, a Charlie Chan film began and Caroline got up and left the theatre. Alveena nudged Gladys hard to wake her up, and the two women hurried out.

"You didn't have to do me like that," Gladys complained. "I'm gonna have a bruise. You must have the pointiest elbow in the world. Like a fire poker, it was."

"Hush! Let's see where she goes next."

Caroline walked across the street to the newsstand, and purchased some movie magazines. She turned around suddenly, and they were caught. "Oh….hey, Caroline," Alveena said. "Doing some shopping?"

Caroline smiled happily. "Just magazines." She hugged them to her bosom.

Gladys took charge. "Honey, do you mind taking your mother-in-law back to the campground? I gotta do some stuff in town. Um, errands. And…and the dentist, I have to see the dentist." With that, she thumped Alveena unnecessarily hard in the middle of her back and pushed her forward. Alveena shot her an evil look before turning back to face Caroline.

"Well, I was going to stop at the house, first," Caroline replied, fiddling with the edges of the magazine pages. "If you don't mind doing that…"

Alveena said it was fine, and waved Gladys off. The ride to the small house where Joe and Caroline lived was much smoother than when Gladys drove and before long, they were inside the little two-bedroom clapboard house on Cherry Street.

Caroline was a reasonably good housekeeper, Alveena had to give her that. The place was tidy, if a bit too modern for her taste. Joe's salary as manager at the department store was no fortune, but it was enough to keep the two of them in style. A big Zenith radio, plenty of knick-knacks like Kewpie dolls and china pigs. A Hoosier cabinet in the kitchen and an ice-box. Everything a lot more modern than the farmhouse, where Alveena still had a pump at the sink, and kerosene lighting. Electric power hadn't yet made it out the country roads. Even their tent at the campground was more up-to-date than the farm.

Caroline disappeared down the hall, and Alveena made use of the bathroom. When she returned, she could hear Caroline's voice coming from Daisy's bedroom. Since the little girl died, her room had become a shrine, with nothing touched or changed, and all kept immaculately clean. The door was only partially closed, and Alveena pushed gently on it. Caroline was in the rocking chair, one of the movie magazines open on her lap to a photo of Shirley Temple.

"See?" she was murmuring. "What did I tell you? You still look just fine." She glanced up as she became aware of Alveena in the doorway and held up the picture. "Don't you think so? Now that her teeth have come in?

She was so worried when she lost her baby teeth. They had to put in a plate to cover it up, but now her big-girl teeth are grown in and she looks just fine."

Alveena found it difficult to speak and her voice came out faint. "I…I didn't know you were such a big fan."

"Well, of course!" Caroline put the magazine down in exasperation. "Oh, Mamaw, I figured it out a long time ago. Did you think I didn't know?"

"Didn't know what?" Alveena began to feel a little light in the head.

"About Daisy! Why, it was such a relief! To know my little girl is doing such a wonderful job out in Hollywood, cheering people up from these hard times. Why, even the President says she helps people forget their troubles. I'm just so proud of her!"

Alveena's hands began to shake and she sat down suddenly on the end of the small bed. "Caroline, what are you talking about? That's a picture of Shirley Temple. The actress. She's not Daisy."

"Oh, I know, I know – it's a big secret. The studio has built up a background for her. It's fine." Caroline smiled even more, and a fire lit her eyes. "I couldn't understand, at first, why they took her away. But now I know. She's helping America get back on its feet. I can't be selfish." She faltered then, letting the magazines slip to the floor. "It's hard, sometimes," she whispered, wringing her hands together. "I miss her so much."

Alveena couldn't speak. Caroline smiled, slyly this time, and got to her feet. "Want to see something?"

Moving to the closet, she opened the door and pulled out a small trunk. Alveena knew that Daisy's clothes had been packed away in there, but when Caroline opened it, she saw that they had been replaced.

"I'm making her some new clothes to wear when she comes home," Caroline murmured, gently taking out the frilly dresses for Alveena to see. Even Alveena, who was not a movie fan, had seen enough photos of Shirley Temple to recognize a white and red polka-dot dress, and one with tiers of ruffles. Caroline must have made them herself. They weren't perfect. Some of the seams went awry and the piping on the polka-dot dress was poorly aligned, but obviously much work had gone into them.

Did Joe know? How could he not?

Caroline continued laying out the clothes – dress after dress, small patent-leather shoes, hair bows – and smiled at them fondly. "I know it might be a while, but she'll come home someday. When times are better. I want her to feel comfortable, with nice things like she has in Hollywood." She looked around the small, perfect bedroom. "I prob'ly should repaint the walls. Her bedroom in California is light blue."

Alveena got to her feet and stared down at her daughter-in-law. 'Lord,' she prayed, 'forgive me. Please forgive me my hard feelings. And help this poor girl.' Reaching down with a shaky hand, she stroked Caroline's hair. "My dear girl," she said. "My dear, darling girl. It'll be alright."

Caroline smiled up at her. "Yes, of course it will!" Something changed in her eyes for a moment, a split second when Alveena could see terror hiding behind the bright smile. "I just have to be patient, that's all. Just be patient, and someday my girl will come home to me." She returned to the rocking chair and turned her attention back to the magazine photos.

Oh, dear Lord, Alveena thought. How long has Joe known about this and hidden it from me? And how do we help Caroline? Forcing her to face the truth might break her all over again. And in mounting horror, Alveena watched as her daughter-in-law continued to rock, back and forth, smiling at the pictures, and humming *Baby, Take a Bow*.

The Two-Bit Punk
1937-1946

1937

JUDGE PARMALEE SURVEYED THE YOUNG MAN standing in front of him. He saw a skinny fella with a bad haircut, a poorly-fitting suit, and slightly nervous demeanor. Only slightly nervous, and not a bit afraid, which wasn't exactly a promising sight. Judge Parmalee liked his young men nervous, whether they were guilty or not. And Murphy Yount was guilty – that was for sure.

He glanced at his papers. "You've been here twice before," he reminded Murphy. "Last year and the year before that. Always the same thing – disturbing the peace during camp meeting. What's the matter? Don't you like camp meeting?"

"I love camp meeting," the young man assured him.

"Then why you cuttin' up over there?"

"Well, sir, there ain't no cuttin' up to be done at the farm." The man standing behind him made a derisive noise.

"Mr. Yount?" the judge asked. "You have something to say?"

The older man, unshaven and ramshackle, said "This boy's just a mess of trouble. At the farm and ever'where else."

The judge pursed his lips. Verle Yount was known in the community for his general antagonism toward everything and everybody. It didn't come as much of a surprise that Murphy could do nothing right in his uncle's eyes.

He turned his gaze back to Murphy. "To return to the case in hand," he said, "you and your rowdy gang broke into the Shack, stole ice cream and soda pop, made a mess, and left without closing the door behind you. Raccoons got in and made a bigger mess. What do you got to say for yourself?"

"Sir, we was hungry. And being it's the end of camp meeting for this year, we figured no one would be buying them things, so we used 'em up."

"And you were the ringleader, by all accounts."

"Yessir, I guess so. I was the one who knew the stuff was there."

"Last year, you and your friends went joy-riding in Harold T's jalopy, right through the passways, which isn't allowed, and pretty much terrorized a lot of sleeping folks. And the year before, you rocked several tents."

"Really, sir, we was just havin' some fun. No one got hurt. Rockin' a tent is just somethin' you do to show you like someone who stays there. Some of the guys were sweet on a couple girls, so..."

"And you didn't care that it woke up sleeping babies and other folks who need their rest?"

Murphy's shoulders shifted a little under the too-big suit coat. "Guess we didn't think about that."

"I knew your folks, young man. They were good people. It's a crying shame what happened to them, but that's no excuse for your behavior. And now you've got your uncle running the farm so's you got a roof over your head. How do you think this behavior reflects on him and your parents?"

Murphy's steady gaze wavered a bit but he didn't reply.

His uncle did, though. "Judge, I been trying to get this boy to behave ever since I arrived. He ain't been nothing but trouble. I done wore out my arm beatin' him, but he still gives me nothin' but grief. He's good with animals, I got to say, but else'n, he's just a pain in the neck, no good at all. He's a punk, Your Honor, nothing but a two-bit punk, and he's gonna end up a greasy spot in the road." He folded his hands in front of him as if he'd said his piece.

For a long moment or so, the judge didn't speak. Then he said, "Okay, I believe in letting the punishment fit the crime, so here's what goes. Murph, you made a mess at camp meeting, so you can help clean up. Not just the Shack, but the grounds, too. There's always a lot to do at the end of camp meeting – burning trash, mowing, just goin' round and checkin' for anything that could become an issue over the winter. You're hereby assigned to help the trustees for the next two weeks with whatever they tell you to do. You fail to show up, I'm tossing you in jail for contempt of court."

The senior Yount let out a cry. "And get out of his chores at the farm? Now you're punishing *me*!"

"You already said he's no use to you on the farm. So, which is it? He is? Or he isn't?"

Verle shut his yap.

The judge looked the youngster in the eye. "My advice to you, Murphy, is mebbe you should go into the Civilian Conservation Corps once you done your two weeks. They got a good record with young men who are tired of being down on the farm." He held the boy's gaze a bit before adding, "Now, I don't want to see you back here again, you understand?"

"Yes, sir. Thank you, sir." Murphy stood a little taller, and the ghost of a smile crossed his face.

Well, maybe there was hope for him, Judge Parmalee thought. A kid like this could go in any direction, but maybe there was some hope for this one. He hoped so, by Jingo!

1939

The camp officer stared at Murphy Yount, seeing an earnest young man, dressed in the Civilian Conservation Corps standard work clothes which had become a little small on him. A decent young man, Officer Darwin thought, well-liked by the other fellows, hard-working, and good with his hands. So, why couldn't he stay out of trouble?

"You know the penalty for fighting," he said to Murphy. "You've been warned before."

"Yessir."

"What started it this time?"

"We don't like each other, sir."

Officer Darwin waited for a further explanation but got none. Yount had already admitted to throwing the first punch, but if he wasn't going to explain why, Officer Darwin's hands were tied. "You've been in the CCC for two years now. If we're forced to release you, where will you go?"

"Don't know, sir."

Officer Darwin looked at the papers in front of him. "I see your allotment goes to your uncle. Will you head back to him?"

"No, sir. I don't really like farming, and 'sides, he got married to a widow woman with a passel of kids. They ain't no room for me there."

"It says here that you'll inherit your parents' farm in two years, when you're twenty-one."

"Yeah, but what am I s'posed to do? Kick my uncle out? He'll do more with the farm than I ever will."

"Maybe he'll buy it from you."

Yount gave a short laugh and shook his head.

Officer Darwin gave the whole situation some thought. After a long moment, he said, "You've done well here, Yount. In general. I'd hate to see you go. Can you promise me this will never happen again?"

"No, sir." The young man shifted his feet, and his face reddened. "Not meanin' no disrespect, but Smith just yanks my chain. We're bound to always bump heads. I've tried keeping away from him, but . . ." He stopped any further comments and simply added, "Maybe it's time I move on. Might be best."

Officer Darwin thought about the instructions he had received just the other day. "How about this?" he said. "I'm being transferred next week. Been assigned to head out to Catesville, to begin work on a new camp there. We'll have a lot of work to do – clearing trees, putting up buildings and tents, improving roads. What if I can get you assigned to come with me, as part of my squad? That would get you away from Smith, and keep you in the Corps. Things are changing, Yount. A young fellow like yourself could be useful, *if* you can keep out of trouble." He leaned back in his chair, clasped his hands across his midriff, and stared right into Murphy's eyes. "What do you say?"

Murphy could barely keep his elation under control. "I'd like that, sir! More'n anything! Can I bring my dog?"

"*Your* dog? I thought she was the camp dog. Since when is she yours?"

"Well, Little Girl has kinda become my responsibility. I feed her, bathe her, all that."

Office Darwin shrugged. "Okay by me. Just so's you keep your nose clean for a week or two, until we get our papers. Oh, wait! I have to decide on your penalty. Hmm. Let's say you're assigned to work all your recreation hours for me, helping to get ready, until we leave. Got it?"

"Yes, sir!" The young man left, a smile all over his face. Officer Darwin made some notes in the boy's folder and turned to the next case. His aide handed him the next set of papers, and murmured, "Glad you did that, sir. You know the reason they fought?" Darwin shook his head. "Smith got the dog falling-down drunk, and then tied a dead rat to her tail. When Yount found out, he went berserk. In a way, you can respect a guy like that."

"Maybe. But losing his temper isn't going to do him any good in life. 'specially if we're headed where I think we are."

"You think we're gonna get in the war?"

"I surely do. And young fellows like Murphy Yount are going to be doing the fighting. He'll need to keep a cool head for that."

1941

Lorna Keith gazed at the young man in front of her. He was a good-looking fellow, alright, if you liked the type. Healthy and fit, nice features, a shy grin, but also dressed badly in cheap work clothes, and about a month overdue for a haircut. Lorna had had many more attractive young men seeking her attention, men who came from good families, who had good jobs, and money and education. But there was just something about this fella, though, this Murphy Yount, that was just so appealing.

At the moment, he was squatted down eye-to-eye with her little brother on the front porch of their tent, showing off his service registration card, and explaining that he'd been down to the draft board that afternoon. "All the men over the age of 21 have to do this," he explained to little Rory, who hung on his every word. "You will, too, when you get this age."

"So, what happens now?" Lorna asked. "Are you in the Army?"

"No, just registered. I'll be getting' a letter soon, tellin' me to come in for a physical. If I pass that, I might get called up and I might not. If'n I do get called up, I have to serve one year."

"Assuming we don't get caught up in the war. Then, it'll be more." She folded her arms and leaned against the porch pillar. He'd certainly pass the physical. Years of farm work and CCC work had built up his shoulders, back and arms. He had a flat stomach and long powerful legs, and good hands, the hands of a man who was capable. The kind of man you'd want to be standing next to in an emergency.

"Naw, I don't think we will," he said. "Too many folks remember the last one. But if we did, *boy howdy*, I'd wanna serve." He grinned up at her, that boyish element in the man.

Lorna didn't want to think about the war, but who could avoid it? Every day, the news carried stories about what was going on in England and France and Africa. Murph and the CCC had been working in Catesville for two years now, building a military training camp. Newly-enlisted men had begun moving in, training during the day and over-running the town on weekends. Quite a few had found their way out to camp meeting, and all the local girls were as excited as Christmas morning.

She could remember Murphy from years ago, when they were just kids and he had a reputation as a bit of a troublemaker. What kind of hell, she wondered, was he raising these days?

They began walking along the passways, with Rory tagging along until he came across a group of his friends. As he ran off with them, she asked if Murph wanted to go get an ice cream cone at the Shack. "No thanks," he said, grinning. "Them folks have long memories." They headed out for The Bog instead, that low-lying back corner of the campground, where the ground tended to be a bit marshy. There was usually less of a crowd out there. She found herself holding hands with Murph as they walked along, and he told her of his life in the CCC camp, and his plans to go into carpentry work.

"I got a farm," he said, "but I rent it out to my uncle. Not much money, but he does all the work, so that's fair." He did a lot of carpentry work for the CCC and hoped eventually to have his own business. "I'm fixin' to go out on my own," he said, "but now's not the right time. Even at the camp, we're short of building supplies right now. The government's grabbing it all up. So, it's looking like I'll be 'round here for a while. Sure hope I can keep seeing you after camp meeting is over." He slid his arm over her shoulders, and she obligingly slowed her steps, until they stopped behind an old oak tree and kissed. *Mmmm*, she thought. *Good kisser. Very good kisser.*

The next two weeks sped by, and she and Murph spent as much time together as possible. He was only able to come out in the evenings or weekends, but they had so much to say to each other, so much to learn about each other, that each moment was precious. As Big Sunday dawned, and she returned from the spring with a bucket of water, her father called her to come out and sit on the porch with him. She settled on the porch swing, while her father relaxed in an old rocking chair with a fresh cup of coffee. After a bit, he said, "You seem to be gettin' kinda serious about this fella."

Lorna flushed. It wasn't like her dad to talk about personal stuff. He pretty much stuck to the topics of chores, church, and once in a great while, a compliment on her cooking. "Yes, Dad," she said. "I like him more every time I see him. He's a good guy."

"You more than like him."

She dropped her gaze and stared at her hands clutched in her lap. "Yes."

He sighed and shifted in his chair. "I'd like you to hold off makin' any serious decisions, Kitten. You're young, both of you. Wait."

"Do you not like him?"

"He seems a decent fella. Seems to have finished sowing his wild oats. You know he was a terror, years ago. But really, what has he done since then? Been in the CCC for four years. Four years! Most fellas only stay a year or two. Why hasn't he found a real job yet? Times are getting better. I'd like to know he can support a wife, before you start thinking about becoming one."

Now it was her turn to sigh. "He's thinking about enlisting."

"All the more reason then to wait. We're heading into somethin', I believe, Kitten. I see it coming closer. We can't let Hitler take over all of Europe. If Murph enlists, he might get sent overseas. I don't want to see you become a young widow."

"*Dad!*"

"It's gotta be said. Wait. Please."

"He hasn't even asked me yet."

"He will. I see all the signs. Just don't rush into anything, I'm begging you."

She couldn't look him in the eyes. She felt on the verge of tears, and if he was, too, she'd completely lose control. Her dad had never begged her for anything before. He had instructed, insisted, and imposed his will, but never *asked* her to do what he wanted. Parents didn't ask their children to behave, was his view. They expected compliance. So what he was saying now was that he knew this was out of his control. That was a liberating thought, but it also brought home to her the weight of responsibility.

If Murph did ask her to marry him, she'd say yes. That much she knew. Could she wait, as her dad asked? She didn't want to, and she trusted Murph to come through, to find a way to support them. He may have been a punk back in high school, but he was her punk now, and she loved him.

Murph would be there within the hour for the Big Sunday church service, and a family gathering afterward. Would this be the day he proposed? Only time would tell. A real short amount of time.

1944

Dear Tommy,

Well, hello from your big bro Kenny and all the 82nd. I was sure glad to get your letters and all the others that have been piling up for me. Can't say where we are, but tell everyone I'm okay and getting a little break and will answer every letter soon. I guess you know things have been pretty hot over here. Maybe the less said, the better.

As for me, I'm okay. Tell Ma I'm getting plenty of grub, she shouldn't worry. We're back in training right now and out of the action. I guess y'all are getting ready for camp meeting. I can just see Ma cooking and baking like a fiend, boy what I would give for some of her fried chicken and peach pie. I know you will be happy to eat my share! Sure wish I could be at camp meeting too, listening to music and watching all the pretty girls go by. Say 'Hey' to the best-looking ones for me.

TOMMY, DO NOT READ THIS NEXT PART OUT LOUD TO THE FAMILY

Ma says you've been talking about enlisting early. She says you're getting crazy ideas about lying about your age, and God knows, you're a big enough fellow to get away with it. DON'T BE A DAMN FOOL. I know you want to do your bit, but for chrissake, don't do it. You're only 16. It ain't like you see in the movies. There's no glory, just a lot of hell.

All us guys try to write home something cheerful, and sure a lot of it's true – there are some great guys here and we have fun when we can – but the rest is pure hell. It's dirt and mud and blood and puke and seeing your friends get shot up and wondering when it's going to happen to you. Men who've been shot up don't just fall to the ground and close their eyes, like in the movies. Their eyes stay open, Tommy, and they're screaming and calling to their mamas and trying to crawl away and looking at their bleeding stumps or their guts that have splattered all over everywhere. And if they've been hit by a grenade or a bomb, it's even worse. I've seen bits of bodies you wouldn't believe. So, don't be a damn fool and enlist. With any luck, this will be over before you're 18. I pray to God it is.

War will kill your soul. You get so used to horrible sights, you can't even feel any more. I seen it in the guys around me. I see it in myself. You remember Murph Yount? He married Lorna last year when he was on leave, remember? He's in the 82nd too now (they keep regrouping us). Steady guy, always has a good word, kills Jerries like the rest of us, but wouldn't hurt a fly otherwise. Always has a soft spot and a bit of food for any stray dog that comes around (my God, you'd hate what happens to animals in war).

Our last couple of days in France we were assigned to clean out a couple of villages the Jerries had torched. You'd cry just to see how they destroyed these places, and the state they left folks in – women, old men, babies, cripples – but none of us was feeling sorry for any dead Germans we came across. We had too many bodies of our own to collect.

And then we came across these two Jerries who'd been burned to a crisp, sitting against a tree trunk, helmets on the ground next to them. They were completely blackened, their faces like mummies, their fingers burnt off, smelling like oil and burnt pig. We walked past them, and one began this loud buzzing noise. Scared the shit out of us! Then he and the other began moving back and forth, like they was trying to get our attention. A couple of the guys started laughing a little at those poor, putrid ~~fucks~~ fools who were too stupid to know they was dead.

Then someone behind me shot them both, right in the foreheads, and they tipped over sideways and went quiet. I looked around and it was Murph. He stared back at me and said, "I wouldn't leave a dog like that." And then he just kept on walking and he didn't say a word to nobody for three days.

I don't know, Tommy, I don't know what this war is gonna do to me and guys like Murph. I just - <u>Don't do it Tommy!</u> Do not enlist. Not until you have to. And pray that this war is done by then, or I don't know if there will be any reason at all for folks to keep fighting. Maybe we'll all just be animals by then. Sometimes it feels like that's already happened.

So, stay away from that recruiting office, you hear me? I'm still your big brother and I'm telling you, I mean it. I'll beat the shit out of you if I have to. Just stay where you are. Keep the home fires burning, and don't drive Ma crazy (and don't tell her how much I swear now, she'll wear me out!). I'll do all I can to come marching home as soon as possible. Go to camp meeting, kiss a pretty girl, and say a prayer or two. I love you, kid. Your big bro, Kenny

1946

Judge Parmalee stretched out his legs in front of him and relaxed in the swing. Lordy, it was hot out! He fanned his face with his hat and clapped it back on his head and took another swig of cold tea. The weather was always hot at camp meeting, but this year was worse than ever. Or maybe it just seemed that way. At the beginning of the summer, everyone was happy as coon dogs that the war looked to be 'bout over. Hitler dead and the Germans surrendering, but the Japs just couldn't seem to quit. And now this news last night, President Truman announcing some big bombing in Japan, a military base called Hiroshima.

Would it make any difference? The judge sure hoped so. It was hard enough, knowing how many GI's would never come marching home. It was time for the fighting to end. At least, some of the soldiers who'd been in Europe or Africa were returning. Every day, he saw more and more young men on the streets.

Even here at camp meeting, they were walking the passways or sitting in the arbor. Sometimes he recognized this young fellow or that, newly home and back in the bosom of his family. Some of them proudly wore their uniforms still, crisp and clean, emblazoned with ribbons and medals and military patches designating their units. Others couldn't get into civvies fast enough, quick to let their hair and whiskers grow out.

Most of them drank too much and swore till the air turned blue. Some – too many – came back with missing legs and arms and eyes. Some came home only to die. And there were those who couldn't let go of the violence. The judge was already seeing too many court cases where some veteran got drunk and took to beating his wife or kids or getting in fights with other men, unable to accept that peace had arrived.

Most of 'em would settle down, given time. He'd been a veteran himself, part of the Old Hickory division during the first World War, and he'd taken part in some pretty hot fighting on the Western Front. He knew it took a while for the brain to rid itself of the rot of war. Most of these fellows would make it back to a normal life. A few wouldn't.

He watched the folks walking along the passway, nodded to those he knew or recognized. A few men respectfully doffed their hats in respect, a few others stopped and spoke. But most walked on, arm-in-arm with their wives, calm and peaceful as the sun began to lower, and the day's heat eased. A man in uniform caught his eye, about halfway up from the Bog, walking with a pretty woman pushing a baby carriage. The fellow's gait was uneven, a sort of halting step with his right leg. Likely been wounded. The judge would have taken him for a young man, judging by the width of his shoulders and his proud, military posture, but as a ray of sun slanted across the man's face, he could see heavy lines across the man's forehead, and dark circles under his eyes. Not so young anymore, or at least not young in spirit.

Judge Parmalee, in that moment, recognized the fella. What's-His-Name, Murphy Yount, that everyone called 'Murph'. Oh yeah, he recognized him. The two-bit punk. Always in trouble back then. Well, that was the thing about camp meeting. Over the years, you could watch folks grow up. See how they turned out. Some kid you first knew as a snotty-nosed brat might turn out to be a business owner or decent farmer. Some little beauty might end up fat and sassy, with a houseful of kids. You could never know in advance how someone might develop. He'd seen miracles and he'd seen disasters.

He kept watching as Murph and his wife drew closer, until they were nearly right upon him. The younger man walked tall and proud, and his wife smiled up at him adoringly. Well, maybe it all worked out okay. The judge liked to think he'd done the right thing by steering Murph all those years back. As the couple drew even, the soldier tipped his hat to the judge, and Judge Parmalee took his own hat off and held it against his heart in respect. Looked like the two-bit punk had amounted to something after all. He had, indeed. By Jingo.

The Writer and the Hot Rod Jockey
1950

I THOUGHT LITTLE WEEK WOULD BE MY best bet. Away from the normal distractions of housework or the radio, and alone in my tent on the outer ring of the campground, maybe I could get some work done. Things were quiet during this first week of camp meeting. People were still moving into their tents, getting settled and renewing old ties, and I thought it could be my saving grace. A quiet time to finish writing the story I'd been working on for two months already. My editor was starting to get the fidgets.

So, each morning, I set up my trusty old Remington on a rickety wooden table on the back porch and tried to write. Mostly I ended up just staring across the field toward the old white church with its fancy scrollwork. Tore up every page I began.

Honestly, my brain just never felt emptier. My ideas had dried up like a smear of spilled ketchup, all brown and yucky, a gummy mess not the least bit appetizing. All I could think about was my upcoming rent payment and how I wasn't going to be able to cover it if I didn't finish this darned story soon and get paid for it.

Well, all this dithering had to stop. I set up again Saturday morning, determined to do this thing. Time to just pound it out.

Yes, start writing.

Any time now.

Any time.

Phooey!

"Lady! Hey, Lady!"

I looked up to see a skinny boy, maybe about fourteen years old, wearing faded overalls rolled up to his knees and a dirty white t-shirt. He glared at me and said, "You ever gonna get going? I'm tired of waiting!"

"Huh?"

"I'm getting fed up! You've had me behind the wheel of that car for almost two months now. When you gonna let me drive?"

I shook my head in disbelief. This simply could not be. Before I could say anything, though, a woman's voice said, "Well, I don't think he should drive. He's just a kid. Of course, what do I know? I'm only the mother."

The woman sauntered into view and casually lit a cigarette, leaning against the porch railing. I knew her immediately - slim skirt, white blouse, pink hairdresser's smock. Elaborately coiffed hair. "Not to even mention," she continued, "the race is on a Sunday. I work on my feet five days a week, trying to give perms to women who have about three hairs on their heads. I clean the house on my day off. All I want is for my family to be together on Sundays, especially during camp meeting, but no, now they want to run off to the races."

She tipped her head in the direction of a man who came out my tent door, holding half a bologna sandwich, and a bottle of Coke. The woman continued. "It's not enough he comes home from the filling station every day, with black gook under his nails, and greasy clothes. Now you've got him working on engines for those hot rod jockeys, filling up my back yard with all kinds of car parts and wrecked cars and tires and such. I work on my feet all week long, and – "

"Nag, nag, nag," the man said. He was small and wiry, bald, wearing a dirty mechanic's coverall. "Same old song. Your life is so tough. You think mine is any picnic? Running a filling station out at the crossroads, with barely enough traffic going by to keep things afloat? That racing crowd is the only thing helping me to make ends meet. And then I come home to the same old meals over and over. Tuna casserole, tuna salad, tuna a la king. Whyn't ya ever fry some chicken, or make a meatloaf, fer Pete's sake? It's getting so I can't look another can of tuna in the face." He turned to me. "Why'd you make her that way, huh? And while we're at it, why'd ya have to make me bald?"

"Now wait a minute," I said, finally stung into utterance. "Y'all can't be here!" I glanced around to see if any other people were observing this little trio. "You're not even real!"

"And we never will be," the boy argued, "if you don't finish this story and let folks read it. I want to live! You ain't even give us real names. I'm just The Kid, she's The Mother, and he's So's Your Old Man."

"I don't give names until the story is done," I said with vast dignity. "Until I feel like I really know you. Now if you don't mind, I can't get any work done with you here."

"You're not getting any done *without* us here, that's for sure." The Kid plunked himself down on the ground. "I ain't leaving 'til you finish."

"Me neither," said So's Your Old Man. "I'm a-stayin' here until you grow me some hair."

"Well, I don't see why I should stick around," said The Mother. "I'm barely in the story at all. You just put me in there to be an irritant. When I think of how you have me working on my feet all week long..."

"OKAY! You don't want to be in the story? Fine!" I snapped my fingers and just like that, she disappeared.

So's Your Old Man jumped to his feet. "Don't worry about the hair, Lady! I'm right happy to be bald!" He backed away and then turned and ran around the end of the tent row. The Kid, however, just stared me down. He knew I couldn't cut him from the story.

"Okay," I sighed. "Why don't we go down to the track and watch things for a while. They've got the qualifying races today. Maybe I'll get some ideas. You can help."

The racetrack was brand-new. Mr. Theodore Berry had gotten tired of looking at his abandoned cotton field between the road and the river and decided to put in something that might actually make some money. All over the South, in small towns and large ones, people were going crazy for racing. Ever since Bill France, Sr, and his cohorts in Daytona had established a professional stock car racing organization, tracks were springing up everywhere.

The cars had to be exactly as they had come off the showroom floor. No modifications. Local races could be entered by professionals *and* amateurs, which tended to promise strong local attendance. Plus, there wasn't a whole lot else to do in much of the South in the summer. Not for fun, anyway. School-time sports were over, the county fair and the circus only happened once a year, and it was hard to stay excited over a horseshoe match.

So, Mr. Berry created his track. A crew had been out there all summer, clearing the land and bulldozing down into the red clay soil to create banked turns and two long straightaways. A pond in the center of the infield helped drain water off the track, so it didn't get too muddy and rutted. Of course, dirt-track racing was a dirty business. A cloudy red haze hung over the field when the cars were running, along with the fumes of gas and oil, and the vivid stench of outhouses in the sun.

Well before we reached the track, we could hear the throb and whine of car engines. The qualifying heats hadn't yet begun. Race cars were still arriving, many of them older cars from the thirties. Tough little beasts that didn't weigh too much. The '34 Ford coupe was a favorite, with a steering wheel big as a washtub, and no windshield, just wire mesh to keep dirt clods from coming through. They had numbers painted on their sides, and only a few arrived on trailers. Most were just towed behind some pickup truck, with its back end piled with spare tires, replacement parts, tool kits – and usually three or four fellows who were racing hopefuls or mechanics.

Advertisements had been put in all the local papers and slapped on the sides of barns and trees and just about anything that didn't move. Everyone knew the facts by heart. A mile-long track, races of fifty to one hundred miles, including a consolation race for those who had just missed qualifying for the real races, and a purse for the top ten drivers in each race.

Events were to get underway at 1 pm, which of course, was the outstanding crux of the matter for the church folks in the area and at camp meeting. Was it right to operate such a business on a Sunday? To be selling tickets and bottles of Coca-Cola and bags of peanuts, to be tearing around a track as fast as a car could go, to be yelling from the grandstand and likely betting on a favorite driver? Lots of folks said no, but many, many more would say yes.

I had expected to see a fair number of onlookers for the qualifying races but found myself astonished that so many turned up. The Kid's excitement was palpable. He could hardly keep himself from running right down to the pit crew area, but I reminded him we were just there to watch, for now.

"We've got to figure out your motivation," I said. "What is it that's driving you to get behind that wheel? What exactly is it you want?"

"I wanna drive fast, that's all. Fast as I can. Faster'n anybody else. Like him!" He pointed at a man who'd just completed a heat. The fellow climbed out of the car and pulled off his helmet. He was a real hot rod jockey, all right, with a DA haircut, and smartass grin. The Kid watched as the guy shucked off the top half of his mechanic's overalls, revealing a pack of cigarettes rolled up in his t-shirt sleeve.

Right there, I could see The Kid's motivation – to be like that guy – tough and confident and reckless, all at the same time. And why not? You didn't have to be rich to be a stock car driver. You didn't have to be well-educated or well-connected – just had to drive fast and turn left. It was all about the pride, not the prize money. Not that there was much money in stock car racing anyway. Most of the drivers would be lucky if they made enough with their winnings to just stay in the game. Maybe win five hundred dollars and spend most of that on tires and gas and repairs. Tonight, they'd sleep in their pickup trucks because they couldn't afford a motel room. They'd live off canned beans and bottles of Cheerwine, because all their money went to fixing up their cars.

I could imagine it all and soaked in the details. My editor would love it. The boys who read "Adventure Life" magazine would love it. If I could only get the darned thing finished.

I left after an hour. The Kid remained behind, glued to the scene, but I'd had enough. I needed to get home and get writing while all the vivid impressions were fresh. I thought a lot about the hot rod jockey we'd noticed – I could name him Slick for now – and considered ways to include him in the story. Should he be a hero or a jerk? A mentor or a rat? Did he drink? Womanize? Cheat? Could he have an injury that would keep him from racing, giving The Kid a chance to sneak in?

The story was suddenly full of new possibilities. I could make him a little younger. A bit more handsome. He could have the face of Montgomery Clift. I hurried back to the tent and began writing, furiously pounding the keys for page after page after page. I was on a roll. I had my inspiration and I was off to the races. Ha!

It rained that evening, of course. Up in the sleeping loft, the drumming of raindrops hitting the tin roof worked its magic and I slept soundly until about two in the morning, when I woke up, thinking vaguely that I might need to go to the restroom. I tried to talk myself out of it. The row of individually-owned privies was finally gone, replaced by a few communal restroom buildings scattered around the edges of the campground. It was a bit of a walk in the dark. And the harshly-lit cinderblock buildings tended to be full of moths fluttering around, making a person nervous to park their behind.

I had just decided to go back to sleep, when I heard a new voice, right behind me, *in the bed*. "How ya doin'?" it said.

I don't know what the world's land speed record is for getting out of a bed, down a ladder, across a room and out on a porch with the door pulled shut behind me, but I'm pretty sure I beat it. "Who the hell are you?" I shouted through the open-slatted wall.

"Sorry if I woke you," the voice said, and I opened the door to see him. Slick. The guy I'd been noticing all day and imagined into my story. "How's tricks?" he asked pleasantly.

"What were you doing in my bed?! Get out of my tent. This is not that kind of story."

"Maybe it should be. Why do you write boys' stories, anyway? I'd think a dame like you would write romance. Or maybe something for True Confessions."

"Boys' stories pay better." I snatched up a sweater and wrapped it around myself. "What do you want?"

"Just trying to help." He gave me a thorough once-over and strolled to the ice chest and pulled out a beer. Which surprised me, as I hadn't stocked any beer. Camp meeting rules didn't allow it. "I been thinking. Maybe I shouldn't be a complete bum. Maybe bad with a little bit of good. Complex characters are more interesting, don't you think? More memorable." He took a long swig of the beer and added, "I'm leaving soon anyway. Got drafted."

"What? I didn't write that into the story."

"Surprised the hell outta me, too. The whole thing is crazy anyway. Why are we getting into another war when we just got done with the last one? What do I care about Korea? But yeah, come Monday, I'm supposed to catch the bus and head on out for basic training. Maybe it's just as well. You're making me the kind of guy that The Kid shouldn't emulate. And there's this girl...Lucy. We've been getting close. I'm probably not the kind of guy she should hook up with, either. Right?" His gaze met mine and I had to look away. "Yeah, that's what I thought.

So, fine. Just make me memorable, okay? Because pretty soon, I might just be another unknown soldier."

He left while I was still thinking about the ramifications of it all, the fabulous poignancy I could put in. I would fire up the old Remington and get typing. Put ideas down as fast as I could, while I still had them.

But first, I needed to get to that restroom.

Next morning, The Kid showed up while I was still eating breakfast. "You get anywhere last night?" he asked.

"Keep your shirt on," I mumbled around a mouthful of scrambled eggs. I made him wait until I had finished eating, cleaned things up, and carried my supplies out to the porch. I handed him the typed pages I'd completed.

He just skimmed. I could tell by how fast his eyes were moving. "Jeez," he sighed, "you changed everything. You've made it all about Slick, 'stead of me. That's not fair!" He threw the pages to the ground. "This is MY story! I'M the star, not that hot rod jockey! Besides, you're writing for a magazine for *boys*. You can't forget about the market."

"That was before. This is big. I think this could be a whole novel. I've always wanted to write something more serious. This could be my *Red Badge of Courage*, or maybe *Call of the Wild*. Something people will remember!"

"Aw, I hate that junk! You promised I could drive that car."

"I never promised."

"You put me behind the wheel and left me there for two months! I deserve better from you."

"Look, I'll put you in a different story..."

"Forget it." He waved his hand in disgust and ran away. I had completely lost control. That happens sometimes. A story just gets away from you. Rips itself right out of your hands and goes down its own road. Usually, those end up the best stories. But not always. Maybe this was a mistake.

One of the things I knew about writing was that the characters had to feel real. They had to have their own dreams and desires and passions, and something had to stop them, prevent them from achieving those dreams. Maybe a foe, maybe something in nature, maybe a string of events – but in the best stories, the something that stopped them was really their own selves. Fears, doubts, stubbornness, pride. Because that's usually what stops real people in their real lives.

I knew. I'd stopped myself many a time. I'd built a career, measly as it was, out of reliably upbeat, funny stories. Things a boy could read and enjoy, and then forget about the very next day. But truth was, I dreamed of writing something memorable. Maybe even *being* someone memorable. I'd built myself a life, too, that stayed safely in its box, content to watch other people daring to try, noting their failures and their successes. That's what I did. I *watched*. I lived a life filled with watching others, so I didn't have to risk doing something myself. I sometimes thought it was a pretty stupid way to live.

Little Sunday came around and I decided to go to the prayer meeting at the arbor. Every bench was crammed full, and all the grassy space surrounding the arbor was filled with folks on blankets and chairs, listening to the preacher. I knew that down at the racetrack, the drivers would have begun to arrive. They'd be working on their cars, tinkering with the small details, checking the tires and the radiator one more time. Gradually, they'd build up their nervous energy so as to have plenty on hand when that green flag dropped. I knew I'd head down there as soon as church service was over, but in the meanwhile, I needed to build my own courage, become a little cold-hearted so as to achieve the ending I had already written in my mind.

The text of the sermon was Proverbs 19:21. "Many are the plans in the mind of a man, but it is the purpose of the Lord that will stand." Oh, swell. Just when I decide to play God myself, with my characters, I'm reminded that, in the end, none of it is really in my hands. Here's the thing I always wondered – if God's will be done, then is it right what He puts people through? If He is the Father and we're the children, does there ever come a time when the child should question whether the parent really knows what He's doing? And if I, as a writer, want my characters to be real people, is it wrong for me to put them through things and into situations from which they'll never recover? These doubts and questions plagued me. I knew the characters were fictional, but as I wrote, they always became real for me.

After service ended, I hightailed it out of there and joined the steady stream of cars headed toward the track. Somewhere along the ride, The Kid joined me on the front seat, staring intently ahead to where a cloud of dust already hung above the action. I wished he hadn't shown up. This wasn't his story anymore, not really. I didn't need him to sit in judgment on me.

We saw Slick almost as soon as we got there, standing by his car, with his crew swarming around. Lucy was there too, just as pretty as I'd written her, sweet and lovely, the girl next door. She hovered nearby, trying not to get in anyone's way but clearly hoping to get a moment alone with Slick before the race began. He saw me and walked over. Tossing a coin to The Kid, he said, "Whyn't you go get a coupla Co-colas for you and Lucy?" Then, taking me by the arm, he said, "We gotta talk."

I allowed him to pull me over to a quiet spot, under the grandstand. "I know what you're planning," he said. "A big dramatic moment, right?" I started to explain, but he waved it off. "No, I get it. The girl gets pregnant, the guy panics, he gets reckless behind the wheel and bam! He's a dead duck. I understand. I really do. But here's the thing." He looked into my eyes and spoke gently. "She's a nice girl, Lucy is. I don't want her to have to go through that. I mean...have you thought what it will be like for her after the story is over? Pregnant, alone, no money, nobody to take care of her? I just can't stand it. Kill me off, that's okay. Like I said, I'm probably headed that direction anyway. But don't do it to her. She doesn't have to be pregnant. You can change that. Don't make me that much of a louse. Center the story on The Kid again; he deserves it after waiting so long. What do you say?"

I'd like to say I did the right thing. Not just the right thing for *me*. Does God ever have this dilemma? Does it break His heart sometimes?

The Kid came back, obviously more star-struck than ever, and now also carrying an obvious crush for Lucy. I led him to a space on the grassy bank where we could see everything and watched as Slick headed back to his car. I watched as Lucy tentatively walked up to him and whispered in his ear. Watched as his face changed, as he turned and put his hand on the roof of the car for a moment, watched as he resolutely climbed in. I sat up there in my heaven and watched.

The race began. Excitement grew as the crowd cheered for their favorites. The Kid became almost breathless, pounding his fist on his knee as the drivers battled it out for the lead position. "He can do it," The Kid said. "He can win. He's the fastest guy out there, faster than all the pros. He's really good. And someday, I'm going to be just like him."

For the first time, I couldn't watch, and after a while, The Kid noticed. "You're gonna let him win, right? Don't let me down again. If I can't be in the race, it's only fair if he wins. Otherwise, what's the point?" We could see Lucy in the grandstand, shouting Slick's name and urging him on. "She's so pretty," The Kid said. "Isn't she? She told me she and Slick might get married. How about that?! Will they? That'd be neat."

Down on the track, things were heating up. Dust rose, engines screamed. This was the big money race, for a top prize of maybe five thousand dollars. Big-name drivers led the way, the men who'd already made reputations for themselves at Wilmington and Charlotte and Atlanta. Some of the cars had already spun out or been eliminated in one way or another. As the intensity rose, so did the summer heat. A rumble of thunder competed with the rumble of engines, and people began glancing from the track to the sky, trying to keep an eye on both.

And then it happened. The leader, number 21, Punk Walters, spun coming off the second turn, and so did the second car, trying to avoid him. Slick was right behind, barreling through the clouds of smoke and dirt, and passing them both. Then suddenly, he hit Turn Three and maybe he couldn't see, or maybe his mind was on something else, but in any case his car missed the turn entirely, flew up the bank and through the air, rolling upside down as it landed and bursting into flames. People screamed, drivers went crazy trying to avoid the whole thing, and The Kid began running toward the burning car.

I tried to stop him. I'm not a monster. He didn't need to see that, the flames ripping through the car, black smoke billowing. I knew Lucy had already fainted in the stands. Someone would help her, she'd be okay. I barely knew her, but The Kid was flying across that field, joining firefighters and crewmen as they tried to beat out the flames.

At that moment, the storm broke loose. Thunder cracked and the skies opened. The fire went out in a cloud of steam, but it was too late. I was there as they pushed the car over, as they pulled out the blackened body. The Kid dropped straight to the ground as if he'd been shot.

I ran to him and bent down to touch his shoulder. He jerked away from me and covered his head, shuddering and choking, crying and swearing. "Damn you!" he screamed. "*Damn you!* Don't you write this stuff! Don't you do it! I hate you! Get out of my life! *How could you write such a thing?!* Don't ever write about me ever again! I'd rather die."

So…I just never sent the story in. Every now and then, I pull it out and think, Okay, I can fix this, but I never can. Instead I wrote a different story, an upbeat kind of story with a different boy, who ends up behind the wheel and wins by a fluke. This other boy was happy, my editor was happy, I was able to pay my rent. Big hairy deal. Was it worth it? Putting my characters through that? Putting myself through that? Allowing them to become so real for me that I felt destroyed when it was over? Maybe this writing gig just isn't for me. I don't like it. I don't. And I don't want to play God anymore.

The Lake
1963

EVERY SUNDAY AFTER CHURCH, DAVID PAYSEUR drove his family out into the countryside, past the old farm, and up to the picnic grounds on the bluff. They spread blankets on a sunny spot where they could eat lunch and see how much things had changed that week. Inch by inch, an enormous lake was growing, filling in the river valley since the dam was built.

For the past two years, his great-granddaddy's farm had been disappearing, a bit at a time. First, the electric power company had come through with their surveying equipment and serious-faced men holding clipboards. Then there'd been a haggle over price and property lines. His widowed mother turned to him to deal with all that. "This would have been yours, next," she said, her eyes rimmed with tears. "Your daddy always told me not to sell it, but no one foresaw this." But he had no other choice, David decided. He'd lose the farm anyway, once the dam was constructed, and the land flooded. Might as well make the best deal he could get.

Evelyn, his wife, was all for it. "It'll be better," she said, making little attempt to hide her elation. "We can buy a new house, closer to town. In a neighborhood, so the kids will have friends to play with and I'll finally have people to talk to. You know I hate being so isolated out here on all this land. A modern subdivision is my idea of Heaven."

It sure wasn't his. He wondered how she could be so happy to give up all the space – the wide, open skies, the sight of growing corn stalks, the sense of freedom. But then, Evelyn had been a city girl, born and bred in Charlotte. Sometimes, he supposed, she missed her own childhood, so different from his.

So, he'd made the deal, and moved out. He and his mother went through every item in the old farmhouse, deciding what to keep, what to sell, what to give away. Boxed up generations of memories. And then went back, every Sunday, to see what was gone next. The power company didn't bother to strip the house, they just pulled it down. David was there the day they fastened chains to the porch pillars and tore them loose, watched as the roof collapsed, as the walls hit the ground in a cloud of dust. The house groaned as it fell, and so did he.

In later visits, they saw tree trunks that had been toppled and left in the dirt. No big need to haul them out, they'd just rot under the eventual lake. Meanwhile, the dam was constructed, huge earthen walls covered with acres of concrete – enough, it was said, to build a sidewalk all the way to the Pacific Ocean. David's farm, of course, was not the only place torn down, and his wasn't the only family to come visit each week once the water began to rise. It just felt that way, a very personal disaster. In actuality, hundreds of people were affected as entire mill towns were razed, churches and graveyards relocated, and bridges demolished.

And then the dam was finished, and the waters began to rise.

At first, it just looked the way it often looked in the spring when the river was high and about to overflow its banks. Then it did overflow, and the creeks backed up and people began to really see all they were losing. Not just land, but a way of life. The ferries and bridges across the river ceased to exist, leaving just one new bridge across the center of the proposed lake. A person might now find themselves having to drive twenty miles to get across or around the lake.

The water just kept creeping up. Flooding his fields, crawling across the foundations of the house, obliterating even the road that led to it until the closest he could come to his family's farm was the high bluff of Wib Little's land, a quarter mile away. Wib invited the locals to come and picnic on Sundays, and Evelyn and the kids began to look forward to these outings. Wib even put in a couple of outhouses and sold soft drinks and boiled peanuts.

"We're watching history being made," he said, enthusiastic about the idea. David always had to get up and walk away at that point. To him, the lake was like a big sheet someone had pulled up over a body after the death struggle. It was big and bland and *in the way*, and it covered up the river he loved.

And then, that was it. The lake reached full pond level just shortly before camp meeting in August, and it was all anyone could talk about.

"Bootlegger's Alley is gone. Just dives right under the lake and never comes up again."

"Kenny Hill's gonna open a fillin' station there and sell bait and sandwiches to the fishin' crowd."

"He'll never get rich doin' that. He should sell hot dogs too."

"I don't like the spot they moved First Baptist to. Got no shade trees around it. Church socials are gonna be in the blazin' sun."

"My daddy figures maybe now they'll finally improve the road from Charlotte, so people can drive up on the weekends."

"People ain't never gonna drive up from Charlotte! What for? A big ol' lake with nothin' on it."

"'You realize they put in ten access areas for boats, but only one for swimming? I ain't got a boat."

"Ya better get one, boy."

"The swimmin's no good anyway, the lake bottom is so mucky. That good old clay soil turns into a foot-deep of slurry at the bottom."

"Crawford Story caught a mess of bass last week, out in one of those narrow little coves that used to be Long Creek. There's plenty of good fishin' to be had."

"Sure was pretty last winter, drivin' across the bridge in early morning, the fog just a-settin' on top of the water."

"Won't be pretty this winter, driving across that bridge. Gonna be a mess of construction equipment goin' in and out of that steam plant location. They're gearin' up big time now."

"The racetrack's closed down, y'know. The lake flooded turns Three and Four."

"I wanted Daddy to get one of those leased lots the power company's offerin' and put a cottage on it, but he says when pigs fly."

"They're sayin' it'll provide power to four counties, by the time they're finished."

"Yeah, well, let's just hope we ain't all glowin' in the dark after they finish that nuclear plant."

"I like it. It's so peaceful, especially early in the morning, or just before sundown. So quiet and calm."

"I miss the sound of the river. The river talked to you. The lake doesn't."

"Talked to you! Huh, sometimes it dern near yelled at you. I seen a lot of damage done by the river in flood. The river wasn't always a friendly thang."

"They're sayin' the lake covers more'n 32,000 acres. And 211 of those were mine."

"We had a flock of geese show up around Easter. More'n thirty of 'em. Thought they looked right pretty, 'til we saw what they left behind. Now we're not so crazy about 'em."

"Well, it's different, that's for sure. Not at all like the river."

"You c'n say that again."

At least the campground was safe. The final shoreline of the lake came within a half-mile as the crow flies, and they'd been promised it wouldn't rise any further. The road past the campground was safe too, maybe even safer than before since there was actually less traffic on it now. The Bennetton-Mooresville highway was the only one that crossed the lake, so that was what most folks used, and Campground Road became just a minor byway, even though it was the original road to Painter's Creek, and all the old churches were out that way.

Seemed like throughout history, progress had passed right by Painter's Creek. To its detriment, perhaps, but definitely to the benefit of the campground. Roads, railroads, residential lots, business development – they'd all gone in other directions, leaving Painter's Creek drowsing in the shade. And the campground right along with it, still intact.

"You've got that right," Evelyn said when David expressed this thought. "Everything progressive absolutely avoids Painter's Creek like the plague. We're in the Dark Ages here. And camp meeting the worst of all. Dirt floors! No bathrooms! No window screens, and flies everywhere! Let me tell you, just the mud alone this year is driving me 'round the bend."

He tried not to be resentful. Camp meeting was in his blood. He'd been coming there every summer since before he could remember, and so had his folks and grandparents and every generation prior to that. Sometimes it seemed like he and Evelyn had absolutely nothing in common. He brooded about it – too much, maybe. Even his boss had commented about David's moodiness.

Of course, part of the problem was the heat. There was no getting around it, this summer had been hot, really hot, and rain every day during camp meeting so far, with no cooling relief, just more steamy air. The passways were muddy ravines, and although the children had all been warned to rinse their dirty feet before they entered the tent, half the time they forgot. The straw spread across the dirt floors grew damp and musty, the whole place smelled.

And Evelyn was pregnant this summer, seven months along. They hadn't planned on another baby. Four children were plenty, and the youngest already seven years old, but there it was. Her only consolation was that she was due at the same time as Jackie Kennedy, the President's wife. Evelyn adored Jackie. "She's my ideal of a classy, modern woman," she'd said more than once, and she modeled her hair style, her clothes, and her manners on Mrs. Kennedy. Even tried to imitate the woman's low whispery voice – though not that Yankee accent, thank the Lord.

Wednesday had been another hot one. David had spent most of the day at his office. He and Evelyn had reached a compromise – she and the kids would spend daytimes at home, where the kids could cool off under the sprinkler and she could cook on a modern stove – then they'd meet at the tent to eat supper. The evenings weren't so bad, for the air cooled down quickly once the sun had set. David felt bad that the kids missed out on most of camp meeting, but Evelyn could be very emotional when she was pregnant, so he didn't argue.

He was just beginning to put his papers in order before leaving the office when the phone rang. "Jackie had the baby!" Evelyn's voice wobbled with distress. "It's way too early! They're saying on the radio that he's – it's a boy – he's only about four and a half pounds. Oh David, her baby might *die*!"

He tried to calm her down. "It's not good for you to get this upset, honey," he said. "Try not to worry, I'm sure they'll have the best of care for the President's son." She would not be comforted. Finally, he told her to just sit tight and he'd be home as soon as possible.

The house was in an uproar by the time he got there. The two boys were out in the wading pool, arguing about something or other. His second daughter, eleven-year-old Mary Lou, was doing her best to persuade her mother to sit down and put up her feet. Evelyn wandered the kitchen, alternately poking at the chicken frying in the pan and fiddling with the radio dial to find any news updates. When she saw him, she said, "I think Jackie herself is alright, but I can only imagine how upset she must be."

Evelyn's left arm wrapped around her belly, as if trying to hold her own baby in tightly, and Mary Lou implored her again. "Sit *down*, Ma. Your ankles are all swollen."

"Where's your sister?" David asked his daughter. "Where's Laurel? Why isn't she here?"

"You said she could go to Kilgo's Kanteen with Betsy and Donna. Donna's mom drove them."

David took charge, sending Mary Lou out to supervise her younger brothers. He turned off the stove and forced Evelyn to sit in the big chair in the living room with her feet propped on a hassock. "This is ridiculous," he said "I know you admire her, but – "

"We're the same age! If she could have a miscarriage, so could I!" Diane rocked back and forth, holding her stomach.

"You're not going to have a miscarriage."

"You don't know that! I might! With this hot weather and all these storms, it could happen! Everyone says barometric pressure changes can cause one! Maybe that's what happened with Jackie! Oh, why don't they do an update?!"

Gradually, he did manage to calm her down. He pointed out that no news was good news and that there was every chance that the baby would stabilize. Eventually she settled into the chair and began to doze off. He finished cooking the chicken, told the kids to dry off and get dressed, and set the table. Evelyn woke in time to eat, and everything seemed pretty normal again until the evening news came on. The President had been flown to Hyannis Port where his wife had delivered, and they'd both been able to see their son, but now the baby was being taken to a hospital in Boston, as a 'precautionary measure'.

"You see?" David asked. "They're giving him the very best of care." Finally, he persuaded her to turn the television off for a while so they could take the kids to camp meeting. At thirteen, Laurel lived for those evenings when she could walk around the passways with her friends, giggling and whispering, while the boys liked to hang out at the Monkey Stand, debating which cheap toy they would persuade their folks to buy for them. Mary Lou, always their dreamer, just sat out on the back swing, listening to the new transistor radio she'd gotten for her eleventh birthday a few days ago. She was crazy about this new British group, the Beatles.

Evelyn settled on the front swing, discussing Jackie's plight with her neighbors. Each time another friend or acquaintance came by, she took the opportunity to bring up the subject all over again.

It was times like this when David missed the river the most. Since he was a boy, whenever he got stressed out, he'd head down to the riverbank and watch the water sliding by. He never got tired of watching it rippling over rocks and tree roots. The river had been narrow where it passed through the farm, deeper and a bit more turbulent, always in motion. It seemed to wash away all his worries. A person looking at it couldn't help but realize that it had always been there, long before anyone lived on the land. It made one's problems seem puny and unimportant.

The lake just didn't do that. The lake was proof that things could change in a cataclysmic way and he couldn't do a single thing about it.

He sat by Evelyn and gradually managed to change the subject by talking about plans they were making in the new house. When they decided to leave the farm,

Evelyn had fallen in love with a new subdivision going up just west of downtown Bennetton. *"Lucky You,"* the sign on the highway had read. *"To be coming home to this modern, spacious ranch-style house, with acres of space inside and out! Sliding glass door! Wall oven! Brick patio! Family room!"*

They'd chosen one with four bedrooms and a large flat yard and he'd been working all summer to get the lawn established. The yard was ugly, he thought. No trees. They'd all been bull-dozed out of the way when the subdivision was built. One neighbor's yard ran into another, nothing much yet to distinguish property lines. The kids loved it. Plenty of space to play ball or re-enact their favorite TV shows – *Gunsmoke, the Jetsons, My Favorite Martian.* He and Evelyn bought patio furniture and put in spindly little saplings, but it just felt naked and raw to him. *Everything* felt naked and raw.

The next day, Evelyn seemed better. The news was more encouraging than otherwise – Jackie was resting comfortably, the baby was getting everything that a doctor's care could provide. They had named the boy Patrick. David went back to work. Evelyn took the kids to a matinee. In the evening, they hung out at the campground again and stayed in the tent overnight. And at last, the rain stopped.

But Friday morning, Evelyn turned on the radio first thing and heard the news. The baby had died at four that morning, having lived only 39 hours. Evelyn immediately got upset. "Jackie never even got to hold him," she said, staring at the radio, tears in her eyes. "She didn't ever get to see him again – he was in that hospital in Boston and she was still in Hyannis Port. Oh my God, I feel so sorry for her!" She rocked back and forth on the kitchen chair, one slippered foot tucked underneath her, the other resting on the damp straw on the floor.

"I'm so sorry," David said. "But Evie, you can't go on like this. For crying out loud, you don't even really know the woman! It's ridiculous to carry on like this, upsetting yourself. If anything's going to bring on a miscarriage, it's this frenzy you've worked yourself up to!"

"Oh, *David*! How can you? This is the worst thing that can happen to a woman, to lose her child. How can you be so unfeeling?" She wrapped protective arms around her mounded belly. "Jackie will never be the same!"

The radio droned on. The President had flown from Boston to be at his wife's side. "At least she still has Jack," Evelyn said. "He'll be there for her. Thank God for that. *He* cares about his wife."

That stung. "I care about mine, too!"

"Not as much as you care about that damn river!"

"What?! How did we go from Jackie's baby to the river?" He stared at her, completely bewildered.

"I don't know!" She got to her feet and began shoving things around on the kitchen counter. Opened up the percolator and started filling it at the sink. "I don't know! I just know I'm *sick* of you moping around all summer, moping around all the last *two* summers. Oh, the river is gone. Oh, the lake is so terrible. Oh, the good old days have all gone away." She started to spoon coffee into the pot, then turned suddenly with the spoon in her hand, sending coffee grounds flying in all directions. "I'm *sick* of it! You think I'm too caught up in the Kennedys? Well, you – you're too caught up in the past!"

She turned her back to him again, bracing herself against the counter, and began to cry. Hard.

Oh, Lord, he thought. I can't stand to see her cry. He put his arms around her. Pressed his face against her hair. "I'm sorry," he said. "Look, it's all going to be alright. Come on, baby, sit down."

Evelyn allowed him to steer her to a chair. "It's the *sixties*. We're sending men into *space*," she choked out between sobs. "There's a bright future ahead, if you can just let go of the past."

He didn't argue, although her logic made little sense to him. He just wanted her to calm down and stop worrying him. He hated conflict. "Honey, it's all okay. I'm sorry if I go on too much about the river. I'm sure the lake will seem just fine once I get used to it."

She sniffled and took a long shuddering breath, and wiped her eyes on a paper napkin. After a moment, during which she visibly drew herself together, she said, "I'm sorry too. I get so upset. I *know* you care about me. Really, I do." She managed a tremulous smile and put her hand into his. "I just feel bad for her."

Whoosh! Another quick directional change in the conversation! But he ought to be used to that by now. He kissed her forehead and said, "Hey, I know what. Why don't we pile all the kids in the station wagon and head up to the mountains for the day? It'll be cooler up there."

"What about the office? Don't you have to go in?"

"I'll work it out. I could go in on Saturday instead, for once." He looked down at her and reached out to smooth her hair. "I have to take care of my wife today. And we can talk about the baby's room – we haven't finished the nursery yet. On the way back, we can stop at the paint store. What do you think? Blue or pink?"

Evelyn achieved a real smile this time and held his hand against her cheek. "Maybe we better go with green." She stood up, one hand against the small of her back, and called up the stairs to the kids. "Hey, y'all! Wake up! We're going to go for a drive today."

As she moved toward the boxes of cereal, David took a deep breath. As scattered as Evelyn's thought process was, he had to admit she was right about one thing.

He'd been mourning the river for too long. It was time to face the fact that life changed. You couldn't stay mired in the past – and the past wasn't even always that fantastic. It was just familiar. No unknowns. But *over*. Time to deal with that.

He could hear a rooster crowing outside, from the farm beyond the campground. A familiar sound that he rarely heard any more. He could enjoy it for the moment, but now he needed to look forward, not back. To enjoy, perhaps, a little serenity and calm. Calm like the lake which spread out across the land, smooth and benevolent and dependable. That's what Evelyn needed from him now, and he could be that. In his heart, he knew that the river would continue to flow through him, just as it would always flow through the lake, connecting past to future. But from now on, silent and unseen.

The Yankees
1975

Dear Mom and Dad,   Oct 21, 1975

We have been here a week now, and are all settled in. Here are some photos of the cottage. It's small, but big enough for just the two of us, and you can see we have a gorgeous view of the lake. The leaves have only just begun to fall, which seems so strange since back home, they're all down, raked, and burned at the curb.

Painter's Creek is a REALLY little town, almost just a figment of the post office's imagination. One grocery store, one drug store, two gas stations. There's an elementary school that's pretty old, built in the 1920's, and that's about it. The nearest bigger town, Bennetton, is twenty miles away, and it's about the same size as our town back home. What's different is that it's surrounded by countryside, instead of other towns.

Bennetton has most of what we might need, although no movie theatre, no shopping mall, etc. For that, we have to go to Charlotte, about 35 miles away. At least there's no traffic! Mark's job is about seven miles away and he can get there in less than ten minutes. Only one traffic light that whole way! And he doesn't pass a single business except for a gas station, and only about three dozen houses. Mostly it's just fields and trees. Dad would probably love it here.

The first morning after we got here, Mark and I went to breakfast at this family-run place. Good food and I had my first introduction to Southern cooking. I tried liver mush (shaped like Spam but tastes a lot better) and grits (tastes like nothing else I can think of, looks like white oatmeal but not sweet, good with butter and salt on it). Dad would like the food here too.

It's going to be a challenge, trying to cook any of the things Mark's mom taught me. The ingredients just can't be found. No ricotta, no Italian sausage. I asked the guy at the grocery store for olive oil, he just stared at me and showed me a bottle of olives. Like I'm going to press them myself? Guess I'll be cooking with corn oil.

This week I am job-hunting. The pay rates are a lot lower than back home, but housing costs are lower, too. There aren't any apartments around here, but in Bennetton there are a few and they're about twenty percent less expensive than back home. Mark and I are seriously considering buying a house, because they're much less expensive too, and the property tax is TINY.

His new job is going well. He likes what he does and likes the people, but he has a hard time understanding them sometimes. Their accents are so strong. Not like "Beverly Hillbillies", though. Not twangy. More like s-t-r-e-t-c-h-e-d out. One guy said he wanted to talk to Mark about the Bobble. Mark said "What??" The guy said, "The Bobble. You know, B-ah-b-l-e." In other words, the BIBLE. And they use different words. 'Hey' instead of 'Hi.' 'Y'all' instead of 'You Guys'. They don't even know the word 'pop' at all. They say "co-cola" for every kind of pop. But mostly they just drink really sweet iced tea.

Be sure to write back and tell me how everyone is. I miss you and think about you a lot, but don't worry. Your girl is doing well.

Love, Maddie

Dear Mom and Dad,   November 5, 1975

Sorry I haven't written. Been so busy. I started my new job at the high school, as a library assistant, and I like it real well. Everyone is very nice – in fact, everyone we've met everywhere is very nice. I think it's because the town is so small – they all know each other and have since they were born. And they're curious about us Yankees. We're like aliens to them. Everything seems to circle around the churches and nobody's happy that we're Catholic. One man told me I would go to Hell, but he didn't say it in a mean way, more like he was sorry to give bad news. Like he hoped I would soon recover from a devastating illness.

Speaking of being Catholic, we have been to the church in Bennetton – St. Agatha's. You won't believe this – they are housed in a HOUSE. A tiny two-bedroom house. The Mass is said in the living room. There are exactly SEVEN pews front to back. And – get this – the confessional is in the BATHROOM. I do not lie! Now if you ever needed a reason not to sin, this would be it. The priests do not live here, they visit from other parishes. This congregation is so small it's considered a MISSION church!

So far, I have met only one person at this church who was born in the South. Everyone else is a Yankee like us, from Michigan or Pennsylvania or New York. Plus a few Floridians. And we're all kind of starved for people from home, so we cling to each other like tornado survivors. After Mass on Sundays, a lot of us go to the same restaurant for lunch and have a chance to get really acquainted. I've decided to join the Women's Organization and get to know more of the ladies.

Last night, Mark and I went out on the deck to look at the stars. With no city lights around, you can really see them. You can actually <u>see</u> the Milky Way. It's just so beautiful. And we are finally getting used to how quiet it is around here with no neighbors, or cars driving past. It's like a world of our own. With crickets.

Love, Maddie

Dear Mom and Dad,   January 2, 1976

Glad to hear you made it safely home, despite the snow when you went through Ohio. We have still not had any snow, and yesterday we even did some outdoor grilling, it was so nice out. And sunny! There's supposedly 300 sunny days per year in North Carolina. So different from Michigan!

Thank you SO MUCH for coming down for Christmas. I was really feeling blue about the holidays, so you were more than welcome, and I'm glad we got to show you around a little. So how did you like our little Charlie Brown tree? I know it was kind of pathetic, but we are really trying to save every penny so we can buy a house. This cottage is only available until Easter, after that the people who own it will want to come up on weekends. The lake is beautiful, isn't it? Not many houses on it, just some cottages, so it's very peaceful.

Over at the high school, I have volunteered to help out with the Winter Guard. This is a group of girls who do flag twirling (not baton, like at home) for the marching band, called Color Guard. When marching season is over, they still do fancy routines and compete against other schools and that's called Winter Guard. So far, I'm just helping with their equipment and food and stuff when they're on the road for a competition, but it's lots of fun. I really like the girls and the school. It's small, about a quarter of the size of my high school, and way out in the country. A lot of the kids' parents still own farms, although most of them also have regular jobs as well. A lot of them work at knitting mills. The 4H club is the biggest school club, not counting Marching Band.

For the most part, the kids have pretty good manners and we don't have a lot of big issues. Maybe because it's such a small community – half the parents used to go to this school, too, and they're pretty involved. The football and basketball games get a huge attendance by parents, and there are quite a lot of parent volunteers.

We did have a gunfight on the bus last month – WATER PISTOLS!

What I've really begun to notice is the lack of ethnic groups. You know how it is at home, my school was full of kids who were Polish or German or French or Italian or Armenian, some of them only one or two generations away from being immigrants. And, of course, Detroit always has the ethnic festivals down on the riverfront. Here, there are only two ethnic groups – white and black – and almost all the whites are essentially British-

Scottish background, and they've been here since the late 1700s. I'm sure it's different in the bigger cities, but around here, not much variety. At least the last names are easier to pronounce!

Definitely not much in the way of ethnic food. We went out for spaghetti last week – it was horrible!!!!! Fortunately, I am really learning to like Southern cooking, especially country fried steak and hush puppies.

Love and kisses,
Maddie

PS - the day after I wrote this, before I could mail it, we had an ICE storm. Not a snowstorm, it's ICE. Just looks like sleet, but in the morning, you wake up to an icy fairyland. Every branch and twig on the trees is covered in a thin coating of ice. Beautiful! But the streets are icy too, not so beautiful. Everyone has to stay home, plus the power went out due to electrical lines breaking from the weight of the ice. No electricity meant we had no lights, no heat, and NO WATER, because of the well pump being electric. We had to get buckets of water from the lake to flush the toilet! Good thing we have a fireplace here. Fortunately, the ice all melted by mid-afternoon, and the power came back on before dark.

Dear Mom and Dad,   April 21, 1976

Have you recovered yet? I know you were excited to hear our news. I am feeling okay, but I throw up EVERY MORNING. Funny thing is, once I've thrown up, I feel fine and can go about my day just like normal. The doctor says not to worry about it.

Now that a baby is on its way, Mark and I have gotten serious about looking for a house to buy. We'd love to live on the lake, but most of these cottages are built for summer living and not really meant to be a winter home. They're not insulated very well, and a lot of them have the washing machine and dryer out in a carport, if they have any at all. So, we are looking at non-lake properties too. There just aren't a lot of houses around here to choose from, and we don't want to be too far from our jobs.

Spring is here in NC. The weather is warm, and flowers are EVERYWHERE. Lots of flowering trees and bushes. Forsythias, azaleas, and these beautiful spindly trees called dogwood. You see them out in the woods, mixed in with other trees, with these white four-petal flowers that spread out horizontally, so they look like they're floating in the woods. Just beautiful. I will send you some photos.

Painter's Creek is supposed to get livelier in the summer. Already on weekends, people are beginning to show up at their cottages to fix things up and move stuff in. Mark and I had a chance to go out on a pontoon boat last week, with friends from church. I hadn't really realized how huge this lake is. Over 500 miles of shoreline (that's because the shoreline is really jagged, but still). Hardly anyone else out on the water. I'd love to get our own pontoon boat someday. There's even a marina nearby where we could keep it.

You remember that place we drove past with the old wood shanties? I've been learning more about it. It's called 'camp meeting'. In the summer, people stay there in those little shacks, for 'religious revival'. Lots of Bible thumping, like that Billy Graham guy. They tell me it's really fun. I can't imagine. Another thing that goes on in the summer here is slow-pitch softball at a place behind a furniture store. Can't quite imagine that either but it starts up soon, so we'll be sure to check it out. Not much else to do around here!

All my love,
Maddie

Dear Mom and Dad,   August 14, 1976

It was so good to visit you last week. Our drive home went fine, and all our groceries made it too. I have to admit, we really miss our Northern food favorites. But you know what's weird? After we got back, Mark and I both said we were worn out from how fast everyone talks at home, and from all the traffic. Seemed funny once we thought about it, but these were things we never noticed when we lived there. I guess we're gradually getting used to the South, where people talk slow and there's almost no traffic.

I can definitely say that Painter's Creek is different in summer than in winter. Lots more people here during the summer, staying at their cottages or visiting someone in the area. The lake gets busy, our sad little grocery store is busier, people are mostly happy to be here. But it's HOT. Holy moley, it's hot!!!! And HUMID. Think about how it is at the end of July at home, add ten degrees, and then multiply that by three months. I swear, some days I'm about to melt. Thank goodness our new house has air conditioning.

Speaking of our new house, we have finished the nursery. You can see those curtains in the photos – took me two weeks to make them, but I think they turned out pretty good. And in the picture of our back yard, if you look carefully you can see a tiny triangle of the lake between the trees. We are at the beginning of a street that ends at the lake, so we're close but not close. There's no access to the lake at that end because it's kind of a high bluff above the water. And there's no swimming access around here, but we've been able to go out on our friends' boat a couple more times, so that was nice.

Camp meeting finished last Sunday with a big 'whoop and a holler'. Our new neighbors have a 'tent' there and invited us to visit. You wouldn't believe this, but it really was fun. Kind of like a county fair, in a way. Everyone walking around and visiting and eating homemade ice cream. Lots of singing and bluegrass fiddling. (Dad would have loved it.) Plenty of Bible-thumping and I was asked by MANY people to 'come to Jesus' and join their church. I'm not going to change, don't worry, but it's nice to be wanted!

We've been going to the softball games, too. Theoretically, these are amateur teams, but man, they're good! This is not like church league. And the slow-pitch softball is a lot more fun to watch because you see a lot more action. The man who owns the furniture store (plus a slew of other businesses) sponsors the team and it's a prize-winning team. They compete in the Nationals and even World competitions and have won the nationals a bunch of times. Sometimes I just shake my head – Painter's Creek is SO small-town, yet it has a national winning softball team, and I'm told that 15,000 people attended the final Sunday's preaching at camp meeting. Not bad for a town of only 400 people during the winter.

I have to say, other than missing you guys, I'm really happy living here. Every day is so beautiful (even if it's hot). We never did have any snow last winter, but I really only missed it on Christmas Day. We've made lots of friends, our jobs are going well, we have our own house long before we probably could have afforded one back home. It's been a good move for us. Although I do still really miss you guys. I hope you can come down for a visit after the baby is born.

Speaking of the baby (who is scooting around inside me like a little VW Beetle right this moment), you know what's weird? I hadn't thought about it before but guess what? Our baby will be a real Southerner, born and bred. He or she will grow up in a small Southern town where everybody knows everybody and have Southern friends and drink Cheerwine and eat Moonpies and go to camp meeting (but still be a good Catholic!) and go to Painter's Creek elementary school with the kids of all the business people and mill workers and preachers and slow-pitch softball players in town. Maybe they'll even get Southern accents. Mark and I will probably always be Yankees in a way, but our kids will be Southerners. I kinda like the idea.

Love always,
Maddie

PS Just throwing out an idea. What if you guys moved South? You keep saying things are bad at home, with the recession and all the layoffs and everything. You could buy a house in the new golf course neighborhood here and Dad could move his business down. There's a big flea-market nearby at a place called The Music Hall, and you'd be around to see your grandbaby growing up. Again, just a suggestion – well, maybe a bribe – but do think about it. You know we'd love it. And, hey, people around here are getting used to us Yankees.

The Fire
October, 1983

THE WOMAN AND THE GIRL SAT IN THE CAR *at the foot of the long driveway.*

"Well? Get out!" the woman said, and the girl did so, carrying an over-stuffed backpack.

"Does Dad even know I'm coming?" the girl asked. "His car's not here."

"I left a message on the machine. You know where the key is."

The girl trudged slowly up the drive until she came to the side door. She reached under the doormat and pulled out a key and held it up for the woman's inspection. Immediately, the woman gunned her engine and disappeared.

The girl stood there for a bit, and then put the key back.

With a sigh, she hoisted the backpack onto her shoulders and set off across the back lawn and into the woods beyond. A narrow footpath led downhill to a creek and she followed the muddy water for about half a mile until she crossed over at a shallow spot where she climbed up the bank and across a field. Soon afterward she came upon a railroad track that ran through an evergreen forest. She followed this for maybe four and a half miles. She saw no one and no one saw her.

Camp meeting that year had been lackluster. Not as many younger people were showing up, it seemed. Oh, they'd cluster around the Shack on Saturday evening, buying cheeseburgers and milkshakes and homemade brownies, but the crowds were definitely not so big as in previous years. It had been that way for a while now. Maybe the days for camp meeting were over. There just wasn't the same enthusiasm.

Even the older folks were beginning to have their doubts. Each year now, stories circulated about teenagers going out to the woods to drink and do drugs and have sex. Last year, there'd even been a woman in a bikini who danced while men threw money. The trustees ran her off, but folks had been scandalized that something like that could even happen. And the place looked rundown. Tents weren't being repaired like they should be, and even the grounds weren't being maintained affectionately as they'd always been. It seemed like folks just had other things to do, and air-conditioned places to do them in, and they didn't want to hang out at the campground on steamy August days.

Some folks blamed the new man-made lake. It had certainly become a vacation spot, with visitors swelling the area all summer long. Painter's Creek was still a destination, but now for another reason. Expensive homes were beginning to go up, and the golf community was thriving down near where the racetrack had been. For certain sure, things were changing, and some folks thought not for the better.

After that season's camp meeting had ended, the trustees met for a long session. They discussed everything, with the hope of improving attendance and encouraging folks to fix up their tents. There was little agreement among those at the meeting. Cyrus

Abernathy, the head trustee, summed it up when he said, "Either people care about the campground or they don't. We can't *make* them care. And if they don't care, all the rules in the world won't improve things. Let's pray for an answer."

The girl trudged on. Trains came through on those tracks only twice a day, coal cars on their way to the steam plant. She stopped when she reached the old church and helped herself to a drink from the outdoor spigot. There was no one around on this cold, gray Saturday afternoon, and she was able to slip quietly into the woods where leaves were beginning to turn, but not yet fall, and walk another half mile to the campground.

The tent was in the middle row on the north side. She'd stolen the key to the padlock a month back, and it hadn't been missed yet. Quietly, she let herself in. The air was stale and musty, and everything felt a little damp. She climbed up into the sleeping loft and pulled a child's sleeping bag from her backpack, along with an extra pair of socks. Darkness had fallen. She made herself as comfortable as she could, ate a Snickers bar, and settled down for the night with a flashlight and a book. Madeleine L'Engle. *A Wrinkle in Time.*

Cyrus Abernathy sat down for supper with his wife Venetia. Wearily, he told her, "Not a good meeting. We didn't accomplish a thing."

"Give it time," Venetia said. "Things have a way of working out." She set a plate of pork chops and fried okra in front of him, and they said grace. Afterwards, she said, "Don phoned. He had to go to Hamburg suddenly, there's some kind of problem with the shipments. Won't be home till the 27th."

Cyrus shook his head. "I'd hate to have to travel as much as he does. Used to be, if you worked in textiles, you hardly had to leave the county. Now, seems like I hear something every week about another mill closing."

After dinner, they watched the news. A big storm had torn through Texas a few days ago – people were still digging out. "Expect a few windy days here," the weatherman said, "as that front blows through."

Venetia said, "Do you think we should take in the hanging baskets and the porch swing?"

"Nah. Won't be that bad."

The girl woke up in the middle of the night, freezing. So far, the autumn had been mild, but in the black of night it sometimes got pretty cold. She climbed down the ladder and looked around with the flashlight. In one corner was an old wooden crate, and there was plenty of trampled straw on the floor. From her back pocket, she pulled a lighter. Tomorrow she would figure out what to do.

Around 2 in the morning, Cora Dellinger's dog woke her up, whining as if he had to go outside. "What is it, baby?" she asked, running her hand over the dog's head. "I let you out before." She heard a couple of dogs barking outside, a little way off. "Oh, you think you need to go hang with your rowdy friends? No way, José." But now that she was awake, she had to use the toilet. She did so and stood at the sink washing her hands. Half-asleep, she gazed through the window and saw an orange-ish light in the sky. What could that be?

She hurried into the kitchen to look out the back window, then she went to the back door. As soon as she opened it, she smelled the smoke and her brain snapped to attention. *The campground was on fire!* Immediately, she placed two phone calls – one to the volunteer fire department, one to Cyrus Abernathy. Then she got dressed.

The fire truck was on the spot within minutes, and cars belonging to various volunteer firefighters began converging on the southeast field. By this time, the fire was roaring through the tents on the north side, and the fire chief made a call to the four nearest fire departments, most of them volunteer, and another call for a couple of bulldozers to knock down tents and create a fire break.

Cyrus and Venetia arrived shortly thereafter. They had already phoned the other trustees and word began to spread from neighbor to neighbor, with people hurrying to the campground to see if their own tent was on fire. Cyrus swore under his breath when he saw the only road blocked by onlookers and right away, he drafted a couple of men to help him direct traffic. Venetia organized coffee supplies out on Cora's back porch where they were sheltered from the wind, and together they did their best to keep bystanders from crossing the road.

The fierce wind that whipped up helped spread the fire from tent to tent, and toward the woods beyond. The only blessing was that it kept the arbor from being threatened. The flames could be seen from a mile away, and the orange light in the sky was visible from the lake. Many prayers went up. By tremendous effort and cooperation between the different fire companies, they were able to get the fire out by morning, although they'd be watching for hot spots the next couple of days.

Crowds of people came by the rest of the week, people whose tents were destroyed, people whose tents were damaged. People whose tents were just fine but wanted to see the carnage. People who'd never been anywhere near the campground but who stopped by to enjoy the drama. Fire Chief Yarmouth, a 27-year veteran, was pretty sure within 24 hours that the fire had started in Tent 207, Cyrus Abernathy's tent, and for a while, rumors were rampant that it had been an act of vengeance, due to his stiff enforcement of rules against drinking and loud music after 9 pm. However, Chief Yarmouth eventually made a statement that it appeared the fire may have been caused by a transient seeking shelter, or maybe teenagers experimenting with drugs.

He said, "There were no accelerants, nothing to indicate an intent to do damage. Most likely accidental...although if we find the person or persons responsible, we will still file charges. Those tents are private property and nearly a hundred of them are destroyed or seriously damaged. That's more'n a third of the entire campground – so you can bet we're serious about finding the perpetrator."

Meanwhile, the cleanup began. Volunteers arrived by the dozens to clear lots and drag away the burned lumber, as well as curled and blackened tin roofs, and mounds of ashes. Women organized food supplies for the volunteers, building contractors offered the use of their back hoes and bulldozers, the local newspaper printed a lurid selection of photos of the damage and quoted many campers mourning the loss of their tents.

"My great-granddaddy built ours in 1910."

"We've had ours for four generations."

"All the furniture in ours was hand-made a hundred years ago."

"Nothing left. It breaks my heart. This is more than a burnt building, it's like they tried to destroy my soul."

The trustees met and decided to give the tent owners two years to rebuild. That was considered sufficient time for some effort to be made, despite the cost. Truth was, the rebuilding began almost immediately, and many decided to take Chief Yarmouth's advice to make their new tents a bit more fireproof, with concrete floors and sheet-rock between the walls. Many who had never bothered before to hook up to the campground water system decided to do so, and discussions went forward regarding the need for some kind of security force.

Before they knew it, the trustees were being bombarded with suggestions and offers for improving the campground facilities – better lighting, better bathroom facilities, maybe some picnic tables and gardens. Several of the huge old oaks on the north side had burned beyond saving, and a local nursery donated a number of fast-growing Bradford pear saplings. That pleased the crowd, and many said, "They'll look so pretty in the Spring."

There was certainly plenty to do. Cyrus found himself working hard every day, all day long, so he was surprised to see his son Don show up – had the time flown that quickly? Could it really be the 27th already?

Father and son walked the perimeter of the campground, with Cyrus pointing out the path of the fire. "The irony is," he said, "folks have suddenly realized they'd miss the old place if it was gone. Been a long time since the community has really pulled together in this way. If you could say there was one good thing to take from this catastrophe, that would be it."

Don commiserated with him on the loss of their tent. "I guess the new one will be alright," Don said, "but I'll miss those height marks we used to have on the door frame. And Granny's big ol' rocking chair." He kicked at a pile of fresh lumber stacked by the new concrete floor pad and then looked at his dad and said in a softer tone, "I can't get hold of Tiffany. She took off and I don't know where. Landlord says she was behind on her rent. I don't honestly care what my ex does, but she shouldn't keep Chelsea from me."

A cold chill ran down Cyrus' back. He asked softly, "When's the last time you heard from Tiffany?"

"I don't know. A few weeks past, before my trip. She left a message on my machine, but it was pretty garbled. Sounded drunk . Something about the beach, about how she deserved a better life."

"And you haven't heard anything from Chelsea since then?"

"No. But I'm sure she'd call me if she needed anything."

Cyrus took his son's arm and forced him to meet his gaze. "Son – after the fire…about a week later…a body was found. Burned, pulled apart. We think dogs got to it. Didn't find all the…parts. Couldn't identify it, other than they think it was a young girl. Nobody reported a missing person. Son…are you sure Chelsea's with her mother? She wouldn't have run away?"

The two men stared at each other, as their faces paled to white.

The Fussbudget
1998

GRANDMA IS FUSSING ABOUT GETTING READY for camp meeting this year, even though she has it organized down to the last baked bean and roll of toilet paper. She's been going every year since she was born, 1932, and so I guess she knows what's needed, but she really gets into the whole 'tradition' thing. I'll try to stick in something new, like my Walkman or Gameboy, and she throws a hissy fit.

"That's not what camp meeting is about," she says, packing her sun tea jar and a bag of lemons. "It's about family, and Jesus, and knowing why the good Lord put us on earth. Now where did you put the Skip-Bo cards?"

I find the cards, give them to her and tiptoe away. Grandpa is sleeping in the living room in his wheelchair with all the shades pulled and I lay on the floor in the half-darkness. The wide wood boards are cool, but hard, and I can feel my ribs and hipbones grinding against them. My breasts are coming in at last (or should I say going out?) and they mortify me. *Mortify* is a good word. I learned it in Ms. Crawford's English class. It means death, as in 'my breasts embarrass me to death', or 'my breasts make me want to die', or 'my breasts are just killing me'. All the clothes I own are now divided into two groups: Shirts

That Show Too Much Boobage, and Shirts That Don't. Nothing worse than walking into a room and realizing too late that your breasts are pointing at people.

It must be kind of like that for guys when they get an unexpected boner. Boner is a funny word, too. At first when I heard it, I kept thinking of Banjo, that little cocker spaniel that Grandma used to have. He would wag his stumpy little tail and I liked to grab it and hold on. Underneath the skin and muscle, I could feel his tailbones. But I guess boners aren't exactly like that.

Grandpa wakes up. He does this with no sign of waking, just suddenly his eyes are open. "Where's your Grandma?" he says. "Time for the baseball game." And it is, too. Grandma turns on the TV and they both watch the game. Grandpa falls asleep again during the fourth inning. Grandma watches the whole game anyway, and now and then when it gets exciting, she grips Grandpa's arm.

When I think about it, I've been going to camp meeting every year since I was born, just like Grandma, but fourteen years just isn't the same as sixty-six. She keeps telling me how much it's changed, but when I look at the old pictures she has on her wall, seems exactly the same to me. There's the big arbor in the center of the campground and the rings of tents that have been falling down and rising again since the 1830's. You can always tell which ones are new by the yellow wood. And, of course, the Shack where all the action is.

In fact, the only changes at all that I can see are the fashions. Short-shorts and pointy eyeglasses in the fifties, halter tops and bell bottoms in the seventies. That, plus our family keeps shrinking. In the photos of when Mumma was a kid, over twenty relatives stood on the porch. Now we're down to seven. That's another thing that makes Grandma fuss. "You'd think people could take two weeks a year to spend with their families," she mutters for the hundredth time. "It just ain't right how families get all spread out these days."

"Yeah, but it cuts down on the murder rate," Aunt Jody says, popping her gum and grinning at me. The day we move into our tent, she babysits with Grandpa and my half-sister Kinsey at the house until everything's settled and then brings them out in the evening – him in his wheelchair, Kinsey in the stroller. It's almost like Grandpa and Kinsey are the same age nowadays. They both wear diapers and sleep a lot.

In the evenings, Aunt Jody likes to sit on the swing on the front porch of the tent and say hey to all her old boyfriends when they walk by with their wives. She quit bartending and now she's learning to be a mortician. That's another word a lot like *mortified*, only it means an embalmer of the dead. "Funeral director, if you don't mind," she says. "It's about a lot more than just laying out corpses, you know. I plan to really change things, too. None of this depressing organ music… Hey, Dwayne." She smiles slowly, her lips with their shiny peach color sliding back over her square, white teeth. "How y'all doin'?"

Dwayne (or Bill, or Travis, or Eddie) always smiles nervously. Aunt Jody hasn't changed much since the time when she posed for that centerfold and the wives always make angry faces when they see her sitting there in her short shorts and little cotton tops. She has real good legs for a woman over thirty, they're brown as peaches with little golden freckles on the thighs, and she likes to cross them real slow.

"For example," she continues saying to me, while her eyes follow Travis (or Eddie, or Bill, or Dwayne), "if a person liked to listen to Elvis Presley when they were alive, why not play Elvis music when they die? I'm not talking about the lively stuff, like *Viva Las Vegas*, but you could play *Kentucky Rain*, couldn't you?" She stops to wipe some drool off Grandpa's chin. He smiles and looks vaguely at her. "And clothes, too. If a person wasn't the type to wear a suit, why not bury him in a golf shirt?"

"I don't think I'd like to look at dead hairy forearms," Grandma snaps, "and if you're wanting people to take you seriously as a funeral director, maybe you should button your shirt a little higher. I c'n see clear to China."

Grandma tries to talk Aunt Jody into taking a day off from learning about extracting bodily fluids. "Why?" Aunt Jody asks. "You know we'll only end up fussing at each other."

"We could talk about things."

"No, Mama. We never talk. We just fuss." Aunt Jody checks her hair in her compact mirror and winks at me. "I'll just come in the evenings. I'm on a low-fuss diet these days."

During the days, Grandma watches over Grandpa and cooks stuff for the preachers' meals. I don't think they could even have camp meeting if she wasn't there to make hush puppies and fried chicken and 'nanner pudding. I hang out with my friend, Ashley, and help with the younger kids during Vacation Bible School. Not that anybody asked me if I minded doing it; somehow, it's always just expected that the girls will help. Nobody expects it of the boys, which seems unfair to me. They just hang out at the lake all day long, fishing and sometimes skinny-dipping. One day, Ashley snuck off to the lake to watch them. She told me about it later, but it made me feel so fussed inside my chest that I said I had to go help Grandma with the snap beans. I don't want to think about that stuff yet.

Lots of people show up for Little Sunday, the first weekend of camp meeting. Mumma and Brian spend the whole weekend and we all go to the arbor to hear the preachers and the singers. The Lighthouse Boys are here again this year, and June McSwain, and the Elizabeth City First Methodist Choir. Of course, what everyone really waits for is Reverend Nightlinger from Mt. Olivet. He's the Bible-thumpingest preacher we've got around here and there's never any telling who might decide to give up their sinful ways and come to Jesus. Some folks have done it three or four times already.

Ashley and I get permission to sit on one of the end pews, near the back. It's real hot out and everyone's got their cardboard fans going. Taylor Witherspoon keeps looking at me a lot. He's one of the few boys taller than me, so that's kinda nice and Ashley keeps nudging me and giggling. Taylor wears glasses and they make him look real smart, and he has this sort of slow grin that just does something to me.

After the preaching is over, we go walking with a bunch of others down to Ashley's tent. I get all embarrassed and don't know what to say to him, but Taylor just keeps talking about school and playing the trumpet in the marching band, and we sit together on Ashley's swing. When he goes to stand up, he puts his hand on my shoulder first. It makes a little thrill run right down my arm and out at my elbow.

It's hot, really hot, even at night and Grandma lets me sleep on the upstairs porch. It's not much cooler but I like to watch the whole place slowly settle down and go to sleep. Then it's just me and the crickets and moths and the stars. The moon rises right up over the arbor. It's the prettiest sight.

Sometimes the boys will gather quietly, whispering and passing a cigarette, and walk through the campground. I lay still as can be, my face pressed into the pillow that still smells of Grandma's iron-on starch and try to hear what they're saying. Boys do fascinate me, I have to admit. They're so different from girls and get to do lots better things. I know all about how girls have more opportunity nowadays. Aunt Jody is always telling me that, but it still seems like boys have more interesting lives. The only thing Aunt Jody ever did interesting was when she posed for that centerfold, and Mumma has never done anything interesting at all. Grandpa helped blast holes in the mountains for roads, and Brian is a volunteer fireman and even stupid Lonnie Sigmon down the road drives a dirtbike in moto-cross races. The most exciting thing I ever did was ride the elephant when the Cole Brothers Circus had their show over to the elementary school. It's not a lot to look back upon.

Each night the number of visitors grows. Ashley and I get dressed up in the evening after supper. She put a lot of Sun-In on her hair this summer and it really looks good. Mine is all curly from the humidity, so all I can do is stick it up in a big bushy ponytail. I finally got Mumma to let me wear mascara, though, so we both look lots older than last year. We walk round and round the campground, over and over, smiling at the boys and looking to see if they're smiling at us.

Friday night before Big Sunday, the crowds are really big. Grandma has been cooking all day at the Shack. "It's too much," Mumma fusses at her. "You can't work all day in that hot kitchen, they shouldn't ask it." Grandma's mouth makes a real straight line and she begins folding napkins and stomps around, putting the silverware straight. Mumma sighs and sits by Brian, who's pushing

Kinsey back and forth in the stroller. Brian is always a little nervous around Grandma. He offers her a chair, saying how hot it is and doesn't she want to sit down.

"No, Brian, I'm fine. Didn't you just hear me say I'm fine?"

"Yes, Miz Abernathy, but . . . "

"Then don't be a horse's patootie."

"No, Miz Abernathy," he sighs, running a finger around his collar. I almost feel sorry for him.

Grandpa sits in his wheelchair. Lots of folks come by to say hey and Grandma sits next to him, her eyes sparkling. She talks and laughs and pats Grandpa's hand. He smiles and taps his toe to the country music playing on the radio. Every time somebody new walks up, she tells him in his ear who it is. "The Sherrills," she says. "You remember, Junior and Kat."

"Junior and Kat," he repeats, nodding and smiling. He enjoys the homemade strawberry ice cream. Grandma spoons it carefully into his mouth and kisses him on the cheek. "Jenny?" he says loudly. "Jenny? Jenny?"

"I'm right here, Frank."

"Jenny! Where's my Jenny?" he says loudly, and people across the way turn to look.

"Time to go," Aunt Jody says, and undoes the lock on his chair wheels. "Mama, he gets worse every day. You've got to start giving some serious thought to what you'll do . . . "

"When I want your opinion, I'll ask for it, missy."

"No, Jody's right," Mumma insists. "You have to face facts, Mama. You're not as young as you used to be and Daddy's a lot of work. You can't keep on lifting him and bathing him. You're going to hurt yourself one of these days."

"Well, I'll be dipped in crumbs and fried in Hell before I'll let one of my daughters tell me what I can and cannot do!" Grandma's eyes are blazing and her short, curly hair seems to be standing up on her head. I can see the glare of the setting sun behind it outlining her skull. "We get along just fine, Frank and I, and if I need help with him, I have plenty of friends who'd be glad to give a hand. *Glad* to. Don't you be worrying about us. Y'all just go back to your air-conditioned offices and busy, busy lives and let us take care of ourselves." She glares at Mumma and walks over to Grandpa, putting her hand on his shoulder.

"Jenny?" he says. "Don't fuss. You're always fussing."

In the morning, Grandma is in a bad mood. She said she'd teach me how to fry eggs, but it's not going good. I can't seem to get the knack of cracking the eggs open. "Like this," Grandma says, doing it one-handed into the electric skillet out by the back door. Only this time, the yolk breaks. Usually, she'd just flip it over, cook both sides, and make a fried egg sandwich out of it, but this time she makes a hissing noise with her tongue and tosses it out of the pan and into the grass. I don't know what to do, so I try to pick it up with a paper towel. "Oh, don't mess with it," Grandma says, her voice sharp and tight. I leave it where it is on the grass next to the path, and later I see a dog run over and eat it. "I just don't know any more," she mutters. "Nothing's what it was." I decide that cereal sounds fine for breakfast. I'm not sure exactly what she's talking about, but I know there's no dealing with Grandma when she's in one of her moods.

It rains lightly that afternoon. I usually enjoy rain at camp meeting. Other years, Grandma and I would sit in the upper room and play cards. Little puffs of rain-cooled air would slip in between the open slats of the wood walls while her hands shuffled the cards, red fingernails flashing. I like thinking about how once upon a time she was fourteen and playing cards with her grandma during a warm August rain. "Gin," Grandma would say, and slap down a fan of cards.

But there's no card game this year and she's fussing something terrible. Grandpa's getting heat rash on his – well, under his diaper – and Aunt Jody decides to take him home with her to stay in the air-conditioning. Grandma's so mad she could spit, and I decide to go for a walk with Taylor.

Under the pine trees, it's hardly wet at all. Our shoes squelch a little bit on the red mud. Taylor holds my hand. I hope he thinks they're wet from the rain and not from sweat, because all of a sudden, I am mighty nervous. I've been thinking about Taylor just about every minute since he touched my shoulder and worrying that maybe Reverend Nightlinger is right about the lusts of the flesh. Mine is all goose-bumpy. Then Taylor leans down to give me a kiss, and I just about die. His lips are soft, and warmer than I could imagine. They make a terrible throbbing start up in my own and I want to lean into him something fierce. Then all at once, I start to shiver all over and we each step back. Gosh, I think, what do I say now – *kiss me some more?* Instead we hold hands again and walk to the Shack. My hair is getting all frizzed up with the rain, but I don't care. Taylor kissed me.

That night it's even hotter and we can hear thunder rolling up from the lake. It's gonna be a whopper of a storm, so Grandma and I take quilts and pillows and a flashlight to the upper room, close under the tin roof. Grandma brings a jug of lemonade and some cookies, too. We nestle on the old wicker loveseat, reading stuff from the National Enquirer to each other. I like the ones with pictures of celebrity fashions, especially the ones showing the best-dressed and the worst-dressed. "You'd think they could do better," Grandma says, "with all the money they make. Look at that tacky dress. They had style, in my day."

The rain begins really coming down, just about deafening us as it drums on the tin roof. Grandma's perfume seems stronger up here. Avon's Topaz, which she has always worn till I can't think of anyone but her when I smell it.

"Grandpa had a good afternoon, didn't he," she says, more of a statement than a question. I think about how it seems like he has no chest anymore, he is so curled over on himself. "I wish he could have stayed longer, he'd have liked the singing, I think."

For once she's not fussing. I roll over on my back with my head in her lap and my knees pulled up. "You met him here, didn't you?" I ask. I've heard the story a thousand times, but I have to get Taylor out of my head.

"He was visiting the Hendersons," Grandma says, her eyes closed. "He was just out of the service, almost 30 years old. I was only eighteen. He'd never seen a camp meeting before and they had to explain to him about why the cabins are called tents, and suchlike. I was working at the Shack and he told Carl Henderson he'd never seen a woman with such a flat backside. I overheard him and said, quick as a shot, 'that's because I don't waste time the good Lord gave me just sitting on it.' He told me later that was what decided him to get to know me better. That I could give him a setdown like that without missing a beat."

She strokes my hair for a while, and I listen to the rain now drumming soft and steady. And she says, "We were married before Christmas." Lightning flashes and I can see Grandma's red lipstick looking dark against her white skin. I roll on my side and mush my face into her stomach. The housedress she's wearing smells like sunshine and warm breezes. "He was so good-looking," she says. "I thought he hung the moon."

She looks down at me, sternly. "Always set your standards high, Jayelle. Don't date any stupid boys, you hear?"

I nod against her warm belly. "Yes, ma'am. I mean, no, ma'am. I mean, I won't."

"Your grandpa was a self-educated man, an intelligent man. He read everything he could get his hands on." After a minute, she corrects herself. "*Is* a self-educated man." Lightning flashes again, with thunder right on top of it and we both jump. "Mercy," she laughs. "Mercy, Maud. Good thing ol' Banjo isn't here. Remember how afraid he used to be of storms? Used to whine and fuss until one of us had to go sit with him in a dark closet."

"I miss Banjo. He was a good ol' dog," I say and loop my first finger around Grandma's belt, tug at it a little. "I felt bad when he got old, he got so shaky and nervous. He shrank down to nothing." I twine my other fingers in Grandma's belt, too, taking hold. And then in barely a whisper, I say, "Just like Grandpa. Disappearing bit by bit, same as Banjo did."

"Not quite like Banjo," Grandma says, her voice quiet and tired-sounding. "Banjo just wanted comforting when he got sick. You didn't need to worry about leaving him his dignity. You didn't need to . . . " She hushes up suddenly and looks out the window. Thunder booms real close by and seems to shake the tent. She strokes my hair again. "Everything's changing," she says in a real low voice. "I hate it for him."

The storm stops. As if it had wanted to go out with a bang, like 4th of July fireworks, it pounds out a final volley of thunder and lightning and then goes quietly away. Grandma and I go downstairs to the porch for some fresh air. Rain drips from the trees. Even though it's after midnight, lots of people are awake, talking and excited from the storm. Grandma picks up her pot of geraniums that had tipped over and presses the earth back down around their roots. "You'll be fine," she tells them. "Sun'll be back tomorrow."

Big Sunday brings the biggest crowds of all. Everyone dressed up in church clothes and carrying picnic lunches. Grandma goes all out, with slow-cooked barbecue, fresh-made slaw, silver queen corn on the cob. She doesn't have any truck with people who take the easy way out, bringing in tubs of KFC or cardboard boxes from the supermarket deli. She says, for the hundredth time, "I just don't understand how people can let all their traditions die out." She puts her best tablecloth on the big rough table that Grandpa built in the downstairs room a long time ago, and sets out real plates, not paper ones that can be thrown away afterward. Mumma has made lemon chess pie and Jody puts a jug of daisies in the middle of the table.

Grandpa is asleep in his wheelchair, but he wakes up when we're ready to eat. He still likes to eat Grandma's cooking, even if we have to cut it up real small. I take Kinsey out of the stroller. She's cutting teeth now and drools all over my good blouse. When she grins, all that spit makes a bubble. Brian takes her on his knee and we all hold hands to say grace. Grandma adds at the end, "Lord, let us have many more times at camp meeting, if it is Your will, Amen." She tucks a napkin under Grandpa's chin.

We begin passing food around. Out of the corner of my eye, I spot Taylor Witherspoon sauntering past and looking to see if I'm looking at him. I *am* looking at him, and that throbbing in my lip starts up all over again. Nobody seems to notice, thank goodness. Mumma and Jody are giggling over some private joke, Brian's feeding the baby. From the next tent, we can hear music. Elvis Presley, singing *The Wonder of You.*

"That's be a good song to use, don't you think? I'm going to make a list."

"Miz Abernathy, did you hear that the Baptists are debating about whether to use cushions on the pews now?"

"People are too soft nowadays."

"Yes, ma'am. Well, maybe if they were softer, they wouldn't *need* cushions, heh heh."

"Pass me some more of that slaw. It's awful good."

"Honey, who's that boy out there? He keeps looking over."

"Anyone want some cornbread? It's fresh made."

"Jenny? Where's my Jenny?"

"I'm right here, Frank."

Christmas Eve
2005

SHE WOKE EARLY ON THE DAY BEFORE CHRISTMAS. After tossing and turning most of the night, it seemed futile to continue to lie there and fret, so she just got up. There was still so much to do – pies to bake, final gifts to wrap, rooms to clean and always laundry, laundry, laundry. Might as well get going on it. Within another 48 hours, the whole thing would be over and she could put Christmas 2005 behind her and not think about it again.

Not think. That's what Liza wished she could do. Not think. Not feel. Just focus on the task in hand and not remember. Stop going over again and again the thoughts that were wearing a path in her brain. Had she done enough? *Had she been enough?* Ten years of trying to be the person she needed to be, rise to the challenge, and all the while knowing she could never quite succeed, never quite stretch herself far enough to meet everyone's needs, let alone her own.

Mom was gone. That was it, the final good-bye, there was nothing further she could do. Ten long years of illness and suffering and the slow spiraling-down of abilities. Ten years of strokes and falls and increasing physical limitations, ten years of dominoes slowly toppling one on the other. Ten years of herself helplessly watching it happen.

Oh, *shake it off*, Liza told herself. This is Christmas Eve. Start the coffee. You have a million things to do for those still living, and children who look forward all year to this night. Twenty people arriving tomorrow for a celebration that most of the adults would dread. They'd put their grief aside for one day to make the children happy, but, oh, Death was so much more poignant at Christmas, the supposed time for joy.

Stop, she thought. *Put your feelings away.*

She had time for one cup of coffee, then the kids woke up and her husband James appeared, all showered and dressed and heading for the office. He gave her a sympathetic kiss and reminded her he'd be home by early afternoon so they could go to the Christmas Eve service at the arbor. Another family tradition that couldn't be skipped, not even this year. She added a note to the long list of To-Do's. *Quilts for pews. Thermos. Hot cocoa. Find Laura's mittens.*

The kids were full of loud, happy chatter, heating Eggos in the toaster and skirmishing gently over the butter and syrup. Thank God for children, she thought. They were her only bright spots these days.

Gradually the morning passed, filled with chores and errands, and she was able to focus on her many different jobs and see that things were getting accomplished. The kids helped. Kelly made sure that everyone had finished wrapping gifts and put them under the tree. Jake walked the dog and brought in firewood from the stack outside. Laura at last found her mittens and had the fine task of assembling everything needed for their traditional Christmas Eve games and snacks.

For several years now, they had attended the 4 o'clock service at the arbor and afterward gone out for Chinese food, inspired by the kids' favorite Christmas movie, *A Christmas Story*. When they returned, they'd play Mexican Train or Skip-Bo and reminisce about previous Christmases and read *The Night Before Christmas* before they put out cookies and milk for Santa, and a couple of carrots for his reindeers. Even though none of the kids really believed in Santa anymore, they still enjoyed the tradition.

Last thing before bed, they'd change into new Christmas pajamas and hang their stockings. Now that Kelly was officially a teenager, she had balked at the idea but Liza persuaded her to go along with it. "Just this one last time, Kelly," Liza said. "Please." And Kelly agreed.

Since Dad had died – oh, had he really been gone eleven years? – Mom had stayed overnight with them on Christmas Eve. She'd gone to the service, sang along to the music – even though in the later years, she could no longer remember all the words – and allowed each of the children to unwrap one gift from her. Their other gifts would wait for morning, but from her they'd have one 'big' important gift to open that night.

But not this year. That seemed to be the mantra that was developing. *Not this year*. She and her sisters repeated it to each other as they figured out how to carry on. Only a week since Mom had left them. The funeral had to be squeezed in between holiday events. It felt so wrong. How could they celebrate the season while they were mourning their mother? How could they continue their tradition with this huge hole in the family, when nothing would ever be the same again? Dad's death had been hard enough, but it occurred in late winter, when everything was already drab and depressing. Not at Christmas, when they were supposed to feel joy.

Oh, don't go there! Liza forced her thoughts and feelings back down deep inside and focused on seeing that the kids were all bathed and dressed and ready for church service. It would be cold at the arbor. So different from the summer events during camp meeting. Cold and damp, although there would be plenty of lights and music. Usually some kind of Christmas play, too. Not a Nativity play, at least not every year, but something to remind people of the 'reason for the season', and shine a focus on the birth of Christ, of the sense of love toward our fellow men, of faith in our Savior, of the certainty that there was a plan for all of us.

It sure didn't feel that way right now. No. She had to shut her feelings off.

Finally, it was time to head over to the campground. Laden with blankets and supplies, Liza and her family made their way to the pews inside the arbor. On the stage, a small set had been erected. A fake fireplace and mantelpiece, with stockings hung from it. Two rocking chairs, some potted poinsettias, a small Christmas tree. Off to one side, the electric organ had been returned from its winter storage for this one day, and Cal Greenway was already softly playing some old favorite hymns.

People filed in, laden with their own quilts and blankets to drape over pews and tuck around babies and old folks. Folks nodded to Liza, the same ones who'd attended the funeral and filled her kitchen with casseroles and cakes. She knew they sympathized, but she couldn't meet their eyes or her own would overflow yet again. Her sister Nancy arrived with her own family and joined Liza's group in the same pew, and their other sister Alice sat with her two children in the pew behind them. Now she was surrounded by family, yet she felt so alone, so sad, missing her mother so much it was like a blow to the stomach.

The minister spoke, music was sung, she did her best to join in. James sat on her left, his shoulder solid and strong next to hers. Laura to her right, curled up against Kelly who put her arm around her younger sister. Jake sat on the other side of his father, his impish nature subdued for once. This year's Christmas play was about a father and son, long estranged, coming together at last in a moment of forgiveness and love. Saved by a Christmas miracle.

But no Christmas miracle for Mom. Just one medical emergency after another, as though she'd been endlessly falling down stairs. And then gone before Liza could get there, between one breath and the next. There's been no final moment, no chance to say one more time that she loved her, no last hug or kiss. Instead, she'd been caught in horrible holiday traffic, stuck on a highway while trying to get to the hospital. Alice and Nancy had been there, thank goodness for that, but Liza had failed to arrive in time.

Failed. That's what it felt like, although with the logical part of her mind, she knew it wasn't true. She'd done her best through those ten years, to take care of Mom's needs, to follow up with doctors, to count out pills and practice physical therapy. She took Mom on outings and brought the kids over, checked in frequently with the staff at the assisted living facility. But it never felt like enough. And wasn't. Not when Liza also had a part-time job, three school-age children to manage, and a husband and a house to care for. She was pulled in twenty directions all the time, and it was never enough. How many times had she made an excuse or felt sorry for herself with so much to do, and now Mom was gone and she couldn't do one more thing for her. *Oh Mom*, she thought. I'm so sorry. I didn't do enough and I didn't see the end coming, and I *didn't know it would feel this bad.*

Tears threatened to overflow. I can't do this, she thought. I can't put on a happy face for the children, I can't even put on a calm one. I'm a wreck, and I just want my Mommy. And I'll never have her again.

The play ended and the minister began speaking again. She couldn't follow his words, she could only sit in her own misery and beg God to have mercy. She closed her eyes, feeling the congregation around her, feeling the cold that seeped in around the edge of her collar and up the sleeves of her coat. She sat with her hands on her lap and just tried to breathe.

A sense of warmth crept over her shoulders, very slight at first, and then a bit more. A hand, warm and slender, slid into hers, palm against palm, fingers interwoven. Mom's hand. She'd know it anywhere, those long slim fingers, the soft skin. Mom's hand, which had held hers in every crisis and every triumph of her life. Mom's hand, warm and alive, seeming to tell her "It's okay. I love you, and I know you did your best. I know you loved me, and you're going to be alright."

She didn't dare open her eyes, didn't chance breaking the spell. Was this real? Her imagination? Was it only her memories coalescing to bring back the physical sensation? No matter. She didn't care what the answer was, she just allowed herself to feel. To embrace this miraculous moment of having Mom back just once more. To believe that Mom had understood, had accepted, had not only forgiven any of Liza's shortcomings but had not seen them as shortcomings at all.

Liza didn't know if such a thing were possible, but one thing she felt sure. If this was something Mom *could* do, she *would*. She would reach out one last time to ease her daughter's suffering, to think of someone else before herself.

Her eyes were still closed as she felt the warmth of that hand spreading throughout her body, warming her soul. Mom *loved*. That was the whole substance of her life – she loved and was loved. If Liza could carry that into her own life, then it would be as if Mom never left. The legacy, the tradition would go on. Even as the sensation left her hand, and Liza opened her eyes at last, she knew she would remember this moment the rest of her life and find solace.

And now the final song was sung. This time she was able to join in and hold hands with James and Kelly. As the song ended, she turned to hug Alice and her kids, and passed hugs down the line to Nancy's family. She hugged everyone within reach. It was alright. Yes, they would all be alright. Their celebration tonight and tomorrow might be more solemn, certainly different from last year, but somehow, she no longer faced it with dread. Mom would live on in her children and grandchildren, and they could celebrate the joy she'd brought during her lifetime and – yes, even clasp sorrow to their hearts without it having the power to overwhelm them.

Thank you, Mom, for coming to me, Liza thought. And thank you, God, for letting her. She glanced around at the old solid structure of the arbor, where her family had seen so many years come and go, and it felt like an embrace. Something that would last.

Love without end. Amen.

Big Week
2018

RAY CANSLER COULDN'T SLEEP. For half an hour, he'd lain rigidly at Mary Lou's side, trying to avoid tossing and turning so as not to wake her up. But he just couldn't get back to sleep. Finally, he eased himself off the air mattress, used the bathroom as quietly as possible, and went out onto the tent porch.

The campground was almost silent. He could hear the leaves rustling in the trees, the *whirr* of many electric fans, and one bird merrily chirping, but otherwise the place was quiet. At 4:57 in the morning, it certainly should be. He set himself down on the left-hand end of the swing, the end which didn't creak so bad, and cautiously started it going.

"Dad?"

The voice came from above. His daughter Bethany, on the balcony right over his head.

He called up, softly, "Why you up so early?"

"Feedin' the baby. Hang on, I'll come down."

Within a minute or two, she came through the back door, cradling Ava against her shoulder. "And why are *you* up so early?" she whispered, grinning.

"Restless, I guess." He started to make room for her on the swing but she shook her head and took the rocking chair. Ava, a small round bundle with a shock of dark hair, stirred briefly and went back to sleep. "You shoulda put her back in bed. She needs her sleep."

"Nah," Bethany replied. "She's so milk-drunk now, it'd take a bomb going off to wake her. Besides," she added, giving the little noggin a kiss, "I like to hold her. She hardly lets me anymore, now that she can crawl."

He gazed at his daughter in the half-light. Long and skinny as ever, with a tousled braid hanging over her shoulder, wearing a nightshirt and a pair of flip-flops. She was the mother of three, but still looked about 13 years old to him. He whispered, "You want some coffee?"

"Not yet."

They both swayed in silence for a few minutes, her in the rocking chair, him on the swing. Ray didn't mind waking early. He enjoyed having the day to himself for a little while. He resisted the urge to reach for the baby – it would be a shame to interfere with the lovely image before him – but he surely would have liked a chance to hold her. Seemed like his grandkids got past the holding and burping stage so quickly! Five-year-old Arlo and three-year-old Mack were constantly going, going, going all day long. The only chance he had for lap time was just that little bit before they went to bed, and then the competition among the adults could be fierce. Mary Lou, especially, held on tight to story-time rights.

Well, he couldn't complain. It had been another great week. A *wonderful* week. Bethany and the kids arrived on Tuesday, with her husband Hank coming in the evenings. Hank was one of the McLeods, and he'd taken Bethany and the kids over to his folks' tents for their big gathering yesterday. Before then, however, Ray and Mary Lou had been able to spend lots of time with their daughter and the three grandkids – going out on the boat, watching them play in the wading pool, teaching Arlo and Mack how to crank a fishing reel. And, of course, taking them all to church service and singing. What a joy to bring his family into the arbor and let all his friends see what a fine group they were.

He said, keeping his voice low, "Arlo sure is excited about starting kindergarten. He's been talking about his teacher. Mrs. Raspberry this, and Mrs. Raspberry that."

Bethany started to laugh but stopped herself so as not to wake the baby. "Mrs. *Rosen*berry." She kissed little Ava's forehead and went on. "He's over the moon. But poor ol' Mack hasn't caught on yet that Arlo's going and he's not. He's gonna miss having his brother around. But it'll be good for him, too. Get out from under Arlo's thumb."

Ray was about to comment on the complicated relationships and pecking order of brothers, but Mary Lou came out onto the porch at that moment, bearing two steaming mugs of coffee. She set them down, unceremoniously confiscated the baby, and joined Ray on the swing.

"The boys are awake," she murmured to her daughter. "No – don't get up – Hank's fixin' them some cereal."

Bethany settled back in the rocker and sipped appreciatively from her mug. Through the open door, they could hear the boys' piping voices and Hank's rumbly laugh.

Mary Lou settled the baby more comfortably, and asked, "So how'd it go yesterday?"

"Oh, you know the McLeods." Bethany stretched her arms and legs in front of her and gave a big yawn. When she had thoroughly finished, she said, "About thirty of them packed into those three tents and everyone talking at once. You don't dare make eye contact with anyone or they launch into some long fish tale and you can't break away for at least twenty minutes." She smiled at the memory. "But they're entertaining – you gotta give 'em that. The boys had a great time running around with all their cousins. I wish we lived closer so they could get together more often. Oh, by the way, they're doing their big family photo before lunch, so can we schedule ours for right before the preaching? So there's at least a half chance the boys will still be clean?"

Ray spoke up. "Do you think you might ever move back here? Things are changing. We even have a decent grocery store now, and they're building all kinds of new housing developments."

"Yeah – I see they're breaking ground right here, next to the campground. Big ol' housing development."

He snorted. "I wouldn't buy there. They're supposedly leaving a greenbelt between the houses and the campground, but let's face it, during the summer, they'll be fighting a lot of traffic. And even when it's not camp meeting time, this road gets backed up pretty bad as you approach the stoplight. They need a turn lane."

"I know. Who'da thunk that Painter's Creek would ever have traffic jams? But, really, Dad… I don't think you should pin any hopes on us moving back." She drained her mug and continued, "We both like our jobs, and for me, right now, things are perfect. I work mornings and can be with the kids the rest of the day, and I would never be able to find a part-time job around here that pays as well."

The baby began to stir, and then broke out in a huge smile when she saw her Grammy's face. "Good morning, Ava," Mary Lou crooned. "How's little Miss Binkers?"

"Little Miss Stinky-britches, you mean. Come on, Toots." Bethany gathered up her daughter and headed into the tent.

Mary Lou took Ray's hand. "You had to know that wouldn't fly," she said.

Ray sighed. Yes, he knew perfectly well that Bethany and Hank would stay in Raleigh. Hank had some high-tech job at Research Triangle Park, and Bethany was a forensic archivist – whatever that was – for a private foundation. They owned a beautiful old house, three stories high and completely renovated, in an attractive neighborhood with gorgeous towering trees. There was no reason for them to come back.

That was the problem, he mused, in raising your kids to be smart and independent. They outgrew their need for you, and eventually the shoe was on the other foot. Not that he and Mary Lou were dependent on anyone. Not yet. Not like Mary Lou's parents had been for quite a few years. It was just that he wanted to see the kids more often.

Wade and his family lived nearby, thank goodness. He and Mary Lou spent many happy hours going to school events – concerts, ball games, art shows. Probably not a week went by that they didn't see at least some of that gang. And the kids were often over to spend the night.

But I'm greedy, he thought. I don't want to miss out on those experiences with Bethany's kids. After all, who knew how long he'd be around to play Grandpa? He was already 72, so he might not even see all his grandkids grow up. Probably wouldn't. And besides, he needed something to do.

Four years ago when he retired, he'd been glad for the free time to travel a bit with Mary Lou or go fishing as often as he wanted. He'd revamped the garden and tinkered a bit in the garage. But even so, he had time on his hands. And no time to waste.

Maybe he and Mary Lou should make a change. They'd considered it after her parents died. Buy a condo near Bethany's, where they could stay for a couple of weeks at a time, while still keeping their house here in Painter's Creek. They knew other retired couples who did that.

Of course, Raleigh wasn't *that* far away. Three to three-and-a-half hours' drive, depending on traffic – but there was always lots of traffic. He and Mary Lou often went for the weekend, but he didn't like crowding Bethany for more than a couple of nights. If they had their own place, they could stay longer. And just looking for a condo meant an exciting project.

The only thing that had held them off was money. The inheritance from her folks wasn't enough to buy a place outright, and he couldn't see getting a mortgage at this point in his life.

But what if they sold the tent?

The campground tents sold for a surprising amount of money. For one thing, it wasn't often that a tent came up for sale. Maybe one or two a year changed hands. And lots of families had outgrown the tent they owned and needed more space, or had never had one but always wanted the chance. He knew he could make enough to help pay for a condo, but what if…

"Earth to Ray," Mary Lou said, elbowing him. "Where've you gone to? You're a million miles away."

"Just thinkin'." Ray got to his feet and helped Mary Lou up. "We better get us some breakfast. It'll be time for preachin' soon."

They finished eating and got cleaned up, all ready for Big Sunday service. Wade's family arrived and the ten of them gathered on the front porch. Wade set up a tripod and once everyone was in place, he set the timer and stepped over next to his wife. As usual, the younger kids wiggled and squirmed, but Wade took several sets of shots and announced that he'd gotten some really good photos.

"Okay, well, let's shake a leg," Ray advised. "If we don't go now, we won't be able to get seats together." They made their way to the arbor and found a good-sized crowd, but by squeezing together a bit and holding the youngest kids on their laps, they managed to fit together in one pew.

"This is fun," Mary Lou said, hugging Mack.

Ray agreed. *Lord forgive me*, he thought, *but I'm so proud of my family*. Seated behind them were five generations of McLeods, Hank's family, from 92-year-old Miz Florence, down to the newest sprout, little Blake, just three months old. The extended family filled four pews but, Ray thought, *they ain't got a thing on us!*

First up was the Methodist church choir, and then Reverend Harkey stepped up to the podium and began preaching. Ray tried to listen, but his thoughts were racing around like a pack of wild dogs. More and more, he liked the idea of getting a condo. There were lots of things to do in Raleigh – the museums, parks, an arboretum. Mary Lou would enjoy going to concerts and the fancier stores. And then when city life wore them out, they could come back home to Painter's Creek. They could even leave a supply of clothes there so they wouldn't have to pack every time they went back and forth.

At the moment, however, he needed to put himself into *this* moment. This was the last day of camp meeting, and if the plan he was surmising should take place, this might be his last Big Sunday ever. Would they even come back if they didn't own a tent? Lots of folks did. Either squeezed in with relatives, or just came for the evenings and Sundays. Somehow, though, he couldn't see himself coming back as a 'visitor'. This could be the end of a very long era. Was that what he wanted?

A shifting in the pew brought his attention back. Arlo was working his way down the row of adults to his grandfather's lap. Ray pulled him up and hugged him, and breathed in the scent of his hair. Yes, this *was* what he wanted. To be able to be around these children – and their parents, of course – as often as possible. He wanted the kids to *know* him and Mary Lou, to be completely comfortable with them, as Wade's children were. And for him to know them, to see their little personalities unfold. To be able to spend the kind of time with them that they'd experienced for the past week. It couldn't happen if they only saw each other once in a while.

By the time service was over, Ray had made up his mind. Camp meeting had been a wonderful part of his past, but the days were growing short... and what he wanted to do was embrace the future.

He knew well and good he should talk things over with Mary Lou first, and all the way back to the tent, holding Arlo's hand, he considered a plan of attack.

The Clary family sold their tent last year. Got a pretty good price for it too, so he heard. Of course, his own tent was in much better condition, but it was in the outer row and some folks preferred the inner row. And he should make plenty of mention about the opportunities to attend the ballet – not something he particularly enjoyed, but Mary Lou did. And especially talk about fixing up the condo – furniture and stuff – women always liked that. He could envision much scouring of consignment shops. Mary Lou loved a good bargain and she was a wizard at restoring old furniture. And might be they could get a three-bedroom condo, so that Wade and his family could come for overnights. And if he would just get to work and refinish that old coffee table…

"Ray – what are you doing?!"

He snapped to and realized he'd walked right past the tent. Mary Lou was staring at him in amazement. "Uh, sorry," he mumbled. "Hey, what's for lunch?"

"You'll find out when I put it in front of you," she snapped. "Now let go of Arlo. He's gotta go with his folks." She nodded at Bethany and Hank, who were preparing to head over to the McLeod tents for their group photo.

Ray sheepishly handed over his grandson. Wade's wife Stephanie would help in the kitchen, along with their daughters Allison and Becky, so he and Wade decided they were best off out of the way, on the front porch. As they sat in the swing, half-watching young Colin playing catch with another kid, Ray decided to test the waters.

"Well, it's been a good camp meeting," he said, drawing the words out slowly and stretching for emphasis. "Just about perfect. Guess I won't see many more like this one."

Wade turned to look at him. "Are you alright?"

"Yeah, sure…just thinkin'." Ray shrugged. "Just, you know, wondering how long this will continue. All good things come to an end. I mean, at some point, the kids'll outgrow this place…"

"Are you kidding? They love it here." Wade squinted a bit at his dad. "What's all this about? Are you sick or something?"

"No, for gosh sakes! I'm fine! Just thinking out loud."

"Well, don't. You're freakin' me out."

Ray could see this wasn't quite the approach he needed. He had to think it out a bit more.

Over the fried chicken and mashed 'taters, he tried again. "Hey, have you heard what the Clary's got for their tent? 'Course, it was pretty in pretty bad shape…"

"Yeah, but did you see what the new people did? Tore the old one down," Wade replied. "What a heartbreaker."

"And that eyesore they built? I'd die of shame," Mary Lou said. "Twice as tall as any of the other tents in that row. Fancy porch. Sticks out like a sore thumb."

"Yeah, well, my point is…"

"Granite countertops, I heard," Stephanie said with a grin. "Scandalous!"

"Yeah, but Bob Clary said…"

Bethany passed the peas and said, "I heard they've got manufactured wood floors. Now, shoot, does that make any sense? Pine floors, sure, but manufactured wood floors? Kinda ridiculous."

"But that's not the issue – "

"Well, what *is* the issue?" Mary Lou turned a stare his way. "You've been chewin' on somethin' all day. Spit it out!"

All eyes turned to him. Ray cleared his throat and said, "Well…I was thinkin'… maybe…I just mean *maybe*… it's time to sell the tent."

And that's when all hell broke loose.

"Sell the tent!"

"Noooo!"

"What would ya wanna do that for?"

"But we *love* the tent!"

"If anything, we oughta buy a second tent!"

"Have you lost your mind?"

"Wahhhhh!" (This from Mack.)

"Alright, alright, alright! Sorry I brought it up!" He handed Mack a strawberry to distract him, then said in an even tone, "I was just playing with ideas. Mom and I had thought about maybe buying a condo near y'all in Raleigh – still keeping the house here – and going back and forth – and selling the tent would, you know, help with the cash flow. Just an idea."

Mary Lou smacked his arm. "Well you mighta give me some warning. We only talked about buying a condo, not about selling the tent. Sakes alive! I always thought we'd be leaving the tent to the kids." She glanced around the table. "Y'all want it, don'cha?"

"Yes! Of course! *Don't get rid of it*!"

Hank, ever serious, said, "Maybe we could buy it from you. Keep it in the family that way."

Ray shook his head. "No, no – if we're gonna pass it on, it'll be for free. I just thought – well, who knows if you'll even want to come here once Mary Lou and I are gone?"

"*I'm* not going anywhere," his dear wife said. "Have you got plans I don't know about?"

Right behind her, Wade said, "This is the second time today you've said something about not being around. Is there something you haven't told us?"

"Oh, for cryin' in the sink!" Ray roared. "I'm not going anywhere. Nothing's wrong with me. I'm just trying to figure out how to buy a condo without going into debt!"

"Why do you even need a condo?" Bethany asked, trying to keep Arlo and Mack from throwing peas at each other. "You can always stay with us."

"But I know we're crowding you when we come. And, bless you honey, but all them *stairs* you've got…" He raised his hands in surrender. "Just thought it might be an answer. Didn't mean to start World War Three!"

"Nobody's mad," This from Stephanie, the family peacemaker. "We're just surprised."

"Oh, heck with that!" Mary Lou got up from the table and began clearing plates, even those that people weren't finished with. "*I'm* mad. You don't go making decisions like this without talking to me first!" She stomped her way to the kitchen sink and, a moment later, a Beatles song came on. *Back in the USSR.*

"I *didn't* make any decisions," Ray grumbled. "I just floated an idea – and it's landed on me like a ton of bricks."

Hank clapped him on the back. "Come on, let's go for a walk and you can throw more ideas around. I promise, I'll – "

"Oh, no, you don't!" Mary Lou turned and glared at them with her hands on her hips. "Any conversation on this subject is to include me."

Ray dropped his head in his hands. *Lordy, why had he ever opened his big mouth?* Soon all the adults were sitting around the table, throwing in their own two cents about what he ought to do. He didn't like *any* of the suggestions. They all seemed to hinge on him having to lean on the kids. Either sell the tent to all of them, or let Hank buy a condo and rent it to him, or just continue to horn in on Bethany ("We don't mind – we'll put the boys together in one room and you can have your own space!"), and from there they went to forgetting about the whole condo idea and just staying in rental units on an irregular basis. Or hotels. Didn't they know how he hated hotels? Mary Lou even brought up the idea of selling their house in Painter's Creek and buying *two* smaller condos, one here and one there, at which point he looked at her as if she were talking a foreign language. What a mess. What a mess!

Finally, at his wit's end, he said, "Okay, okay –
enough! I've heard your ideas. Now it's up to me and
Mary Lou to talk it through and come up with a decision.
It's *our* decision."

Mary Lou walked over and addressed the whole
group. "Well, I'm sorry to say it, but we need to start
cleaning up. Bethany and Hank have all their stuff to
pack to go back home, and we need to clear away all
this lunch mess and pack the groceries and things. It's
the end of camp meeting for this year, and we have a lot
to do."

They all kind of shuffled off, glancing over their
shoulders at him. As soon as they were all out of sight,
he heaved a sigh, got to his feet and went over to the
storage space beneath the stairs. He pulled out the boxes
that would hold the framed photos, all those photos he'd
hung at the beginning of Little Week. That dad-blamed
chore he had to do every year. Hang the pictures, lug
the furniture, fill the air mattresses, repair the screens,
store all that stuff in his garage all winter. Was it even
worthwhile? He was getting old, damn it! All he wanted
to do was sit in the sun and play with his grandchildren.
Was that too much to ask?

He took the photos down one by one, swathed them
in bubble wrap, and packed them away without barely a
glance at any of them. He felt sick at heart. It seemed like
such a brilliant idea. Maybe that would be his epitaph: *It
Seemed Like a Good Idea at the Time.* And to top it all
off, Mary Lou was pissed as hell. He hadn't managed to
get her that riled up in a good while.

Well, dadgummit.

He wrapped another photo, glancing at her out of the
corner of his eye. She was cleaning out the cabinets and
boxing things up and he could tell from the stiffness in

her movements that she was mentally arguing with him the whole time. The Beatles' White Album was on full blast, Side Three. Maybe when it got to *Mother Nature's Son*, she'd calm down. Of course, a couple of songs after that was *Helter Skelter*…so maybe she wouldn't.

The tent seemed jammed with people. The younger kids were out on the front porch – Ava in the baby swing, all three boys playing with some old Matchbox cars that had belonged to Wade. He could hear Hank clomping around upstairs as he and Bethany packed up. He could hear their murmuring voices too, probably debating whether the old man had popped his cork. Wade was directing his girls in loading the truck with kitchen boxes as fast as Mary Lou could pack them, and Stephanie was directly behind him, packing away the jigsaw puzzles and games, and giving him sympathetic glances.

Man, he hated sympathy. He felt quite sorry enough for himself and didn't need any help. Finally, he couldn't stand it anymore, and headed out for a walk.

All along the passways, people were packing to leave. There was always a huge exodus after lunch on Big Sunday, especially those folks who didn't live nearby. He passed a couple of groups doing their family photos out on their porches. Gathered around Maw-Maw and Paw-Paw, they were. Making him feel bad, probably on purpose. An old curmudgeon, that's what he was.

"Ray! Ray Cansler!"

The voice came from behind him. Ray turned to see Bob Clary, who came hustling up to shake his hand.

"How ya doin', ya old coot? Where's your better half?" Bob, who looked like a jovial Santa with white hair and a beard, pumped Ray's hand up and down, and kept pumping it as he continued to speak. "Wasn't sure I'd see you this year. We just came in for the day. Been up in Asheville all summer. Love it up there. Great place. Got a rig in the RV park there. Right on the river. Hey, didja see what they did over to our old place? Put up that big monstrosity! I call it the Tent O'Plenty. Ain't it the worst?!" He laughed and his belly shook up and down.

Ray eased his hand out of Bob's grip. "Yeah, I saw it."

"Well, makes no difference to me. Ain't my worry no more. We live in the RV full-time now. Great thing! A few months here, a few months there. Headin' out west next, gonna stop and see our Karen in Memphis and then on to Colorado, where m'brother lives. Take our time, don't drive more'n four hours a day." Bob saw another friend, waved at him and said, "Gotta go. Give our love to Mary Lou!"

He waddled off and Ray watched him for a minute before turning to head back to the tent. Maybe that was an idea. An RV. His head filled with images of western sunsets and mountain streams. They'd never done any RVing, although he and Mary Lou had gone camping a few times in the old days, with the old-fashioned type of canvas tent and a camp stove. He allowed himself to wallow in a few daydreams until he found himself almost passing up his own tent once again.

Arlo and Mack were on the front porch, with Allison keeping an eye on them. Arlo watched a cartoon on his dad's tablet but Mack was still playing with those Matchbox cars, running them in the sandy soil off the edge of the porch, and singing to himself. "Back inna SS Aw, Back inna SS Aw. Ooh hoo hoo."

Well, Mary Lou would be happy. At least one grandkid appreciated the Beatles.

He slowly went to find her. She was up in the bedroom, briskly folding sheets and blankets and packing them in a laundry basket. As he entered, she gave him a brief glance and continued with her task. Ray fiddled with the doohickey that plugged the air mattress, and let the darn thing flatten out. *Let It Be* rolled out of the CD player. Not his favorite album, but he liked this song. He began singing along. "And when the night is cloudy there is still a light that shines on me. Shine until tomorrow, let it be."

Mary Lou picked up the next lines. "I wake up to the sound of music, Mother Mary comes to me. Speaking words of wisdom, let it be."

They turned to look at each other and she came into his arms. Slowly, they swayed back and forth to the rest of the song, singing along. "Let it be, let it be, let it be, let it be. There will be an answer. Let it be."

His face against her hair, he said, "We'll do whatever you want."

"Oh, no you don't. We'll do whatever *we* want. You think I'm gonna take all the blame if it doesn't work out right?" She tipped her head back to look up at him. "I'm all for getting a condo. It'll be fun. But I don't know about selling the tent."

"Then it'll have to be a mighty small condo. Or one of them tiny homes."

"We'll figure it out. What's so wrong with getting a mortgage?"

"Nobody's gonna give a mortgage to a man my age."

"You're only seventy-two. Not ninety-eight."

"Dad died when he was sixty-eight."

She pushed him away. "Is *that* what's bothering you? For heaven's sake, Ray! Your dad smoked like a chimney. But you're healthy as a horse. A very *healthy* horse. Let's talk to the bank first, and then – "

He pulled her back into his arms. "Ran into Bob Clary. He and Janet are living in an RV these days. Travel all over."

"Well, we can talk about that too. We can *talk* about *all* of it. That's the whole idea, you know. Deciding things together."

"Okay."

"Okay."

Ray folded the air mattress and together they managed to shove it back in its box. As they headed downstairs with the mattress, pillows and bedding, Ray said, "You know, another thing we could maybe do is…" Before he could finish, they rounded the bottom of the stairs, and he saw the grown-ups huddled around Hank's tablet.

"What's up?" he asked.

Hank held the tablet so he could see. This morning's photos were there on the screen. Mary Lou scrolled through as he looked at them over her shoulder. There they were, the whole gang. On the front porch of the tent. He and Mary Lou in the center, with Wade's family to one side, and Bethany's to the other. Another showed just Wade and Stephanie, then one with their kids. Here was Hank grinning at Ava, and Bethany trying to hang onto the boys, and there he was, sitting on the swing with Mary Lou, his arm around her shoulders. And then the two of them, with all the grandchildren crowded in. He felt his eyes go a little misty.

"Yeah. Pretty good," he said, and couldn't say more.

Mary Lou looked at them more objectively. Finally, she said, "We're gonna need a really big picture frame. 'Cuz I'm hanging this whole bunch." She looked over at Ray. "Did you really, seriously, for one darn minute, consider selling this place?"

He blew his nose. Loudly. Tucked his handkerchief back in his pocket and shook his head. "Nope. Not once. Never crossed my mind. I don't know who that fella was. Musta been loco."

He put his arm around her shoulders and was afraid there for a minute that he'd bust out crying. *That* was no good. So he cleared his throat and said, "Well, all I can say is, who wants to go to the Shack for one last ice cream cone? It's on me."

And they all cheered.

Acknowledgements

In this, my first foray into historical fiction, I found many people and places that provided information and inspiration. Among them:

Barbara Kidd Lawing, for many years as the leader of a writers' group I attended in Charlotte, and editor of this book. Not only a great friend, but a true help in achieving a Southern 'voice' for these stories

Terry Brotherton, for encouragement and the factual material in his books, Rock Springs Campground, Volumes 1 & 2

Gurtha Strand, for encouragement and information on cotton-growing in the area

The Mundy House and History Center of East Lincoln County

Florence Shanklin Library Book Club, for the kick-in-the-butt I needed to finally begin work on these stories

Charles Jonas Library, their county research room, and the Adult Writers' Group, led by Kelly Kinard

Lincoln County Museum of History

Eastern Lincoln Historical Society

Lake Norman, Our Inland Sea by Diana C. Gleasner and Bill Gleasner

Rock Springs Campmeeting group on Facebook

Davidson College Lake Norman Project

NC GenWeb project, including the African-American Special Project

NCPedia.org

Lake Norman Magazine, November 2004, Vol. 32, No. 11, article by Carol- Faye Ashcraft

Cover photo by Brittany Green Agosta

Also by CAROLYN STEELE AGOSTA

AFTER THE WINK, AND OTHER STORIES

THE PLEASURE OF YOUR COMPANY

EVERY LITTLE STEP SHE TAKES

ORGANIZED AND LOVING IT

https://www.carolynsteeleagosta.com

www.ingramcontent.com/pod-product-compliance
Lightning Source LLC
Chambersburg PA
CBHW070332260626
47160CB00003B/1020